SAN FRANCISCO FILE

PHIL RIBERA

ISBN-13: 978-0-9962103-4-8
ISBN-10: 0-9962103-4-2

Published by Phil Ribera

Learn more about the author by visiting: www.philribera.com

Interoffice Memorandum

To: Chief of Police - San Francisco Police Department
From: Daniel Patrick McKenna - Homicide Inspector

Subj: Letter of Resignation

I am writing from the County Jail, where I'm being charged with murder. This seems as good a time as any to pen my resignation.

As you are probably aware, my promotion to inspector was not a springboard to the illustrious career I had hoped for. In fact, my 25 days in the Homicide Detail triggered the complete unraveling of my professional and private lives. Now my coworkers think I'm a rat, the public sees me as a serial killer, and my wife and daughter won't speak to me.

I am afraid that you have been misled by my superiors in the department. The real facts of my case are not what you've heard from them or seen in the media.

If you want to learn what really happened, a good starting point would be early October - a couple of days after I began my assignment in the detail.

It was a Wednesday morning as I recall, the day we found the first body . . .

1

Hoffman Avenue Crime Scene

She was an average lady in an average neighborhood, at 9:26 on an average morning. Except, she was dead.

We gazed down at the woman sitting in the driver's seat of a car—her gray eyes wide, as if frozen by their final horrifying sight. Her hair was still damp from a morning shower, and it hit me that she probably didn't start her day thinking she would be San Francisco's sixty-third homicide of the year.

"Car comes back registered to the vic," Moretti said, tossing her driver's license onto a folding table that had been set up by the CSI techs.

I edged around Moretti to view the photo. She was a pretty, young brunette, nothing like the bloody mess crumpled in the Toyota just a few feet away. Lying next to the license was a clip-on ID badge from what looked like a company across the bay.

"Admin Assistant." Moretti said, tossing it back with the rest of her purse's contents. "Humph."

"Single gunshot behind the left ear," said Alan Lam. "Probably a carjacking gone bad."

"What makes you think so?"

The four inspectors turned to glare at me, making me wish I had kept my mouth shut. Apparently, three days in the detail hadn't earned me the chops to ask questions. I was suddenly aware that I'd been the only one to stop at the CSI van where I had signed the scene log and donned gloves and shoe covers. It was protocol, yet these veterans were above such menial tasks.

"Car keys are missing." Moretti used his pen to pick through the contents of the purse, now scattered on the table. "Shooter probably panicked and took off on foot."

I nodded as if I'd been enlightened, but still had some doubts. *Carjacking? What street thug wants to flee from the cops in a Prius?*

And why shoot the girl, even if it was a robbery? She was a twig of a thing, hardly a threat to anyone.

Then I noticed there was no cell phone among her belongings. My twelve-year-old daughter doesn't shower without bringing her phone into the bathroom with her.

These musings ruminated in my head, but I thought it best to keep them to myself. It wasn't my case, and as much as I wanted to demonstrate my investigative competence, I'd have to bide my time.

"The vic's address is just up the street on Elizabeth," said Lam. "Probably couldn't find a closer parking spot."

As they headed up the hill toward the apartment, I was left to guard the scene. It's what I used to do as a patrol officer, but with the promotion and all I had hoped for more involvement.

A dozen onlookers had braved the cold to belly up against the yellow tape. A group of teenagers weighed in on which street gang might be responsible, and two elderly ladies crossed themselves in prayer as they huddled together. A young mother shielded her children's eyes while crossing the intersection, and an Asian man in business attire stood on the other side of the street talking on his phone. News reporters arrived and began filming me, so I tried to appear inspectorly. After a while, I called for a double patrol unit and had them move everyone back a block.

The ME's wagon showed up just as the inspectors were returning from the victim's apartment. Moretti supervised the body's removal while the others directed the collection of evidence and the taking of crime scene photos. One inspector, a grizzled old guy named Lou Cassidy, stood away from the others talking on his cell. He nodded to me as he ended the call, and I nodded back.

Wearing a plaid 80s-vintage sport coat, he sauntered over to explain that they had done an "exigent search" of the dead woman's second floor flat. A passkey provided by the manager had allowed them to check inside for other victims, but nobody was home—dead or alive. Cassidy said that they planned to return with a *paper* later in the day and do a more thorough search.

"Fucking courts," he said. "They legalize pot and flag burning, but make us get a warrant to search a murder victim's house for evidence of who killed 'em."

I was familiar with Fourth Amendment case law; it had been on the inspector exam. But I nodded anyway, making the old guy think he'd taught me something. "There goes a few more wasted hours," I said.

Cassidy described the victim's flat as a mess. "Dirty as a pimp's skivvies," were his exact words. And since Cassidy was the only inspector even talking to me, I decided to run my theory by him.

Pointing to the absence of the victim's phone, and the fact that her frail build hardly made her a threat worth shooting, I asked Cassidy how often the inspectors get these initial presumptions wrong.

He shrugged and picked his teeth.

Still nagged by their hasty assessment, I said, "Random murders account for only twenty-five percent of homicides. Even less for female victims."

"You read that in a book somewhere?" Cassidy lifted an eyebrow. "Look kid, who knows? We might all be wrong, and this thing could turn out to be road rage over how slow she drove her fucking Prius. But take it from an old dog who's been around the hydrant a few times: Keep your eyes open and your mouth closed. Questioning these guys after spending only a minute in the detail will go over like a lead fart. They know what they're doing. They'll figure it out."

I liked Cassidy, but that didn't mean I agreed with him.

He grinned. "Take a breath, hot shot. There are plenty of corpses to go around. We can test out your book smarts on the next one."

"We?"

He grinned again, but it was more like a grimace. "That was the captain on the phone. He's partnering us together starting today."

"Great." I extended my hand.

Cassidy gave it a single lackluster pump and then returned to the veteran inspectors. He was a slow mover with a puffy face, and his jowls dripped 80 proof sweat. Of all of them, he'd be the easiest to work with even though the guy was clearly counting the days until his retirement. In any case, it was Captain Dowd's decision to put us together, and that was that.

As the ME zipped the woman into a body bag, I scrolled over the facts in my mind. The girl was clean, nicely dressed, manicured nails, and even her car was immaculate. But her apartment looking like a pigpen didn't add up.

The missing car keys was the only fact that actually supported an attempted carjacking, but I still had my doubts. I wondered why the killer would take the keys but not the car. Then it struck me; there must have been other keys on the ring. Probably her house key.

If the killer had beat the inspectors back to her flat, it would explain why the keys were taken and possibly even why the place was in such disarray.

I had to find a way into the dead girl's apartment to see for myself.

3

2

Tyrrhenian Sea

With stabilizers as good as any commercial vessel, the 436-foot-long *Serenity* barely felt the shifting tides as she cruised into Cala Coticcio Bay off Sardinia's north coast.

She required upwards of fifty crewmembers, all of whom were housed in quarters that were both separate and invisible to the guests. Aside from the captain and navigation crew, her staff included cooks, mechanics, laundry workers, housekeepers, pool cleaners, servers, maintenance people, staff managers, a helicopter pilot, and a healthy contingent of security personnel.

Sergei Petrenko had arranged the 250-mile trip south from the yacht's home port in Savona for the sole purpose of meeting with the top management of his company and their families. They were his CFO, Marketing Director, Operations Director, General Counsel, and the heads of HR and IT departments. Petrenko's personal assistant had taken on additional staff for the trip, including a French pastry chef, a sushi shokunin, a masseuse, a tailor, a swimming coach, an arts and crafts instructor, and a ventriloquist.

Servers laid out platters of pickled cucumbers and tomatoes as Petrenko poured himself a vodka. His cell phone vibrated and he saw that it was his man in San Francisco. Raising an index finger to pause his guests, Sergi stepped into his private office. "Tell me Mr. Tam, what did you find out?"

Silence hung for a second. "A woman," Tam said. "An American woman by the name of Rhonda Pitts."

"So, you've located her?"

"Yes, sir... however, I'm afraid there's been something of a complication."

Switching the phone to his other hand, Petrenko closed the office door. "I'm listening."

"She's dead. Shot in the head."

Petrenko eased into his leather chair. "And this just happened?"

"Yes, probably an hour or so ago. She was in her car, which was parked a short distance from where she lived."

"A coincidence, perhaps? Some sort of random crime?"

"Maybe," Tam let out a measured breath, "but I don't think so."

"No, I don't either." Petrenko stared into his drink before downing the last of it. "I don't believe in coincidences."

"It looks like a professional hit to me." Tam glanced across the street to the police investigators clustered around the body in the light blue Toyota. "Could there be another interested party?"

"Hmm." Sergei Petrenko breathed heavily into the phone as he contemplated the notion. It was possible. After all, Moscow wanted what they believed was theirs as much as Petrenko wanted what he believed was his. "How did you find the girl?"

Tam walked around the corner to his car. "One of the shipping containers turned up in a warehouse here in San Francisco."

"And this dead girl's involvement?"

"The warehouse is leased in her name," Tam said. "I arrived in San Francisco yesterday, and tracked down the woman's home address only this morning. I was on my way to contact her when I noticed the police activity down the street." Tam paused. "But even with her name being on the warehouse lease, there's no way that this woman is behind the cargo thefts. Whoever killed her must also know that."

Petrenko nodded as he gazed over the port bow to an empty cove. For nearly a decade his Hong Kong private investigator had built a reputation catering to the devilry of the rich and famous. Sergi knew that two traits set Tam apart from other private sleuths: investigative acumen and complete discretion—both of which appealed to the egocentric billionaire.

Tam continued his thought. "So, I'm trying to figure out why they would take her out."

"A message?" said Petrenko, finally. "Perhaps this Pitts woman is somehow involved with the men we want. The men who stole from my company."

"Should I remain in San Francisco?"

"Yes, keep on this." Ice cubes clinked as Petrenko refilled his glass. "Just stay back in the shadows, and let me know what happens."

"Of course, sir."

Petrenko paused. "I'm thinking that whoever killed this woman is also trying to flush out our thieves. Mark my words Tam, this is going to get interesting."

After concluding the call, Sergi stared out at the sparkling sea and thought about who might have hijacked his shipping containers. The thefts were the price of doing business in today's world, but that had become a secondary concern. Foremost in Petrenko's mind now was the question of who else was interested in the stolen containers. Interested enough to kill the American woman.

After the fall of the Soviet Union, the *Sluzhba Vneshney Razvedki* had emerged as a remodeled version of KGB's foreign intelligence service—Vladimir Putin's personal errand boys. And though the SVR was a possibility in the Pitts woman's murder, Petrenko thought that dispatching a hit team onto U.S. soil would have been too risky—even for Putin.

3

985-B Elizabeth St.

My partners had left the lights on in the dead woman's flat, perhaps to make it appear that someone was home. After watching awhile, I could see that the place was still empty.

I had picked up a burger at a place on 24th, and had it balanced on my knees as I phoned Doris. She didn't seem angry that I was still working, but she wasn't happy either.

"Hey," I said. "This was part of the deal; you knew that going in. I'm expected to work long hours, especially if I catch a case."

"How could you have gotten a case already? You told me it would be weeks before you were on the rotation." She paused. "Danny?"

"Yeah, I know what I told you." I licked the sauce off my free hand. "It's not my case, per se. But I've got a hunch that I need to check out."

"You've been an inspector for less than a week," she said. "What the hell are you trying to do, get yourself fired? You've got to be kidding me, 'a hunch.'" She started laughing. It was the sort of belittling cackle that you want to prove wrong.

"My burger's getting cold." It was all I could think to say. Ending the call, I wondered if Doris was right. It wasn't even my homicide case, and I'd be in big trouble if anyone knew I was poking around it. On the other hand, I was sure that Moretti and Lam were barking up the wrong tree. And if I could come up with something to help them—a suspect or even a good lead—it would go a long way toward earning their respect.

I finished my burger and left my Jeep across the street. The manager had just taken a pot pie out of the oven, and seemed annoyed when he opened his door. Flashing my inspector shield, I asked for the key to the girl's flat.

"I already gave you guys a key," he said. "This is the only copy I have left."

I promised to return it when I was done.

Unit B was on the second floor. It had a compact bathroom, and a bedroom that barely fit a double bed. Duel pocket doors separated it from the living room and kitchen.

Lou had been right; the place was a mess. But not like the home of a slob. There were no dirty dishes piled in the sink, no brown toilet bowl, and no scummy film on the shower tiles. The strainer in the bathtub drain had even been emptied of hair. I could tell that Rhonda Pitts had been a meticulous housekeeper.

Having taken my share of burglary reports over the years, I saw right away that this had all the earmarks of a ransacking. The bed was askew and most of her clothes were on the floor, yet I noticed that two sweaters remained neatly folded among the heap—as if they had been tossed out of the drawers that way. The victim's shoes were piled in the corner along with dozens of matching shoeboxes. I had to ask myself why the woman would go to the trouble of saving all the shoeboxes, yet leave the shoes out of them. She wouldn't.

The inspectors wouldn't have done it. Trashing the place would have only made their evidence search more difficult.

I was quickly coming to the conclusion that whoever killed Miss Pitts took her keys after shooting her and then scoured the joint while we were still down the block examining her corpse. They had clearly searched her apartment for something specific, and I was betting it wasn't her shoes.

It was getting stuffy, so I opened a window. As I sat on the bed, I tried to visualize the Pitts woman living her simple life—driving her car across the bridge to work and back each day. She had gotten herself mixed up in something, but what?

Deep voices in the hallway shook me from my thoughts, and then a whispered exchange near the door. I tensed, fearing that Moretti and Lam had returned.

I envisioned the manager leading them to the apartment, grousing about the cop inside who had borrowed his last passkey. Their obvious question being, *What cop?*

For a second, I considered climbing out the window and fleeing down the fire escape. But the inspectors would know from the manager's description that it was me who had bogarted his way into their crime scene.

I moved closer to the door and listened, now sensing that the voices belonged to someone else. Their words were guttural, yet still barely above a whisper. Moretti and Lam would have no reason to whisper.

I slipped my weapon out of its holster and held it against the side of my leg.

8

There was a metallic jangle, a "shush" by one of the men, and then the sound of a key slipping into the lock. It crossed my mind that they could be family members of the Pitts woman. But they could also be whoever had gunned her down.

I gripped the pistol tightly as the pulse pounded inside my head. Just as I was about to throw open the door and thrust my weapon into their faces, I heard something else. Other voices, louder, not whispering, echoing up the stairwell.

The two men at the door froze. An instant later they were scrambling away down the hall. Then, a heavy thud as they threw open the door to the fire escape.

"Police! Freeze!" called familiar voices. But the other two men were already scrambling down the ladder. Moretti and Lam trudged past the door, no doubt having been startled by the men.

I had no idea why the inspectors had returned, but it didn't matter at that point. As they chased after the intruders, I saw my opportunity to slip out of the flat.

From the bedroom window, I watched the two dark figures jump fences westbound through the neighborhood. Clearly younger and more fit than the investigators, their getaway was going to be a walk in the park. By the time Moretti and Lam made it to the back fence, the other men were already on Grand View Avenue.

"I'll go back and call it in," yelled Moretti. Poor guy looked like he was about to hurl his entire dinner. Lam clambered over the first fence, but he wasn't doing much better.

I closed the bedroom window and quickly left the apartment. Slipping the borrowed passkey under the manager's door, I dashed across the street, past the inspectors' car, to my own Jeep. As I turned down Elizabeth, I saw the hunched outline of Frankie Moretti calling for backup on his car radio. I circled the block without spotting the two interlopers, then took Portola over the hill into the Sunset District, where I hit 19th Avenue toward the Golden Gate Bridge.

I was heading home to my wife and daughter, but in all honesty I wasn't too excited about it.

4

Grove Shafter Freeway
Oakland

Glancing up just in time, she brought her car to a jerky stop only inches from the other bumper. She cursed as she tossed her cell phone onto the passenger seat. Reading texts while driving was a stupid thing to do. She knew that. But her freeway speed had been little more than a crawl ever since she'd left the office.

A horn honked and she flipped the bird out the window toward the line of cars behind her. Another stupid move, she thought, given that Oakland was ranked the third most dangerous city in the entire country.

Her fog horn ringtone sounded and she snatched the phone off the seat. "Sarah Brooks."

It was her boss on the line, ordering Sarah back to the office. She looked at her watch, knowing that the traffic was just as bad heading in the other direction.

"C'mon, Tim. It's six-fucking-thirty, and I'm almost home."

"I forgot to tell you about the district chief's monthly 'video chat.' He wants the entire unit back here when he calls in thirty minutes."

Sarah tossed her phone onto the seat for the second time, then took the next exit. She cut over to Broadway and headed back toward the port. She hadn't spotted the white Econoline van following her off of the freeway, and didn't notice as it edged up next to her in the slow lane.

The side cargo door slid open just as the van came abreast of her front passenger door, leaving only inches between them. In the gridlocked traffic, Sarah had little time to react.

The first blast caught the top of the doorframe just as Sarah's mind registered the threat. She reached for her sidearm, but the explosion of glass and shotgun pellets forced her to turn away and shield her eyes.

She instinctively stomped down on the accelerator, propelling the car forward into the vehicle ahead of her and then sideways into oncoming traffic. The next shot blew out her back window.

Horns blared and pedestrians ran for cover. A third blast pelted the rear of her car with pellets.

Sarah finally managed to draw her weapon, but the van had become entangled in traffic and was now behind her. It made a quick right turn down a side street near the Paramount Theatre.

Sarah fought through the disorienting smoke, flying debris, and high-pitched ringing in her ears, to assess her injuries. Noticing only a few nicks on her forehead and face, and a trickle of blood on her neck, she was certain that she hadn't been hit by a bullet.

Her mind raced through the order of priorities as she groped the floor for the cell phone. Should she call OPD for help, or pull over and check herself more thoroughly? Or, should she circle the block, find the sons-of-bitches who did this, and blow their asses to hell?

Choosing the latter option, Sarah cut in front of a bus to make the next right. Her car fishtailed onto 19th Street and then onto Telegraph. Spotting the white van as it flew through the intersection a block over, she paralleled them down William—a narrow street that spit her onto San Pablo. The van had again become bogged down, this time behind a double-parked delivery truck. Sarah was gridlocked too, so she abandoned her Chevy Caprice in the middle of the street and sprinted between stopped cars—her 9mm Sig Sauer in hand.

Again, she was a tic too late. From behind a clot of commuters, Sarah watched helplessly as the van freed itself and continued through the intersection, unscathed. She was too far away to see the driver or the license plate, and there was no way to head it off. Once the van crossed under the freeway, Sarah knew there were a half-dozen routes the driver could take to get out of the area.

The van slipped beneath the overpass and out of her view, its occupants disappearing into the seedy backdrop of West Oakland.

5

SFPD Headquarters

I sat in the outer office staring at the nameplate on the door: *Edward T. Fahey, Chief of Police.*

I'd never actually met the chief before. In fact, I'd never even been to the administrative building on 3rd Street. If you had asked me a day earlier if Chief Fahey knew my name, I would have said no.

Hoping that I'd been invited there so he could wish me luck in my new assignment, I worried that perhaps I had already screwed up. Maybe someone had spotted me at the dead woman's flat two nights prior.

"You can go in now, officer."

I nodded to the secretary as I stood up. She glanced at my pants as if my zipper were down, and I saw a glob of mustard—remnants of a hotdog I had gobbled down before coming into the building.

"Mustard," I said, licking my finger and rubbing at the yellow smudge.

The woman bristled and swiveled her chair toward her desk, as if I had volunteered information she didn't care to hear.

A moment later, the door was behind me and I was standing face-to-face with Chief Fahey.

"Come in. Sit down, Daniel," he said, motioning towards a tan couch set behind a coffee table. *Daniel? Nobody calls me that except my mother. And my wife, when I'm in trouble.*

The chief looked older in person. His blue eyes were sharp, though the rest of him was wrinkled and gray. His nose was bent, like he'd seen a bar fight or two in his day. But he had the calming voice of a priest about to hear confession.

"Sir," I said, tentatively taking a seat.

"Relax Daniel, you're not in any trouble." Fahey sat on the couch only a few inches away, and then rested his arm behind me. "On the contrary," he said. "I've asked you here because I need your help."

"My help?" I felt my back stiffen.

He nodded, almost sadly. "What I'm about to tell you, Daniel... I need your word that you won't share it with anyone outside this room."

My gaze shifted around his office. It was modern, with lots of metal and glass, but it didn't fit the old chief. "Sure, Chief, you've got my word."

"You were recently given a provisional promotion to the rank of Inspector, and I assume by now you've begun your new assignment."

"Started on Monday, sir."

I'd given myself about a fifty-fifty chance of even passing the inspector test, never imagining an assignment in the Homicide Detail. New inspectors routinely start out in General Works handling burglaries, bad checks, and minor assaults.

"It was my decision," said Fahey. "And I put you there for a specific reason."

"Thank you, sir." I reached to shake his hand, but the chief eased back without extending his. Clearly, there was more to our little meeting.

"I know that what I'm about to ask of you is a lot..." His eyes grew intense.

Whatever it was, I already didn't like the sound of it. I was nervous enough just being in his office. I offered a barely perceptible nod.

"It's come to my attention that we have a crooked cop working with you down there. An inspector, I believe, operating as something akin to a double agent."

"In the homicide detail?" My words came out squeaky. "How? I mean, why?"

The chief shook his head. "I don't have a whole lot of facts to go on at this point. Don't have any idea who he is or what he's up to, except that it has something to do with one of our investigations—a murder that has either already happened or is going to happen."

My mind was still playing catch up.

"This inspector, whoever he is, or *she* is, plans to intentionally steer an investigation in the wrong direction to protect who actually committed the killing." The chief ignored his blinking desk phone. "I suppose derailing a murder case would be easy enough if it's your own investigation. But if someone else catches the case, our rogue man will be forced to sabotage it from the outside." Chief Fahey leaned forward. "You understand where I'm going with this."

Uh, not really. My selfish takeaway from the conversation was that when the crooked son-of-a-bitch gets caught, his empty position will make my promotion permanent.

"I'll be happy to wait this thing out," I said. "Let you and the IA people do your thing, and then when the smoke clears I can start--"

Chief Fahey shook his head, stopping me midsentence. "No, that's not what I need from you."

"No?"

"No." His hand slid off the seatback onto my shoulder. "Son, I need you to go in, start working, and do your job without drawing any attention. And then I need you to identify the person."

This must be some sort of joke. I closed my eyes and pressed my palms against my forehead. We were talking about a group of seasoned inspectors. Why would one of them go to the other side? And why was the chief telling *me* about it? I suddenly felt like the secretary in the outer office; I didn't want to hear about his mustard stain.

When I looked up, the chief's forlorn expression convinced me that it was anything but a joke.

"Listen McKenna, it won't be a cake walk by any means. This guy's a cop; so besides knowing the ropes, he'll also be desperate—and that means dangerous. Maybe he's doing it for money, or maybe he's mixed up in something bigger—a criminal organization of some kind. He's already stuck his neck out, and he'll turn on you in a heartbeat if he realizes that you're onto him."

After my head cleared, I said, "This isn't really my sort of thing, Chief. There are plenty of talented investigators around. Guys who can work undercover cases with their eyes closed. Why me?" I was waiting to hear him say that I was the best of the bunch, sharp as a tack, a real up-and-comer.

Instead, the chief gazed out the window for a long time. "As much as I hate to admit it, my options are few. I have no idea who I can trust in there. It could be one of the inspectors, or a lieutenant, or even the captain. What I need is someone fresh, from outside the detail. Someone like you who was legitimately promoted and who won't arouse suspicion."

"But they're already suspicious of me," I said. "Nobody makes inspector and then waltzes right into homicide."

He shook his head. "Some of the promotional tests are still under court ordered consent decree, and ninety percent of my appointments are provisional anyway. In other words, I am free to place people where I need them. Sure, the old salts in the detail will be pissed off that you got something that took them years to achieve, but that'll be the extent of it. You've got a credible record and a solid reputation as an investigator. Nobody will see anything beyond that."

14

I understood his point; using a newcomer to the detail made sense. The problem was, I didn't want to do it. In fact, I hated the idea. I'd never shied away from a challenge; not as a kid being moved from military base to military base, not during my college football days, and not as a police officer. But this was too much to ask.

"With all due respect Chief, how are you so certain that I can be trusted?"

His thick jaw didn't budge, but tiny smile lines at the corners of his eyes tugged upwards. "I did my own background check and your record is clean. You've more than proven yourself on the job, and I'm not second guessing my decision. All I need is for you to accept the assignment."

"Can I take a few days to think about it?"

The chief shook his head. "Unfortunately, this can't wait. I need your answer now."

"*If* I were to say yes..." I took a swallow. "And *if* I came up with some information, or actually figured out who it is..." I felt the noose tightening around my neck. "I mean, what's the chain of command on this? Who would I report it to?"

"Me," he said. "And only me." The chief scribbled a number onto his business card. "This is my private cell phone. Anything you find out, even a suspicion, call me at this number—day or night."

I took the card and stared at it like a death sentence. My throat felt like sandpaper and my head pounded. I wanted to rip it up and leave. "So I won't have any help? No backup? Isn't there anyone else in the loop?"

"You know how word gets around in this place," he said. "I can't risk bringing anybody else in on this. Not even my own command staff."

I numbly slipped the chief's card into my pocket.

"You're working under Greg Dowd, is that right?"

I nodded, still in a stupor.

"He's a nosy little prick," said the chief. "Not one of my favorite people. Just lay low and stay away from him as much as possible."

Captain Dowd and me had history between us, and the guy already disliked me. But I wasn't about to get into all that with Chief Fahey, so I just nodded.

"Don't worry," said the chief. "I'll have your back. And like I said before, you can call my personal number any time. But I need your answer before you leave this office. Will you do it?"

6

168 Russ Street

Curtis Tam thumbed through the manila folder, studying the grainy photograph of Rhonda Pitts—the only person he had been able to connect to the cargo thefts. But with her life now under a microscope and her apartment swarming with cops, his only option was to continue watching the warehouse she'd leased.

The rental car company had offered Tam a metallic bronze PT Cruiser, which would have made surveillance work a nightmare on several levels. He'd opted instead for the smoke gray Toyota SUV, which blended better in the neighborhood and gave him space to recline.

Lighting another cigarette, he stared at the plain gray, two-story warehouse. It was sandwiched into an uneven row of mixed-use buildings on the narrow street. As he cracked the car window to vent the stale air, Tam realized how much he disliked static surveillances. They were a lot like fishing, he thought. Initial minutes of anticipation and intrigue followed by long tedious hours of watching and waiting.

Having just returned from a missing person investigation in India, Tam hadn't been eager to take on another international case. But Sergei Petrenko was a man used to getting what he wanted. He had hired Tam after ten cargo containers had gone missing while in transport across the Atlantic.

Not knowing if the shipping companies could be trusted, Tam had installed trackers on 20 of Petrenko's 270 CONEX boxes before they were shipped from the distribution plant in Riga, Latvia. Painted to match the rusty containers, the solar powered devices were wireless, weatherproof, and magnetically secure up to 150 pounds of pull pressure. As long as their lithium iron phosphate batteries were exposed to even indirect sunlight during the day, Tam was able to monitor their locations in real time. In the event of tampering, damage, or intrusion, he would immediately be notified via text message.

Then, two weeks after leaving Riga, one of the tracked containers was diverted. Tam continued monitoring its movements during transit until the box came to rest in the non-descript South of Market warehouse. But after three days of nothing, Tam had become bored and anxious. He had hoped that whoever else was involved in the thefts would have turned up, but he'd seen no one. The building remained empty and dark.

Mr. Petrenko would expect answers soon, and at this point Tam had none.

After a long hazy afternoon of peering out at the quiet warehouse, the investigator began to wonder if the Rust Street lead had died with the Pitts woman. He checked his watch and rubbed his eyes. Not just hungry, but Tam also needed to use the bathroom and stretch his legs. The smell of cooked food wafting from the end of the block was the added incentive he needed to get out of the car.

Tam stubbed out his cigarette and walked to a pizza joint around the corner on Folsom, where he used the restroom and ordered a slice of vegetarian pie. The young woman behind the counter was dressed in black tights, and had whiskers and a tiny black nose painted on her face. Tam thought it strange, but assumed the outfit was either the restaurant's promotional gimmick or an example of the San Francisco weirdness he had always heard about.

Eating as he casually strolled up the west side of the street, the sporty Chinese man looked like any other young professional living or working in the gentrified neighborhood. Outwardly, Tam appeared to be interested only in his meal. But behind his dark glasses, he carefully scanned the street in front of the warehouse. Then, pausing in front of it, Tam used his smartphone to snap a series of photos: the second floor windows, the aluminum roll-up door, the security lock, the chain-link fence on the south side of the building, and the cluttered storage yard containing stacks of wooden pallets.

"You need something?" Two men had come up quickly behind him.

"Hi there," said Tam, taking a last bite of pizza and then extending his hand to the ruddy faced one. "My name is Calvin Yee. You must be Mr. Taylor."

"No." The man ignored Tam's hand. "What do you want?"

The second man stood off to the side—also Caucasian, but taller and thinner, with slick black hair.

Tam removed his sunglasses and pulled a small notebook from his pocket. "Says right here. I'm supposed to meet Gary Taylor at 168 Moss Street. I'm with Paragon Commercial Brokerage."

"This is Russ Street," said the first man. "Moss is a block over."

"Russ, you say?" Tam frowned at his notes. "Well, if you ever need a real estate--"

The man turned away then used a key to open the roll-up door. Tam pretended to be making a phone call, but turned his head ever so slightly to snap one last photo. He'd gotten just a quick glance into the warehouse where a long brown shipping container sat just inside the loading bay. The back was open and several full pallets were stacked alongside it.

The men glanced back at the lingering Tam, who turned away just in time to appear disinterested. Slipping his cell phone back into his jacket pocket, Tam continued on so as not to arouse suspicion.

He had hoped to record the container's 10-digit serial number, which he could then compare with Petrenko's list of those stolen, but his view had been obscured by a white cargo van also parked inside. Tam was only able to recognize the box as a 12-meter FEU container with a Boaz Integrated Shipping Services logo. The same as those used by Petrenko's company.

Knowing that the similarities alone may not prove it belonged to Petrenko, the fact that the GPS transmitter was still pinging from inside the Russ Street warehouse was evidence enough for Tam. That the man spoke with a Slavonic accent was added corroboration, given the container's Latvian origin and that Petrenko himself was Russian. Things were starting to come together.

The rolling door slammed down—a clear message that Tam was not welcome there. Not wanting to risk drawing more attention, he took a surreptitious route back to his car. It was enough of a misstep that they had seen Tam's face, and he couldn't risk them seeing his car as well.

Nearly six hours passed without any further sign of the men inside. The building was dark, save for the halogen lamp hanging over the side gate. Nobody driving past would even know the building was occupied.

Curtis sat in his car, waiting for something to happen and wondering why the men had kept the interior lights off. Possibilities rolled through his mind, one at a time: The two men could be involved in the Pitts girl's murder, and they are hiding from the police. Another scenario was that they had not killed her, but they were hiding from whoever did.

Finally, at 1:30 a.m., the corrugated metal door inched upward and the two men crept out. They scanned up and down the block and then quickly walked in the opposite direction from where Tam was parked. Waiting until they turned onto Folsom, Tam started his car and drove toward the intersection. He was forced to turn left on the one-way street, but managed to spot the two men getting into a small silver Ford.

On the other side of Folsom, Tam parked in front of a small park and waited for their car to pass. The men drove by a minute later, paying no attention to him. A constant flow of cars kept their eyes focused elsewhere as Tam pulled back into traffic. The silver car made a left, drove a few blocks and then turned left again onto Market Street. Tam made every green light, following at a distance safe enough not to stand out. He continued behind the men as they wound around Buena Vista Park, eventually dropping down into the Haight-Ashbury neighborhood.

It was close to 2 a.m. when they slowed near Club Deluxe—a live music venue that was just letting out. The club's doors opened, and out spilled a diverse crowd—from painted and pierced to older people in cocktail party attire. Most were dressed in costume.

Tam wondered if his two suspects were looking for someone in particular among the crowd, but the little car—which Tam now recognized as a *Focus*—gained speed again and continued on. Finally, the car nosed out into the 'T' intersection with Oak Street and pulled to the curb beside a long narrow grove of trees. A park ran several blocks in either direction of where the men had stopped.

At a discreet spot, Tam parked and shut off his car's lights. He hoped, as he watched the Ford idling quietly in the early morning cold, that he would not have to follow the men on foot. It would be both difficult and risky in the desolate greenway.

Then, the silver compact's interior light came on and Tam saw the two men exit the car. The quiet one with slick black hair carried a small daypack, which he had slung over his shoulder. They opened the trunk for only a couple of seconds, then closed it again. Standing next to the car, the men glanced around as if looking for someone.

Tam watched as their two silhouettes evaporated into the dark park. He sat there wondering if the men were actually involved in the cargo thefts, and if tailing them was even worth the effort.

Flipping on his car's headlights, Tam eased away from the curb and onto Oak. He scanned the narrow strip of grass and trees on the north side of the street, but the area was dark and shrouded in fog.

A sudden flash of light caught Tam's attention, farther ahead of where he'd seen the men enter the park. Like a lightning strike, the burst was followed a fraction of a second later by a muted cracking sound. A gunshot, Tam realized.

The flash had illuminated three silhouettes on a footpath in the park, as oddly spaced as three bowling pins left standing in the wake of a powerful headpin hit—two very close to each other and one about ten yards away. Then, one of them—the guy closest to the shooter—wobbled, tumbled, and fell flat near the base of a large tree. Tam slowed his car, straining to see into the shadows but unable to make out exactly what was happening. He could only discern the obvious: a shooting.

More gunshots rang out, this time in rapid succession. They lit the park like a strobe, accenting the juddering movements of the shooter and the remaining man, who was now running away. All the while, the fallen ten-pin lay on its side across the lane.

Tam couldn't tell if any of the gunfire was directed at him, but he instinctively accelerated away from the threat.

Assuming that the police would be responding soon, he decided against making another pass to get a better look. Putting together a quick summation of the events in his mind, Tam made a mental note: Eight shots had been fired by what appeared to be one shooter. The gunfire had resulted in one man down and one on the run. Tam loosely speculated, though he had no way of knowing for certain, that the shooter was not one of the men he had followed. He was more certain than ever that all of these people, including the dead Pitts woman, were involved in the theft of Petrenko's cargo.

Tam slowed after a few blocks, scanning his mirrors to make sure he wasn't being followed, then calmly drove back to his hotel and memorialized the evening's events into a digitally encrypted report for his client.

"Stay back in the shadows," Petrenko had told Tam. And that's exactly what he'd done.

7

850 Bryant Street

The Homicide Detail is housed in a fifth floor office facing north toward the freeway, which at eight o'clock that Monday morning was snarled with bumper-to-bumper traffic heading into the city. My commute from Marin County to the Hall of Justice had taken an hour and a half, yet I was still the first inspector in the office on the day after Halloween.

Marisol Ocampo had just brewed a pot of coffee, and so my week began with the great smell of French Roast and our secretary's motherly smile. She told me that my new partner had called out sick, which, the more I thought about it, wasn't necessarily a bad thing.

Making my way across the room, I considered my shitty weekend. Restless since meeting with the chief, I'd tossed and turning in bed, unable to quiet my mind. Doris had asked me a dozen times what was wrong, but I kept telling her that it was just indigestion. A part of me wanted to spill the whole story, but I never did. I couldn't admit that in my naiveté, or nervousness, or just plain stupidness, I had succumbed to the chief's beseeching request. I don't really remember what I said, but I clearly recall what happened next. Chief Fahey stood, embraced me, and said, "I knew you'd do it, son." And then the old man clapped his knuckled hand around the back of my neck and ushered me out of his office.

Anyway, me and Doris had been arguing a lot since moving into the expensive house that she *just had to have*, even though it added forty-five minutes to my commute. And I didn't think I could stomach her deriding reaction to the mission Chief Fahey had given me.

With a mug full of coffee at my empty desk, I sat thinking that a month ago Chief Fahey didn't know me from the janitor. Now he was trusting me to conduct the most highly sensitive investigation in the entire department. Whether it was a career advancing opportunity for me or piss poor luck remained to be seen.

Suddenly aware of someone's close presence, I turned to find my boss hovering over me. Captain Greg Dowd was only a couple of years older than me. A colorless guy; tall and gaunt, prematurely gray, with sharp features and close-set eyes. The kind of cop—if you can call him that—who was more comfortable wearing a suit than a duty uniform.

"Where's Cassidy?" he asked.

"He called out sick today. Must have overdone it on the Halloween candy last night."

I could almost hear Dowd's teeth grinding. "Yeah, he probably polished off a whole fifth of candy. Will he be back tomorrow?"

I shrugged. "Most likely." Which wasn't really an answer, but then again, how in the hell would I know?

Since Dowd hadn't mentioned the incident at the murder victim's apartment, I was certain that he knew nothing of my late night visit. Which also meant that Moretti and Lam didn't know that I'd been there, either. All good news to me, since I was sure that Dowd never wanted me in the Homicide Detail to begin with and would get rid of me in a second if he could. The police chief's secret mission notwithstanding, my goal was to stay out of Dowd's way and not give him a reason to transfer me back to a radio car.

"Never mind," said Dowd. "Where are Moretti and Lam? I need them ASAP."

Mrs. Ocampo had been listening from her desk and called over her shoulder, "They had a parole hearing at San Quentin today. Log says they'll be back by ten or eleven."

The captain looked at me as if I was the last shriveled hunk of salmon mousse on the hors d'oeuvre tray. "Fine, whatever. Grab your shit and head out to Oak and Clayton. Lieutenant Blythe, the Park District's watch commander, is waiting for you there. Found a body in some bushes along the Panhandle."

"No problem, Cap."

"No problem?" he snapped. "You don't even know what the hell they've got!"

"Well, whatever it is, I'm sure I can handle it."

Dowd glared down at me. "You'll handle nothing. The only thing I want you to do is examine the scene and let me know what it looks like; homicide, suicide, overdose, natural, or whatever. The rest of the guys will be in soon, and I'll send them out to take over."

"I've got to get my feet wet sooner or later, Captain. Besides, Cassidy will be back tomorrow, and if it's anything of substance he'll be here to work it with me."

"We'll see." Dowd started toward his office then hollered back over his shoulder. "Just give me a call before you get in so deep that you screw something up. I'll get you some help."

It wasn't a firm no, which I figured might buy me some time. Had Cassidy been at work, the sweaty old dog would have been given the case. My only role would have been what's referred to as *the stooge*. All legwork, and no recognition. Cassidy would have gotten the credit, and Dowd would have still seen me as the incapable greenhorn.

And I knew that if any other inspectors had been in the office, the captain would have kept me on the bench. No matter what breaks had come his way over the years, he wasn't about to pay them forward to anyone else—especially me. Dowd always had one eye on the guy being promoted ahead of him, and the other on whoever was moving up the ladder behind him.

So there I was, heading across the city to a dead body—which the odds favored being nothing more than a transient, dead of natural causes. But if it turned out to be something more, I was determined to make headway on it before Cassidy returned or Dowd handed the investigation to someone else.

Maybe I'd even solve the thing.

8

Alta Bates Summit Medical Center

Initial reports of shots fired had been received by the Oakland Police Department's Communications Center at 6:37 p.m. on Thursday. A security guard at the Tribune was the first caller, advising that somebody in a white van had shot out their lobby window. Other reports followed, describing everything from a gang drive-by on Broadway to a possible takeover robbery at the coffee shop on the corner. As police units raced to that area, a mobile caller two blocks away reported a woman running down the middle of Telegraph Avenue waving a gun. Not knowing if the incidents were related, police dispatched more officers to that location. By the time Sarah Brooks was located and identified as a federal agent, more than two-dozen patrol cars had clogged Oakland's downtown district.

One eye slowly crept open, peering sideways toward the annoying beep of a machine only a few feet in front of her face. Sarah slowly rolled onto her back and opened the other eye, which felt like unbarring a rusty door. A handsome couple in their late thirties stood gazing at her from the foot of the bed. They were both black, and for a second Sarah wondered if she had suffered a serious brain injury and that these were friends, family, or people she should recognize.

"Agent Brooks?" asked the woman. She wore a tan pantsuit and had a compact but sturdy build. "How are you feeling?"

Sarah's eyes moved to the shaved headed man next to her. He was tall and sinuous, like he spent a lot of time at the gym. He also wore a suit—charcoal gray with pinstripes.

Struggling to raise herself onto her elbows, Sarah asked, "And you are?"

The woman stepped carefully around a computer apparatus mounted atop a rolling cart, and handed Sarah a business card. She introduced herself and her partner as Oakland police detectives who had been assigned the follow-up on her shooting.

The woman went through a series of questions while the man recorded Sarah's responses on a small electronic tablet. Sarah didn't have many answers for them, recalling only the white Ford cargo van and the fact that one man was driving and two others were shooting at her from the van's side door. Her information did little more than validate most of the witness statements taken at the scene. Sarah hadn't even seen their faces, as the two at the door had worn black ski masks and she never actually saw the driver.

They asked if Sarah had discharged her weapon, which she had not. Brooks realized that all the gunfire had probably caused a good deal of property damage, and maybe even some injured bystanders. The locals cops would want to know whose bullets landed where. Sarah also knew that collecting a gunshot residue swab is protocol in shooting investigations. They'd have already checked her skin and clothing for invisible particles of lead, antimony and barium— blowback from a discharged firearm. She had been down that road before.

"I'm sure your people already tested me for GSR," she said. "The labs will come back negative."

They didn't acknowledge one way or another. But in addition to swabbing Sarah for gunshot residue, they had already taken her duty weapon for testing as well.

The detectives mentioned that they had been by the hospital a few times to speak with her during the weekend, but she had been unconscious. It was suddenly clear to Sarah that she had lost a couple of days. Her throat was dry and her mouth tasted like something had died in it. "Can we wrap this up? That's really all I've got."

"One last question..." The woman stood and slung her handbag onto her shoulder. "Can you think of a reason someone would go after you like they did?"

"No, nothing whatsoever." Sarah's response had come out almost too quickly. She was an aggressive agent, had investigated a lot of cases, pissed off a lot of people. That was one of the reasons she had been transferred from the field to a desk job in Oakland. And then there was the little matter of Sarah indiscriminately flipping off a line of other commuters only a few minutes prior to the shooting, but she wasn't about to volunteer that tidbit.

They stood at the foot of Sarah's bed waiting for her to elaborate, or at least shed some light on this thing that both detectives—and even Sarah—felt had been too planned, too methodical, and too aggressive to be random. It had been personal, and they all knew it.

She also knew that the detectives would have pushed a lot harder had she not been a fellow law enforcement officer. But since she wasn't talking, they were at a stalemate.

"How's Miss Brooks feeling this morning?" a cheery voice called out from the doorway.

Again Sarah leaned up. This time to see a balding man strolling into the room, wearing a pullover sweater and Dockers.

As he began typing into the rolling computer, Sarah asked, "And you are?"

The man leaned down to check Sarah's eyes with a penlight. "Dr. Sandsmark. I was head of your surgical team on Friday."

"Surgical *team*?" Sarah eased herself back into the pillow. "What the hell did I miss?"

"Only five hours of microsurgery and sixty hours of barbiturate-induced coma." The doctor nodded to the investigators, with whom he'd already spoken. "At some point during your attack, a foreign object pierced the underside of your jaw and lodged in your neck. A dangerous spot really, between a vertebral artery and your phrenic nerve."

"Shotgun pellet?" Sarah ran a hand over the gauze cravat that clenched her throat like a turtleneck sweater.

Sandsmark shook his head. "Probably not. Based on the size of the object, the detectives and I hypothesize that it was a fragment of metal from your car's doorframe."

The male detective added, "The blast sent it flying into you with so much speed and force that it might as well have been a bullet."

Sarah swallowed dryly. "How big a piece are we talking?"

"About the size of a grain of rice," said Sandsmark. "Doesn't take much penetration into the crowded neck region, even for a tiny object, to really ruin someone's day. This little thing took a *team* of neurosurgeons and a maxillofacial specialist to remove." The doctor held up a two-inch square plastic ziploc baggie containing what looked like a rusty fingernail clipping.

He handed the baggie to the woman, who placed it into an evidence envelope. She had the doctor sign the envelope, which Sarah knew was for continuity of the evidence chain should the little piece of metal ever end up in a court trial.

"Anyway," continued the doctor, "that's why we kept you quietly sedated through the weekend. Your blood needed a chance to clot around the injury, and we couldn't risk arterial or nerve damage from further movement."

"So, if it's all good now..." Sarah lifted herself to a sitting position, appearing more perky than she actually felt. "When can I leave?"

"Two or three more days of observation," said the doctor, "and you'll be as good as new. You just need to take it easy for a while." He told her to stay off work for a few weeks, get plenty of bedrest, no heavy lifting...

Blah-blah-blah. She had heard nothing other than she'd have to stay longer. "Yeah, well, I'm kind of tired here." Sarah said, holding up her hand like a white flag.

"That's probably enough for one day." Sandsmark nodded to the two detectives and they all made their way into the hall.

Tim Sanchez, Sarah's supervisor bounded through the doorway a minute later. "There she is. How's my favorite agent feeling today?"

"Like shit. And why does everyone keep talking to me in the third person?"

He started to shed his sport coat.

"Don't get too comfortable, Tim." Sarah swung her legs over the side of the bed, stretching the IV tube as far as it could reach. "You won't be staying, and for that matter, neither will I."

"Easy, girl!" Sanchez said, corralling her back into the bed. "You can't escape anyway; two police officers are posted in the hallway outside your room. A precaution, since we have no idea if this attack was random or if you were intentionally targeted."

"I'd be safer at home," said Sarah. "I'll probably die from bedsores if I stay here any longer."

"People don't get bedsores in three days." Her boss slid the chair over to her bed and sat down. "Anyway, I spoke with your doctor in the hall and he says you can go home in a couple of days."

Sarah let out an exasperated sigh.

"He said your prognosis is good," Sanchez eyed the tubes in her arm. "But I'm thinking you'll be on medical leave for a few weeks."

Sarah forced herself up again. "No freak'n way! The doc told me that I was as good as new."

Sanchez handed her a get well card signed by everyone in the office, and he told her that the director passes on his wishes for a speedy recovery.

She rolled her eyes.

Changing the subject, Sanchez inquired about a possible motive. He seemed bothered by the same peculiarities that had vexed the Oakland detectives.

The conversation had become tiresome to Sarah, and she itched to get out of there and into the office where she could take a look at her caseload. Somewhere in those files was the key to the attack on her. She felt it in her gut.

27

"Believe it or not, we can handle things without you for a while," said Sanchez.

"Tim. I'm fine."

"A few weeks off to recuperate." Sanchez grabbed his jacket. "Most agents would be trying to milk this thing for even more time. Hell, they'd be begging the doctor for a disability retirement."

Sarah hoisted the blanket up and turned away as if she was going to sleep. A few minutes later she heard Sanchez bid goodbye from the doorway.

Alone in the room again, her mind raced. Sarah's boss and her doctor's efforts to keep her off work had fomented her resolve to do just the opposite. The minute I get out of here, she thought, I'm going to figure out who did this to me and I'm going to make them pay.

Peeking over the blanket to make sure everybody had left, Sarah reached for the call button.

9

Panhandle

Lieutenant Blithe, the Park Station watch commander, was a squat woman with hair shorter than mine. Stepping away from the cops huddled around the body at the base of a Eucalyptus tree, she swaggered toward me like John Wayne.

"Tiffany Blithe." She gripped my hand and pumped it. "Got a weird one here; male white, clean-cut, thirties, business clothes, wearing a plastic mask."

"Danny McKenna," I said, finally getting my hand back. We headed over toward the tree. "Like a Halloween mask?"

She shrugged. "Shot in the back of the head." Then turned away. "Hilbert and Stanford, you two can clear. Nunzio, you and your partner stay and help McKenna. Whatever he needs, got it?"

The body wasn't in the bushes like Dowd had told me, but propped against a tree in plain view. I noticed right away that the scene looked unnatural. A tall lean guy, wearing black slacks and a white dress shirt with the sleeves rolled halfway up his forearms. No scars or tattoos that I could see. He was fit, judging from his toned arms, and his pointed loafers were the expensive kind. Everything at first glance said *Financial District,* except for the vampire mask.

Initially, I'm thinking the guy probably partied too much at last night's masquerade festival in the Castro, walked home in the dark and got robbed... No, they hadn't taken his expensive watch. And I wondered why he would still be wearing the mask. *Perhaps the killer had put it on him afterwards as a message, or maybe as some sort of ritualistic thing.*

"You let me know if you need anything," said the lieutenant as she lumbered across the grass toward her car.

She'd left the two beat cops behind to help—one with his hands in his pockets, and his partner scrolling through messages on his cell phone.

The crime scene van pulled up and two technicians began unloading their gear. One of the techs was an older black man, and the other a younger white woman—maybe about thirty. I figured that as an inspector, I'll be working with these crime scene folks a lot.

Introducing myself to them, I handed the man one of my cards. The two techs helped me ease the body forward, angling him away from the tree so we could examine the wound. Sure enough, a finger-size bullet hole at the base of his neck. I didn't see an exit wound.

The guy was stiff, a pretty good indicator that he'd been sitting there dead for several hours—maybe all night.

The location of the injury being behind him made me wonder how Lieutenant Blythe knew he had been shot. No doubt the first cops on the scene had bent the dead guy six ways to Sunday in order to find the wound, then stuffed him back into the same position thinking that whoever came to investigate wouldn't notice. *Dumbasses!*

"Any witnesses?" I asked the two cops.

The one with his hands in his pockets—an athletic looking kid with thick eyebrows—pointed to an apartment house on the other side of Oak. "Woman in unit 1-A said she thought the guy was sleeping. Seen him here since she got up this morning."

"Anyone else?"

Nunzio shook his head.

"You mean only one person notices a dead guy in a mask sitting in the middle of a park all night?"

He shrugged.

My guess was that Nunzio and his sidekick had done a half-assed witness search. "Never mind," I said. "I'll check for myself."

I bummed a pair of latex gloves from the crime scene gal—*C. Barnard*, it said on her nametag—and then I rolled the stiff onto his side. Working my hand along the rear of his slacks, I felt both back pockets and then patted around to the front. "No wallet, no keys, nothing," I said. "Not even a phone."

The other patrolman glanced up from his texts and shook his head; as if a stolen cell phone was a fate worse than the bullet.

"News people will be here soon," I told the cops. "Block off this whole section of the park with tape and then start a crime scene log. When the techs finish taking photos, cover the guy up with a tarp."

San Francisco's Panhandle is an eight by one-block greenway that precedes the city's Golden Gate Park. The body was a short distance from a paved path that ran the length of the park, clearly visible to anybody who cared enough to notice. The scene was directly across from the Vista View Apartments on Oak Street, which I could see from where I stood.

Mrs. Furtado in 1-A cracked the door open and glared at me through the security chain. In a Portuguese accent, she said, "I told the nine-one-one people that I didn't want to be contacted. The other policeman already came here, and I told him the same thing." She waved an angry hand in the air. "When I called, I told them, I said, 'don't send anybody to my apartment!' That's what I told them."

"Sorry about that ma'am." I lifted my lapel. "I'm not in uniform, so I'm sure that nobody noticed me coming to your door. If that's what you're worried about."

"What about him?"

I glanced behind me. "Who?"

"The homeless man under the tree. What if he comes after me for reporting him?"

"I guarantee he won't."

With her hands on her hips, the woman asked, "And exactly how would you know that?"

"Because he's dead, ma'am." She sucked in a gulp of air, and before she let it out I asked, "Did you hear any gunshots during the night?"

More fearful now, Mrs. Furtado pinched the door tighter. The space was so narrow that I only saw one eye and half of her wrinkled lips. "No. No gunshots. And if you ask me any more questions, I'll take the fifth. I have nothing more to say."

"Take the fifth," I repeated as the door closed in my face. I heard a series of locks and bolts turning, and I laughed at her response all the way down the steps.

While walking east, I assessed the angles and views into the Panhandle from other residences along Oak. A half block farther, almost to the corner of Ashbury, I spotted a small security camera above another apartment house doorway. I couldn't determine from the position of the lens whether its field of view included my crime scene.

The apartment manager was a string bean of a guy with Bob Dylan hair and thin round eyeglasses. He smelled like he'd just pulled his head out of a bong, but I pretended not to notice.

He seemed a little jumpy, almost overly helpful, and I guessed it was probably lingering unease from when pot used to be illegal. The guy said he had installed the camera after a couple of tenants' cars had been broken into, but since then he'd had no problems. Usually only turns it on at night, he said, and then erases and reuses the disks every other day. Meaning, he still had the previous night's recording—which he readily handed over to me.

I knocked on several other doors, but either nobody was home or they didn't answer. Only one tenant buzzed me in, a muni bus driver who worked nights and had just arrived home. Poor guy had been asleep—which I felt badly about, having worked my share of night shifts. In any case, he hadn't seen or heard anything.

By the time I got back to the scene, the ME was loading up the body and Nunzio and his partner were wadding the tape into a big yellow ball. One of the techs took wide angle photographs of the scene while the other measured for a to-scale schematic.

I waited around a few minutes to examine the dirt where the guy had been, just in case they had missed something.

The crime scene techs finally finished, and as the male half of the team carried the camera case to the van, I watched as the woman bent over for her tripod. She smiled and asked if I needed anything else.

"No, not at the moment. But thanks." I had resisted starting some lame banter, but she had seemed so friendly that I guess I gave in. "So, what does the C stand for, Ms. Barnard?"

Her eyebrow arched as she followed my line of sight to her nametag. "Chloe." She collapsed the leg of the tripod with a loud snap.

Embarrassed, I took the notepad from my pocket. "Okay thanks. Just needed it for my report."

"If there's nothing else, then..." And off she went.

So much for my pathetic attempt at flirtation. I might as well have asked if she comes here often.

It's not like I would have done anything, even if she had shown an interest. But for a broken down ex-football player with a bad knee and a few extra pounds, a little boost to the old ego would have definitely gone into my day's plus column.

An unmarked car pulled to the curb just as I was starting for mine. Alan Lam and Frankie Moretti, back from their parole hearing at San Quentin. "Captain sent us out to give you a hand," said Moretti. "I think he wants us to take over the case."

They had softened to me a bit in the short time I'd been in the detail, and I'd found that they were both okay guys. Though I still wasn't about to give up my first case so easily.

"I got it, seriously. Not a problem."

They looked at each other, probably weighing the captain's directive against the workload already on their plates.

"Besides," I continued. "Cassidy will be back in the office tomorrow. So, no worries. We have definitely got this." That last part was an exaggeration; in reality, I had no idea when my partner would return. Then I changed the subject—described the scene, the victim's wound, and the lack of decent witnesses.

32

Lam listened, but Moretti looked distracted—probably thinking about the lunch they were about to grab when Dowd sent them to babysit me. As I spoke, I found myself eyeing the row of cars parked along the curb.

"Most likely a robbery," Moretti said. "Had a shooting like this on the other side of the park a couple of weeks ago. Perp stole the vic's wallet and keys."

Morning gridlock had mostly cleared, but the one-way traffic on Oak was still slow all the way to Stanyan. Something nagged at me about the column of cars parked bumper-to-bumper along the panhandle side of the street.

Nunzio and his partner walked past, nodding their *see-ya-laters* as they headed to their cruiser.

"Hey," I called out to them. "When do they sweep the streets out here?"

The two uniforms looked at each other for a second, then back at me. Nunzio scratched his head, as if he thought I was going to have him do it. "Mondays on this part of Oak," he said. "They were out here already this morning." Both of them hustled to their car and drove off before I could figure out exactly what else I needed.

Moretti and Lam saw where I was going with it. "You're thinking that your vic's car might still be parked somewhere along Oak," said Moretti.

"And if it was there last night," Lam finished the thought, "It would have been ticketed because of the street cleaning. We'll go have a look-see."

About fifteen minutes later I saw Lam making his way across the grass with Moretti huffing and puffing behind him. "Bingo!" yelled Moretti, holding up a ring of keys.

Lam finished for his partner. "Silver Ford Focus, parked at Oak and Clayton. Keys still in the ignition and a parking ticket on the window—issued at 4:49 a.m."

I pumped my fist. "Nice!"

"Only thing is, the car is a rental," said Moretti. "Budget out of the Oakland Airport." He handed me an envelope full of papers. "Rental agreement was in the glovebox."

I opened it, and without my readers I had to hold the papers a foot or so in front of me. According to the contract, a man named Elvis Lang had rented the car.

Lam said, "You've got things to do. We can standby for the tow truck."

33

"After that I'm sitting down to some minestrone at Scala's!" Moretti glared at Lam, then shooed me on my way. "Go ahead, McKenna. We'll handle the impound for ya."

It was a big help. Now that I had a name to work with, maybe even the identity of my victim, I could actually start investigating. *But could I even trust Moretti and Lam?*

I wished that Chief Fahey had never put the thought into my head.

10

Palace Hotel, San Francisco

Everybody in the lobby had been talking about the playoff game, in which, by the 8th inning, the Giants were still tied. Curtis Tam watched for a few minutes in his room as he waited on the line for an international satellite connection, wondering if American baseball would ever develop a real following in his country.

He had changed hotels earlier that day—a habit he'd acquired during years of counter-surveillance operations. Since witnessing the Golden Gate Park shootout 16 hours earlier, he was determined not to let the predator become the prey.

After another series of buzzing transfers, a woman's voice came on the line: "Patching over now... Go ahead for Sergei Petrenko."

Tam had to holler over the background clamor in order to be heard. "Mr. Petrenko, it's Curtis Tam."

"Apologize for the bad connection Tam, but I'm on the helo and we're about to land in Cádiz. What have you got for me?"

"Another shooting, I'm afraid. Two men I was following—both, I believe, are connected to the stolen container--"

"Containers," interrupted Petrenko. "Two more have gone missing. The company's customs broker notified me last night. It brings the total to twenty-four of *my* shipments now gone, vanished somewhere between Rega and the United States. That's one hundred seventy-five-million-ruble worth of Vodka, Tam."

"Do we have any idea where the switches are being made?" Tam was referring to the digitized tracking numbers—which he had long ago concluded were being altered at some point during their journeys.

"Somewhere out there upon the high seas," Petrenko said with Steinbeckesque flair. "Menshikov and his puppet Privy Council! The more I think about it, I wouldn't be surprised if they actually are behind this whole thing. You know, Moscow is still scrapping and fighting me in the courts like a bunch of alley cats."

Tam had read his client's background information, including an abridged history of the discord between the Russian government and Petrenko's company. Moscow's political landscape was still as much of an enigma to Tam as was the company's disputed ownership—which apparently dated back to the 1991 collapse of the Soviet Union.

"I'm changing shipping companies soon." The clink of ice cubes sounded on the other end of the line, which made clear to Tam the source of Petrenko's dramatics. "One with tracking devices on *all* of their containers."

"I assume you still want me to continue here?"

"Yes, yes, stay on it," said Petrenko. "Both of these newly stolen shipments had been destined to stop at the Port of Manzanillo in Mexico, but they never made it."

"When were they supposed to arrive?" Tam took a pen and notepad from the nightstand.

Petrenko repeated the question to someone who was present with him, then came back on the line. "Saturday, your time. Our records show they'd been loaded onto the MS Versand eight weeks ago—a Liberian registered, German owned freighter."

Tam made note of the registry information and shipping dates.

A momentary silence was broken by Petrenko. "More gunplay, you say?"

Tam proceeded to tell Petrenko the story of the early morning shooting he'd witnessed in Golden Gate Park's Panhandle.

"Definitely stay on it, Tam." Petrenko sounded like a kid playing a video game—less concerned with his million ruble losses, and more excited about getting to the game's next level. "We've got to find out who's behind this, but again, my reputation will be tarnished if it ever gets out that you're working for me."

"Not to worry, sir." Tam finished the thought for Petrenko. "I'll remain behind the scenes and your name will never be connected."

"So what's our next move?"

Tam glanced at his case notes. "I need to find out how this scam works. Presumably, these cargo containers were being logged by the shipping company. At least up until the time they went missing. I'll do some more research and see if I can't get a better handle on that."

"Good, good." Another clink of ice cubes. "Keep me posted, Tam." And the line went dead.

Tam hadn't had a chance to mention his intention to travel to Manzanillo and interview the port security people. He had always suspected that the thieves had changed the freight's ten-digit identification numbers during transit, diverting the containers from their scheduled destinations.

As he sat staring at his notes, a new logic teased at him. It finally crystalized into an idea so obvious that Tam was angry he hadn't figured it out sooner. Assuming that the people connected to the San Francisco warehouse had simply bought the cargo from a ring of smugglers, Tam had never considered that *they* were actually the architects of the scheme. He suddenly realized that the containers may not have even left the ship in Manzanillo. Why had he assumed they would? Once the tracking numbers were altered, the cargo could have easily been rerouted to the San Francisco Bay Area.

Tam pulled up an international marine traffic site on his laptop. From there he was able to map the MS Versand's location in real time, in addition to its scheduled route and speed.

"I'll be damned." Tam sat back with a satisfied smile as he watched the blinking icon on the map. At that moment the vessel was steaming up Mexico's west coast toward its next port of call: Oakland, California.

11

Forensic Video Analysis Unit

I stopped downstairs at Forensic Services, first thing Tuesday morning. They were working on the security camera footage, preserving the disk to a readable format. For me it was a high priority job, because, at the moment, it was one of only two leads.

My first call was to Budget Car Rentals, but they wouldn't provide much information over the phone—only a confirmation of the renter's name: Elvis Lang, and a home address in the Tenderloin. They said I'd need to obtain a court order to get Lang's credit card information.

My victim's autopsy was scheduled for 9 a.m., and as the lead investigator, I needed to be present. Gathering my notes, I was just about to head over to the ME's office when Mrs. Ocampo handed me a phone message. The medical examiner had called to ask why I wanted to postpone the postmortem examination until tomorrow.

"What's this about?" I said to the secretary. "I never asked the ME to postpone it."

Her eyes wavered in the direction of Captain Dowd's office, but she said nothing.

I walked in and set the note in front of the captain. He glanced up at me as I held my hands apart in a questioning manner.

"Cassidy is out sick again today," he said.

"And?"

"And, you're not attending the post by yourself." Dowd went back to his paperwork, but I remained standing in front of his desk. Finally, he sighed and looked up. "Listen McKenna, I told you yesterday that you're going to need help on this. It's only your first stiff."

The captain was way overreaching, and his logic made no sense. I'd planned to witness the autopsy and take a few notes, nothing more. I couldn't see how Lou being with me would make any difference, whatsoever. Besides, I was already ninety-nine percent certain of how the victim died; what I really needed to know was his identity.

I calmly laid out my argument against postponing the autopsy, and to my credit I did it without calling Dowd a useless waste of skin. "Without a name, my investigation flounders," I said.

He smirked at the reference to *my investigation*. Now he gazed at the ceiling as if searching for patience. "Again," he said, "One more day isn't going to make any difference. Let me distill this down to something you can understand..." Dowd articulated each word as if speaking to 5-year-old. "I'm the captain and you're the rookie inspector—*provisional,* at that. It's my call, and you *will* wait until Cassidy gets back. Understood?"

Thirty minutes later I was still chaffing.

A clerk, whom I'd asked earlier to run a records check for me, now stood in front of my desk holding a printout. "Your guy, Elvis Lang," she said. "The Tenderloin address he listed is no good; it's an empty lot. But, I found a previous contact in our records from six months ago—an arrest for indecent exposure."

I felt my face twist into a knot. "Indecent exposure."

"At least it's something." She handed me the printout, promising to track down the arrest file. But when I got back from lunch, the clerk still hadn't found it. She had left a note on my desk saying that the digitally scanned file was not in the database. The note also said that she was going off duty, but that she would leave instructions to the swing shift supervisor to locate the original hard copy of the report.

I spent the rest of the afternoon on the computer, trying to find what I could about this guy who had rented the car we'd towed from the crime scene. He had one arrest for indecent exposure six months ago, and his driver's license had been issued only two years prior. With a bad address and no history to speak of, it seemed as if Elvis Lang had simply dropped out of the sky two years ago.

The other inspectors were gone, and when one of the night clerks tapped tentatively on the doorjamb, I realized that I'd lost track of time. I motioned her inside and she handed me a folder containing the entire Elvis Lang indecent exposure arrest report. When she left, I slipped on my readers and opened the folder to a photo clipped onto the first page. Lang's ruddy face and bloodshot eyes stared back at me. He looked nothing like my buttoned-down financial district victim, which made me wonder if he and his rental car were red herrings.

Lang had been arrested with a woman in the back of a Dodge Caravan with expired license plate tags. A quick computer check told me that the car they were in was never registered to Lang, and that it had since been junked.

My desk phone rang, the screen flashing my home number. "Hey Doris."

"Do you know it's 9:45 p.m. at night?"

"Yeah." I thought about reminding Doris that p.m. usually means evening, but thought better of it. Instead, I asked, "What's up?"

She sighed. "You're still working?"

I glared into the phone. "*You* called *me* at my office number, so, yes, I'm still working."

"Do you realize that you completely forgot Bridget's orthodontist appointment? You were supposed to take her after fifth period today."

"Uh, oh yeah. Sorry about that." And I really was. My mind had been on work, and I had totally forgotten about the appointment. Bridget was in the final stages of two miserable years of wearing braces, and I had promised to drive her into the city for her appointment. Sometimes I forget that these things are a huge deal to a thirteen-year-old. "Tell Bridge I'll make it up to her."

"Sure. That'll fix it." Doris let out a sigh.

I looked around the empty room, making sure that nobody had come in. "Listen, Doris, Lou Cassidy is out sick and the captain has been depending on me to pick up the slack around here. It's an opportunity for me to... Anyway, I caught a case yesterday and it's a big one."

"Whatever." Doris hung up, clearly unmoved.

I wanted to slam the phone down but didn't have the energy. Instead, I picked up the case file on Elvis Lang, and stared at the pudgy, potato faced guy with squinty eyes. I knew Lang was not my victim, but I was working on the hunch that he may have been with my victim in the rental car—maybe even drove my victim to the scene. I mean, why else would the car be parked adjacent to the crime scene with the keys still in the ignition? But without a legitimate address for this Elvis guy, I had to focus on his prior arrest.

As I read through the file, I saw that the indecent exposure charge wasn't the Pee-wee Herman kind of thing I had imagined. Lang had been busted in the middle of screwing a prostitute in the back of the Dodge. Of course, neither of the participants admitted that it was sex-for-money. So, with only two half-naked people in the car and no evidence of a *solicitation,* the cop had to settle for a misdemeanor indecent exposure arrest. Unfortunately for me, the DA never filed formal charges. Dropped the whole thing. The good news, if there was any, was that the hooker had also been arrested and her information was listed in the report as well.

Sha Nay Nay Moore was a name I could never forget, though I had given it a good try. A skinny crack whore when I first dealt with her five years earlier, she used to turn tricks out in the Bayview. All of the street cops in Hunter's Point had run-ins with Sha Nay Nay at one time or another in those days. She was probably seventeen then, so I guessed she was in her mid-twenties when her name came up again in my homicide case.

12

U.S. Customs and Border Protection
Port of Oakland

Sarah felt helpless without her duty firearm, but she knew the feeling would be short lived. She had a back-up at the office.

The duty nurse had called the charge nurse, who had called Dr. Sandsmark—all of whom warned Sarah not to leave the hospital against medical advice. But she had already lost too much time, and her mind was made up not to stay another night. Having scribbled her signature onto the AMA discharge form, Sarah Brooks walked straight past the two uniformed cops and out of the building. That was Monday afternoon.

She'd been patient, waited all of the following day until after everyone had left the Maritime Street office. Now inside, Sarah peeked out the window to make sure she hadn't been seen. Her neck was still sore, and its heavy gauze dressing made it that much more uncomfortable. She would remind herself later to toss the whole contraption.

Flipping on the light, Sarah unlocked her bottom desk drawer and removed a Walther PPK. It held a .380 round, which was essentially a shortened 9mm bullet with less velocity and knockdown power. Her Walther wasn't as effective as her duty weapon, but it was definitely more protection than she'd left the hospital with.

Tucking the handgun into her purse, Sarah lowered the louvered blinds to contain the light. The former file room had been made into an office to accommodate her disciplinary reassignment. Though it had not been called a *punitive transfer*, Sarah had been pulled out of the San Diego field office and placed behind a desk at the Port of Oakland. *Agent Brooks is bellicose, antagonistic, and inimical,* stated her disciplinary report. And the district director had made it clear that the Port of Oakland was the last chance for Sarah. Next stop would be the unemployment line.

Sarah's current cases stood in a vertical file organizer atop her desk. Spreading them out in front of her, she tried to recall the details of each. There were seven cases in all; two closed, four open, and one that had been handed off to the SF office as part of a larger, already ongoing investigation of theirs.

At 2:30 a.m. Sarah checked her watch and poured another cup of coffee. She had read through all of the cases, hoping that the motive for the attempt on her life would have become obvious. But nothing certain had materialized. Sarah had only managed to separate them into three piles: *probable, possible*, and *definitely not*.

The four *definitely not* files included the investigation she had already handed off to headquarters; two other closed case files, the defendants in which had since been deported; and a fourth case of a merchant seaman who had smuggled a suitcase full of cocaine off of a cargo ship, and who was now serving a prison sentence.

Only one case file was in Sarah's *possible* category—a shipping container full of liquor that had been flagged for secondary follow-up inspection.

The final two investigations seemed most likely, and were in the *probable* stack. Both of them appeared serious and far-reaching enough to provoke violence. One of these involved the smuggling of technology workers on H-1B visas from India, and the other was a ring of seafood distributers importing illegal shark fins in refrigerated shipping containers.

Sarah sat staring at the files, wondering if her hunch was wrong and the attack on her was the result of something that had long since dropped off of her radar. Even the possibility that the shooting had been completely unrelated to her government work.

The sound of the keypad buttons being pushed outside echoed in the quiet office. Someone was coming into the building, which gave Sarah only seconds to act. She quickly swept the three most probable case files into her desk drawer, then closed and locked it just as the office door swung open. There stood her supervisor, head tilted and an exasperated expression on his face.

"Tim," Sarah said with a casual nod. "Early start this morning?"

"Not funny, Brooks." Sanchez closed the distance to her desk, eyeing the four files she'd left there. "The hospital notified me that you had absconded."

"I didn't *abscond*, and I don't owe anybody an explanation. It's my life, my health, and my decision. And I'm not staying in the hospital when I feel perfectly fine!"

He glared at her. "Be that as it may, this is still *my* office and you still work for me. And it's my decision that you *will* be taking time off to recuperate. That means you will *not* be allowed to come into the office until such time as you are cleared to do so by the doctor."

"Is this a suspension, Tim?"

"Not yet, but you're definitely pushing it in that direction." He snatched the four files from her desk. "I know what you're trying to do here, and it's not going to fly. Not on my watch. These cases are not your personal property; they belong to the federal government. And this shooting will not become your personal vendetta."

"I have no idea what you're talking about." Sarah slipped the holstered firearm out of her shoulder bag to show him. "The OPD took my duty weapon for testing or evidence, or whatever. And with an attempt having just been made on my life and all..."

"Show me what else you got in there," he said. "Any more files?"

Sarah held her bag open for him.

Satisfied that she had no other files, the stiffness drained from Sanchez's stance. Nodding slowly, he said, "Look, Brooks, I know you've been through a lot. I'm just trying to do what's best for you; not just because of your injury, but I'm also trying to protect you from yourself. You've already got one foot out the door and the other on a banana peel. One more screw-up and there'll be nothing I can do for you."

"Yeah, I get it, Tim." Sarah's eyes rolled toward the ceiling as she took in a long breath. "I know you're trying to help, and I appreciate it. I do. The only reason I came in here was to pick up my off-duty weapon. I'd like to have some protection at home." She smiled. "While I'm off *recuperating.*"

Sanchez returned the sarcastic grin. "Well, just in case..." He held up the files. "I'm hanging onto these. And I'm suspending your police powers until further notice. In other words, you have no authority to investigate anything."

"Like I told you, Tim. I Just stopped by to grab my weapon."

Sarah had hoped Sanchez would leave first, so she could retrieve the pertinent files she'd hidden in her desk drawer. But her boss still suspected that she was up to something.

Standing beside the doorway, he motioned toward it like a game show host. "So, now that you're armed, don't let the door hit you in the ass on your way out. Until further notice, you are prohibited from accessing this office."

Sarah stood, slung her bag onto her shoulder and headed for the door. "Got it," she said with a mock salute.

Sitting outside in the dark parking lot, Sarah slammed her fist against the dashboard. The files that Sanchez had taken from her were insignificant—closed and in the *definitely not* group. They didn't matter to her. But the three still sitting inside Sarah's locked desk were crucial.

One way or another, she had to get those files.

13

Homicide Detail

I pulled into the parking structure the next morning feeling like I had never left. I'd woken at 5 a.m. to find myself still on the recliner in front of the Weather Channel, the deep Scotch I'd poured for myself pounding in my head. I showered in the guest bathroom and left the house before Doris or Bridge got up.

Lou Cassidy glanced up from his newspaper as I walked in, and bellowed, "Danny Boy!"

I nodded, which only increased the pounding in my head.

"*You* look like *I* could use a drink!" He laughed as he put down the paper. "I hear we caught one in the park the other day. Some kind of Phantom of the Opera thing? How'd you manage without me?"

"Already cleared the case," I lied. "Since I didn't have to stop a dozen times for you to piss, the investigation was a piece of cake."

Cassidy howled so hard that he nearly spilled his coffee. He tossed me the part of the paper he'd already looked at, then continued reading.

On the front page was a follow-up article about a federal agent who had been shot in Oakland. I found my case on the third page: No ID ON GOLDEN GATE PARK SHOOTING VICTIM.

The story contained basic facts that anyone passing by the crime scene might figure out, but not much more. There was a quote about the decline of the neighborhood from Mrs. Furtado—the old lady who had taken *the fifth*—and another attributed to Captain Dowd. He had claimed that "*we*" were "pulling out all the stops to solve the case."

What a crock of shit. I wanted to cut out the article and leave it on his desk, along with yesterday's message about postponing the autopsy. But Dowd would probably miss the whole point.

"Climate change," Cassidy suddenly said out of nowhere. "People have got to be real idiots to believe that bullshit. Clearly, it's the Lowe's and the Home Depot stores behind it."

I lowered my section of the paper. "The Home Depot stores."

"Of course! Bastards made the whole thing up just so they can sell more heaters and air conditioners."

He watched my eyes roll. "I'm shit'n ya, kid." He barked out another hoarse laugh. "Now tell me about our case."

Overlooking the "*our* case" part of his question, and the fact that I'm thirty-seven years old and Cassidy still calls me "kid," I ran everything down to him. He nodded a few times, not seeming all that excited about any of it, though he did scribble a few notes.

"Probably a robbery gone bad," he said at the end. "Spaghetti and Rice caught a case like that a couple of weeks ago."

"Yeah, I was there. The woman found dead in the Prius." I grabbed my empty mug. "What's happened on that case, anyway?"

"What, the robbery?" Cassidy was still behind his paper. "The victim's still dead."

I forced an obligatory chuckle. "Did it turn out to be a domestic thing?"

"Nope, just random robbery."

"Random..." I stared out the window. "Then why shoot her?"

"If we knew that, we'd have caught the assholes."

"No, I mean...*why?* Why would they need to do that?"

Cassidy shrugged behind his paper. I didn't bother arguing my point any further. Then again, maybe the girl *was* robbed. For that matter, maybe my guy was too. Even though the rental car thing didn't fit with the robbery, I had to admit that we still hadn't even tied the rented car to my victim. In fact, we still didn't even know my victim's identity.

"The post on my case is scheduled for 9 a.m.," I said. "Dowd had it postponed until you got back."

Cassidy frowned and shook his head before going back to the newspaper. A stronger reaction would have validated my own anger, but, whatever.

At a quarter to nine, we took the elevator to the first floor, walked out the back door, and across the north terrace to the medical examiner's office.

They had already swabbed the victim's hands for gunshot residue, clipped his fingernails for traces of the suspect's DNA, and inked his fingers and palms for a full set of prints. It was weird enough for me coming to these autopsies, bodies all around the room, splayed out naked on metal tables. But to see one of them wearing nothing but a vampire mask was beyond bizarre.

47

The ME finally snipped the elastic string that held the mask in place, and for the first time I was able to see my victim's face. He was a trendy looking man, short black hair combed back, and angular features that gave him a bit of a slippery look.

The postmortem itself revealed nothing new. The guy had been shot at fairly close range, disintegrating his C3 vertebra and splintering the projectile into three pieces. The combined weight of the fragments, which had been contained within the spine, jaw and chest cavity, suggested that our guy had been hit with a 115 grain bullet—probably a nine.

"How close was the shooter?" I asked the ME.

"Close," she said, indicating a circular smoke-colored burn around the frayed entry wound. "Probably within inches."

I saw Cassidy's eyebrows inch upward. Just like me, he had assumed the shot had been taken from a distance, maybe as the victim was running away. But with evidence of a close quarters gunshot from behind, it was starting to look like an execution. *Then what? The suspect propped the body against a tree, then just for kicks put a Dracula mask over the dead guy's face?* Nothing about this case made any sense.

The ME had run the victim's prints over the statewide computer system, and by the end of the postmortem a hit had already come back. She stood under one of the hanging lamps, reading from the single sheet of paper. At one point she rested it on the cadaver's gray scrotum while she removed her gloves.

"Interesting," she finally said, glancing up at me and Cassidy. "The hit we got on this guy is from back in 2011—your victim was fingerprinted for employment purposes."

"Cop?" Cassidy asked.

The ME shook her head and handed me the sheet. "Worked for a liquor distribution company. The ID hit came from Alcohol Beverage Control."

"Gustavs Berzins." I looked from the sheet of paper to the guy on the table. "What kind of name is that?"

Cassidy shrugged.

"Sounds German to me," said the ME.

"Can you give me a time of death?" I asked.

She glanced at a pathology formula on her clipboard. "Liver temp when he arrived here at 10:30 *Monday* morning was 27 degrees centigrade." She had emphasized the word *Monday*, which I figured meant she was pissed off at having to wait an extra day to do the exam. I'm sure she chalked it up to my inexperience, which irritated me even more.

"Assuming a normal body temp of 37.5 at time of death," The ME continued, "and a cooling rate of 1.5 degrees per hour..." She ticked seven fingers. "You're looking at somewhere around 3 a.m., give or take."

I thanked her, and me and Cassidy headed back up to the office.

"Ready for lunch?" Cassidy asked as he thumbed through his messages. "I'm in the mood for German."

My mind went to the image of Gustavs Berzins's wormy intestines and burgundy-colored organs, yanked out, slapped on a tray and weighed like chuck roast at the butcher's counter. "I'll pass."

Cassidy let out another belly laugh as he grabbed his coat and the car keys.

While he was out eating, I spent some time on the internet but found nothing on Gustavs Berzins. I did learn that the surname actually has Germanic roots, according to an ancestry research site. And when written using the correct orthographic alphabet, the name Bērziņš turns out to be the most common surname in the country of Latvia. I had to look up Latvia on Google maps just to see where it was.

The liquor distributor my victim had worked for was across the bay in Hayward, but their phone number was no longer in service. The lack of information on the web made me think that it was probably a front or a shell company.

For the hell of it, I decided to run a check on Sha Nay Nay, the prostitute that had been arrested with the car rental guy. Our system listed dozens of arrests—which I already knew—but nothing since she was busted in the buff with Elvis Lang. It also showed that she still lived in the housing projects out on Reardon.

Night had fallen and most of the other inspectors had left. A few, like me, were sticking around to do some after-hours work. Cassidy was typing some case notes on his desktop.

"Hey, Lou," I said. "Want to take a run out to Hunter's Point with me?"

Cassidy suppressed a belch and unfastened his belt clasp. "Okay, but why are we spinning our wheels over this rental car guy? He might be some innocent schmuck with a couple of DUIs, who left his car parked on Oak while he took a cab home."

My head tilted to his point. Granted, the car wasn't much of a lead, and the car renter's prostitute was even farther afield. But it was all I had to go on.

49

"I really gotta hit the head first." Cassidy grabbed the newspaper he'd already read cover-to-cover, and thirty-five minutes later he emerged from the restroom—pants buckled and ready to go.

We pulled out of the underground parking garage and headed toward Sha Nay Nay's old address in Hunter's Point.

14

North America 3PL
Port of Oakland

It was after eight o'clock in the morning when Curtis Tam parked against the cyclone fence at 20th and Wood Streets. The area beyond it was a flat industrial landscape punctuated by warehouses and abandoned cargo trailers. From his parking spot, Tam could view the entire inspection facility.

Tam had learned that North America 3PL was the centralized station used by Customs and Border Protection to conduct secondary examinations of suspicious cargo. It made sense that freight with inaccurate manifests or discrepant broker/importer entries would draw the attention of the CBP—particularly shipments containing liquor. In the case of Petrenko's hijacked containers, Tam was betting that they would end up there.

The MS Versand was scheduled for a midday arrival at TraPac terminal B-30. Tam had noted six big rigs lined up along 7th street, waiting to clear the terminal's security booth. Safety measures appeared tight, and he saw no other roads or access points onto the dock.

Resigned to stay parked on the public street, Tam spent the morning watching a women's soccer game at an adjacent sports park and reading a newspaper he'd picked up in his hotel lobby. The story about the Rhonda Pitts murder had all but dropped off the media's radar—replaced by the shooting of a federal agent. On the third page, Tam found a small article about the murder he had witnessed in the Panhandle. Still, no identification of that victim had been released to the press.

By late afternoon, the sports park had emptied and a cool wind had kicked up. Tam's computer mapping program still showed the MS Versand in a stationary anchorage in the North Bay—positioned somewhere between Point Richmond and Tiburon.

In the draining daylight, Tam watched a catering truck pull into the parking lot of a shipping company a block away. It seemed a good time for him to take a badly needed break. After getting something to eat and using the park's restroom, Tam returned to his car and continued watching the inspection facility.

Two leathery skinned men walked past him, and something about the way the men carried themselves—fatigued, yet upright, broad shouldered and unafraid—implied dock work.

"Gentlemen," Tam called out as he stepped from his car. "Do you have a moment?"

The two men glanced at one another then back at Tam. Their brown arms were heavily tattooed and both of their brows bore soiled bandannas.

"I'm guessing you're stevedores at the dock, is that correct?"

"Longshoremen," one said with a slight South American accent.

"Local 91," said the other. "Why?"

Tam explained that he was awaiting the arrival of a friend, a merchant seaman, traveling on the MS Versand.

They shrugged.

"It was supposed to dock earlier today, but it's apparently still anchored in the bay."

Again they shrugged. Then, finally, one of them volunteered, "Happens all the time. Sometimes no deep draft terminals are open, or maybe the paperwork is jacked up."

"How long do the ships usually stay parked out there?"

The one with the accent said, "Not much long. We go on strike last year for five weeks, and many ships stuck out there. But now, not so much."

The other guy chimed in again, "A few hours, maybe overnight, but usually not longer." Abruptly turning away, they continued toward the West Oakland transit station.

Another hour passed and the cargo ship hadn't moved. Tam debated whether or not to return to his hotel in San Francisco for the night, then decided to make contact at the inspection facility since he was already there.

Darkness had fallen and huge halogen lights illuminated the exterior of the huge building. There was no longer a line of vehicles waiting to enter, so Tam started up the driveway in his rental car. At the security kiosk, two officers manning the gate seemed indifferent to the private investigator and were reluctant to answer questions about the MS Versand. They certainly weren't about to allow him onto the facility's grounds.

"We're a private company contracted and approved by Customs and Border Protection," said one of the guards—a middle-aged guy with thick eyeglasses. "We facilitate the pick-up and inspection of cargo flagged for secondary inspections. Meaning, we deal with companies and cargo—usually after an x-ray at the dock has turned up something questionable. It doesn't necessarily mean they're guilty of any wrongdoing."

The other guard—a dark haired guy with intense eyes—suddenly leaned across his partner and came halfway out the kiosk window. "Which also means they have a right to confidentiality!"

Tam raised his hands. "Hey, I totally get it. I'm not asking you to violate anyone's trust. Just have a couple of *hypothetical* questions."

Neither responded.

"What if a container full of liquor came off of a ship? Would that automatically require a secondary inspection?"

"Depends," answered the first guard. "Importation of alcoholic beverages is a sticky wicket." The man sat back, interlacing his fingers across his chest. "You got your Alcohol and Tobacco Tax and Trade Bureau. Then there's an importer's basic permit, and you gotta get a Certificate of Label Approval." The guard took a breath. "Also, you got your federal excise tax, on top of whatever CBP charges to inspect your cargo."

Tam continued, "So, if one of these containers was stolen—"

"Intermodal."

"How's that?" Tam leaned further out his car window.

"*Intermodal* containers, we call them." The guy glanced toward the building. "Look, I probably shouldn't even be talking to you. If you have any more questions, you'll have to take them up with the federal guys."

"Can you let me in, just to talk to one of the inspectors?"

The guard stood fast. "Nope. Not gonna happen. B'sides, these are just the uniformed enforcement people here."

"Great, thanks." Tam started to raise his window when the guy motioned to him.

"One more thing," said the guard. "We're not the only centralized examination station for freight coming into Oakland."

Tam's shoulders dropped.

"We're the only one located directly adjacent to the port," he said. But there's actually another CBP inspection facility over on Mariner Square Loop in Alameda." He motioned in a northerly direction. "Anyways, you should really be talking to a CBP investigator."

Tam took a breath, trying not to show his impatience. "And where might I find them?"

"They got an office across the freeway, on Maritime Street."

Tam checked his watch. It was quarter of eight, and commercial traffic in the area had dwindled to a trickle. He'd be lucky to find anyone still around at this time of night.

15

Reardon Heights

Memories flooded back as we drove into the projects; the trash, the abandoned cars leaking oil, the dirt brown rows of dilapidated buildings—all with security bars covering their windows.

The Heights overlooked the shipyard and the old Candlestick stadium—flattened to the ground now, and turned into a hodgepodge of retail and housing. Yet another change in this city that I've never quite been able to wrap my head around.

Anyway, I also remembered the shabby apartment where Sha Nay Nay used to stay.

An old woman came to the door of #104, her sparse gray hair knitted into tiny twigs that contrasted against her ebony skin. She tugged a small green oxygen tank behind her, sucking from a hose tethered to her smock. "Hep ya?"

We introduced ourselves and asked if Sha Nay Nay Moore still lived there.

"She my granddaughter." The woman paused to catch her breath after the trek to the door. "What's that child gone and done now?"

"Nothing that I know of," I said. "We'd just like to talk to her about something that happened awhile back." I assured the woman that her granddaughter wasn't in any trouble.

"Well, Nay-Nay not here. Ain't seen or heard from the girl in over a week."

"Does she stay away like that often?" I asked.

Cassidy mumbled under his breath, "Does the Pope shit in the woods?"

The old woman stood expressionless in the doorway.

I glanced past her into the apartment. It was tidy, and other than the sound of her TV, the place was quiet and appeared empty.

"What about the girl's mother?"

The woman shook her head. "Her mama don't come 'round. She in jail, anyway."

From the way the grandmother spoke, I couldn't tell if we were talking about her daughter or daughter-in-law. Not that it mattered. I wrote my cell number on the back of my card and handed it to her. "Please have Sha Nay Nay call me when you see her again."

The grandmother looked at the card and closed the door without responding. Not angry or rude, but almost as if there was a kink in her air hose and she barely had enough energy to make it back to the couch.

"That was a fucking waste," said Cassidy.

I switched my cell phone back on as we got back into the car, and I noticed a missed call from Doris. I shoved the phone back in my pocket.

"You can just switch the ringer to silent," said Lou, holding his phone under the light. "Got all sorts of bells and whistles; flashlight, camera, video, voice recorder, you name it."

I said, "You sound like my daughter."

"And I got apps," he said. "Tons of apps. You got apps, McKenna?"

"Yeah, I got an app."

"One measly app?"

"Affirmative," I said. "It's called Police Scanner 9-1-1."

Cassidy nearly choked on his toothpick.

I was in deep thought about the case as we continued over the hill on De Haro, and I hadn't noticed that Cassidy wasn't saying much. He finally let out a grunt and shifted in his seat. "So, what's the captain's hard-on for you all about?"

It took a second or two for me to remember back to when it started. "Old history. Dates back to when I was a couple of years on the job, and me and Dowd were working out of Northern Station. We'd both put in for a plain clothes assignment working the muni routes, and I got picked over him."

Cassidy had a pained expression. "That's it?"

"Not all of it." I drove into the garage beneath the Hall of Justice. "Dowd was going to night school at the time, and the muni gig was a cherry schedule with weekends off. The guy wanted the assignment so bad that he tried to pay me to turn it down."

Cassidy laughed. "Fucking weasel had his eye on the gold bars even back then. Tried to pay you. That's rich."

I nodded. "Dowd said he'd 'kick in a little sweetener' if I gave him my spot."

We got out of the car and Cassidy's howling laughter echoed throughout the garage. "A little *sweetener!*" he repeated, laughing even harder.

"Keep it down," I told him. "The captain doesn't need another reason to bust my balls."

Dowd must have been working late, because he got onto the elevator on the first floor and rode the rest of the way up with us. He said nothing to me, but asked Cassidy if he was feeling better.

The elevator stopped at the fourth floor and Dowd started to step off. Then he turned and slapped a forearm across the closing door. "Oh yeah, McKenna, what's going on with that case?"

He was half in and half out of the elevator, and I wasn't sure how much of a briefing he wanted. "Single gunshot, male victim... Uh, clean cut-looking guy..."

Dowd rolled his eyes and glanced at his watch.

I continued, "We think he might be a foreign guy from--"

"Yeah, that's fine," he interrupted. "Now that Lou's back, you can let him take the lead."

"I'd kind of like to run lead on this one," I said.

"What did I just say?" Dowd released the door and stepped out. "It's Cassidy's case and you'll stooge for him."

I knew that any further argument would be futile. Besides, the door had already closed. I just stared down at the floor, as if I might find my shriveled nuts lying there. Cassidy leaned against the back of the elevator, watching me.

I looked at him and shook my head. "I should have taken the goddamn sweetener."

Cassidy cackled all the way back to his desk.

No sooner did I sit down when my cell phone started buzzing. It was Doris again.

"McKenna." I'd answered as if there was a gun to my head.

"Where are you?"

"I told you, I caught a case." I turned away from Cassidy and lowered the phone. "Me and Lou are working leads."

"Yeah. Well, I'm calling to let you know that I'll be going to my mother's for a couple of days, maybe through the weekend. And I'm taking Bridget."

"Okay." I paused. "Can I ask why?"

"Why I'm taking Bridget?"

"No, damn it, why you're leaving! Why in the hell are you going to your mother's?"

"I need a break from you, Danny. Besides, you'll either be working or watching football anyway."

"Doesn't Bridge have school tomorrow?"

"The kids are all off for the rest of the week," she said. "Parent-teacher conferences."

I groaned. "Do we have to go to one of those?"

"*We?* No, Danny. The meeting between Bridget's *parents* and teachers was yesterday. I went."

"Oh."

"Anyway, we'll be back on Sunday night."

"You know this case I'm investigating is a pretty big deal." My attempt at redemption, or pity, was almost whispered into the phone. "I'll probably be working on it all weekend."

"There's a shocker."

"That's not what I meant." Through clenched teeth I continued, "All I'm trying to say is that you don't have to leave. I mean, just to get away from me. I won't be around much, anyway."

"Right. Just don't forget to feed the cat."

After the call, I tried to play it off in front of Cassidy. He'd probably heard enough to figure it out, but for once he didn't make a wiseass crack.

"You got a wife, Lou." I said it like a statement.

He smiled. "Yeah, I got a wife. And I got ex-wives." He stopped smiling. "Why do you think I drink?"

"I thought it was because of me."

He laughed, but not as hardily as I thought he would. "Yeah, well, there's that, too."

16

700 Maritime Street,
Port of Oakland

Sarah Brooks sunk into the seat of her personal car. The department-issued Chevy she'd been driving at the time of the shooting was still being repaired, and nobody at the office was familiar with her cream colored Kia Soul.

She watched in anonymity from across the lot as, one-by-one, her co-workers left for the day. Finally, Tim Sanchez—her supervisor—was the last to leave the office. Sarah waited several more minutes until she was certain Tim was well out of the area, before going in.

Again Sarah pulled the blinds in her office, doing her best to make the building appear empty to passersby. She planned to be there only long enough to grab the files from the locked drawer. They were Sarah's most promising leads as to who her attackers were. But after laying the three cases out on her desk, she found herself transfixed. Now, one of the three cases jumped out at her.

Sarah glanced over the case summary:

```
(3) 20ft. refrigerated shipping containers
unloaded from the COSCO Kobe on 12 October.
Shipment flagged for F/U after manifest
review and VACIS exam. Subj. containers moved
to CES for further inspection. MET manifest
hold and physical examination of cargo
conducted. 1.3 tons banned shark fins seized.
Cargo had been in transit to Three Zhang
Holdings, Ltd. in San Francisco.
```

Sarah knew that shark fins had become a lucrative business, and prices for the delicacy had been driven up by high demand among restauranteurs and wealthy Asians.

The two other cases now seemed much less compelling. A dozen computer programmers here on phony work visas felt tepid, at best. And the "*possible*" file case was even less likely—a single container, flagged because of its commercial liquor cargo, and then ultimately released and allowed to continue on its way.

Stepping into the cool darkness of her office parking lot, Sarah was now more convinced than ever that Asian shark fin profiteers were behind the attempt on her life.

A fine mist had crept in off of the bay, creating a muted halo around the streetlights that illuminated the two cars in the lot. Realizing that there should only be one, Sarah squinted across the hardtop at the gray Toyota 4Runner—definitely not a Fed vehicle. A man sat behind the wheel, but Sarah couldn't discern any more than that.

As she reached for the handgun in her shoulder bag, Sarah's mind raced: Involvement in a shooting here and now would clearly be the end of her career. After Tim Sanchez's warning the previous night, even making an off-duty arrest could be the final straw. On the other hand, if this was about to be another attempt on her life, she'd have no other choice but to defend herself.

Eyeing her Kia, she assessed the distance to where she'd parked. Her car was beneath a lamppost, much closer than the suspicious gray SUV. If she could get to it quickly enough, Sarah was convinced that she could evade the 4Runner—at least until she made it to the closest dock security gate. And once she badged herself though, she'd be home free.

But as much as Sarah wanted to save herself the grief of another Internal Affairs inquiry and almost certain termination, she was stubbornly resolute about exacting revenge—or at least learning the identity of whoever this was.

The 4Runner's interior light suddenly went on, and at the same time the driver's door cracked open. Sarah saw the Asian man, clearly now, as he stepped from the car. He started to say something, but Sarah shouted over him.

"Keep your hands where I can see them!" Sarah had her gun out now, gripping it with both hands as she moved cautiously toward him. "No sudden moves or you'll be dead before you even hear the gunshot."

17

2019 Toyota 4Runner

Only one vehicle was parked out front, which made Curtis Tam wonder if he'd located the right place. He hoped that the woman coming out of the building was a U.S. Customs agent.

Stepping from his rented Toyota, Tam thought about how best to play this. He intended on using whatever clout his status as a private investigator might afford him, without giving up the identity of his employer. In fact, Tam had hoped to avoid the international angle altogether when speaking to the agent.

"Excuse me," Tam called across the lot. "Is this the office where I can find--"

Suddenly there was a handgun pointed at him, and he was being ordered not to move. Tam thought he'd either found the right place, or the really, really, wrong place.

The woman was sturdy, with a fit body and an aggressive bearing. Maybe even angry. No questions had been asked of him yet, so Tam thought it best not to speak. As the woman moved closer, he could see the intensity in her sizable brown eyes. Not an unattractive woman by any means, but Tam's primary focus was on not getting shot.

She stopped halfway across the lot, and something about the woman's stance, grip, and tactics confirmed to Tam that she was law enforcement.

"I'm sorry if I'm someplace I shouldn't be," he finally said. "I'm just trying to--"

The woman shouted over him; something about shotguns and shark fins. It made no sense to Tam.

With his hands still apart, neither raised or lowered but definitely away from his body, Tam tried to explain. "I'm a private investigator, and I'm looking into some missing cargo. You'll find a wallet with my identification and PI license in the breast pocket of my coat."

"Are you armed?"

Tam paused.

"That's a yes or no question," Brooks said. "Are you carrying a fucking weapon?"

"No," he answered. "I am permitted to carry a concealed weapon, but no, I have no weapon with me."

She directed Tam to slowly remove his wallet and set it on the hood of his car. The woman's posture relaxed slightly after examining the documents, and she asked him to lift his jacket and turn all the way around so that she could see his waistband. Then she had Tam lift his pant legs to show that he was not wearing an ankle holster. Once satisfied, Sarah lowered her handgun.

Over the next several minutes, the two played a verbal cat-and-mouse game; both asking questions, but neither giving up more than they wanted to. Brooks's inquiries were centered around Tam's home base of Hong Kong, and whether or not he's a fan of shark fin soup. Tam, on the other hand, thought she was nuts. She seemed irrational and paranoid, to the extent that he wondered whether the woman was actually a federal agent. And when he asked to see her ID or a business card, she balked.

At one point, Sarah touched her fingers to the square bandage on her neck. In the commotion, a dime-size spot of blood had seeped through the gauze.

Tam studied this without speaking, and then asked, "Are you all right?"

Brooks quickly dropped her hand. "I'm fine."

"Yeah? Because your neck seems to think otherwise." Tam motioned toward his 4Runner. "There's a first aid kit in the back of my rental."

18

Southern Police Station

On my way out to Third Street, I couldn't help thinking of how much simpler this would have been in the days when Southern Station was on the first floor of the Hall of Justice. Even though the voter approved headquarters building is only ten minutes from Bryant Street, it's just another one of those changes that I'm still trying to get used to.

Anyway, Lou had called in sick again and I'd begun to worry about him. I had hoped to get a few things done on my case, with or without my partner, but Captain Dowd was causing me all kinds of grief. He didn't want me doing any of the investigation alone—which pretty much meant I'd have to hang around the office, and that wasn't going to happen.

I needed to interview the patrol officer who had arrested Elvis Lang and the hooker, Sha Nay Nay Moore. Even if it meant making an off-the-books run out to Southern Station to meet with him.

I didn't know the cop, but he had a reputation in the precinct as being smart and hard working. Teddy Muniz was assigned to the day shift, and had agreed to hook up with me at Natoma and Russ Streets where he had made the arrests several months earlier.

The guy had a fairly decent recollection of the incident, even though it had been a pretty run-of-the-mill arrest. "Both of them were in the back," he told me. "They were sort of lying on top of the folded down seat. Her pants were down around her ankles and he was straddling her. Thought it was a rape at first, but then I saw that it was just a B-girl and her John."

"Any idea where the John worked?" I asked.

Muniz shrugged, then shook his head.

"What about the car?" I flipped through my notes. "A Dodge Caravan. Any idea who it belonged to?"

"I don't remember." Muniz frowned. "Him, I think. All of that info should be in the report. I remember we had to impound it because the registration wasn't paid up. Don't know if he ever got it back."

I made a few notes in my file. "And the DA dropped the case?"

"I'm pretty sure, yeah."

"Because you didn't have enough for the solicitation charge," I said. "Is that right?"

Muniz shook his head. "No, that wasn't it."

I had closed my notebook, but now opened it again. "What do you mean?"

"I knew it wasn't much of a case," said Muniz, "but I had to arrest them for something. The broad was hump'n the dude right out here in public view."

I felt the frown growing on my face, frustrated with myself for making the assumption. I'd never followed up with the courts to verify for myself why the case had been dismissed. "Then why did the DA drop charges?"

"Politics, I guess." Officer Muniz looked at me like he thought I already knew. "Somebody above my pay grade got involved, pulled some strings downtown, and the case just went away."

Interesting.

I considered confronting the captain when I got back to the office, but he had left for the day. Dowd had already tried to derail my investigation, and I felt that more than just our pained history was behind it. I sat down and made a list of the things he had done to screw with me, and then fished through the pile of shit on Cassidy's desk to find Wednesday's newspaper. Cutting out the article about my homicide, I clipped it to my written list and put them into an envelope for the police chief.

After another hour of computer work, I made a trip downstairs to the Forensic Video Analysis Unit. They were still working on the security camera footage from the apartments across from my murder scene.

"Hope to have it done by tomorrow," was all they could tell me.

When I got back upstairs, a note taped to my desk phone said that my wife had called in to the detail's secretary looking for me—something Doris didn't normally do. She answered right away when I called her back.

"It's Bridget," she said.

"Is she all right?"

"No she's not all right!" Doris sounded on the verge of tears. "She's hungover!"

I slumped into my chair. "What in the hell do you mean she's hungover? She's only thirteen!"

"She went out with some friends earlier and came home drunk."

"For shit's sake Doris, I thought you were at your mom's!"

My wife was silent for a second. "I am at my mom's, you idiot! What the hell does that have to do with anything?"

"It's just that I didn't know she had friends there."

"What? Not that you would know anything about her friends, at home *or* at my mom's, but yes, she has friends up here. So now can we get back to the topic of your thirteen-year-old alcoholic daughter?"

I didn't know which of the two of them I wanted to smack more. "Look," I said. "She's not an alcoholic, she's just... I don't know, all screwed up."

"Oh, that's good. Get that diagnosis from Dr. Phil, did ya?"

A couple of inspectors came in, so I tried to cut the conversation short. "We can deal with it when you guys get home on Sunday. In the meantime, keep a closer eye on her. And don't let her hang out with those kids anymore."

"Really? Ya think?"

19

2111 Lane Street, Suite #101
San Francisco

The Bayview Post Office is housed in a plain brick building on the corner of Lane and Van Dyke Streets.

As soon as Sarah Brooks saw the flagpole outside, she slammed her fist against the steering wheel and cursed. The address was supposed to be company headquarters for Three Zhang Holdings, Ltd.—the consignee listed on the shipping manifest of the illegally imported shark fins. A bullshit corporation with a bullshit address, she thought. There was no suite #101.

Given Sarah's suspended status, she realized she couldn't have done much even if it had been the company headquarters. She was pushing her luck as it was, continuing to follow the leads as if she had authority to do so.

Sarah sat in the post office parking lot, thinking back a couple of nights to the charismatic Asian man she had confronted in front of her office. She now wished that instead of accepting a fresh bandage from his first aid kit, she had tossed his car and searched through his belongings. If there had been evidence of a connection between the Hong Kong private eye and the Chinese holding company, Sarah had missed the opportunity to find it. The more she thought about it, she realized that Tam had been suspiciously evasive—never giving up details about his case, his client, or why he was in the Bay Area.

Out of investigative options, Sarah went inside and buzzed the postmaster with her badge. Sarah quickly tucked it away before the guy got a look at her name or ID number, and then she explained about the company's erroneous address.

"Happens all the time," said the postmaster. "Customers often use the physical address of the post office, and then list a suite or apartment number that corresponds with their PO box number. Makes it looks as if they're operating out of a real brick and mortar building."

"How can they get away with it?" asked Sarah.

"Courts have held that the practice is legal. So, the USPS is required to accept their mail—regardless of whether a parcel says apartment, unit, room, whatever. So long as the number is a legitimate post office box."

Brooks thought for a moment. "Then suite 101 might actually be the postal box rented by the company I'm looking for?"

The postmaster shrugged. "Might be."

"Can you check for me?"

His lips drew back. "Sorry, not without a warrant or court order."

Sarah's eyes became angry slits, but she knew there was little she could do. It would be impossible to get an order from the court and still remain off the grid. Tim Sanchez would have her ass.

Sarah's cell phone suddenly sounded, just as she was about to try charming the postmaster. "Brooks," she answered.

"Paul Bise, Contraband Enforcement Team." The background din of the customs exam station told Brooks where he was calling from. "Sorry to bother you so late in the day, especially after your shooting. We're glad to hear you're okay, by the way. But there's a flag in the system regarding this case we have, and instructions are to contact you immediately."

Sarah envisioned that more cargo had been shipped to Three Zhang Holdings. She knew this might be the break she needed. So caught up in thought, Sarah nearly missed Paul's next words.

"We just intercepted two intermodal containers of vodka—both of which just came off of the MS Versand."

20

SFPD Homicide Detail

Lou came in Friday morning looking like a transplant patient whose body had rejected the new organs. His hands trembled as he topped his coffee from a bottle stashed in the bottom drawer of his desk.

"I got this from the forensic video guys on my way upstairs." Lou tossed me an evidence envelope containing the original Oak Street apartment security footage, as well as a copied version that was now compatible with the SFPD computer system.

I popped it into my drive while Cassidy read the paper and sipped his morning elixir. Right away, I saw that the angle was wrong; a wide shot of the sidewalk and street in front of the building, but no view of the park. Even Lang's rental car was out of the shot. Advancing the disk, I examined another frame, then another and another. They had been taken at thirty second intervals, and the timestamp in the corner showed that it was still only 10:47 p.m. on the night of the shooting.

Though it seemed like a dead end, I realized that the entire night of recorded photographs would still have to be examined. I glanced at my partner. Knowing that he wouldn't do it justice, I made a notation in the file to go through them myself when I had time.

Calandra Moore's phone switched to an automated voicemail, and I left my third message asking her to have Sha Nay Nay call me. After that, I phoned Doris to ask if she was still planning to return on Sunday, and if so, to let her know that I would have a stern father-daughter talk with Bridget about the drinking. But when her cell phone went to message, I just hung up.

Cassidy's coloring hadn't improved during the day, and by afternoon it was obvious there was something seriously wrong with him. When he left work early, I really began to worry. In a moment of weakness and poor judgement, I stopped into Captain Dowd's office to share my concerns. But Dowd was more interested in whether Lou had enough sick leave on the books to cover another absence.

"Sure, the guy's a halfway decent inspector," said Dowd, "but he's a drunk." Then turning back to the papers on his desk he asked, "What do you want me to do?"

I didn't really have an answer, and wasn't even sure why I'd gone in there. Just worried about my partner, I guess.

"And what about the case? Your Dracula mask guy?" The captain was onto something else. "With Cassidy on his ass, it'll need to be reassigned to another inspector."

"But we're moving forward on it," I said. "And besides, Cassidy will be back on Monday. Don't worry about him."

"Don't worry?" Dowd looked up. "You just told me that *you* thought it was serious. Make up your damn mind, McKenna."

I backed my way into the hall. "Trust me, Captain. I've got this."

Dowd squinted through one eye. "I'll give you a couple more days to come up with something. Whether Cassidy's back by then or not."

"Today's Friday," I said. "What can I do over the weekend? How about another week?"

"Five days," he spat back. "Give me something tangible by next Wednesday or the handoff goes to Mendoza and Taylor."

I went back to my desk and stared at the hollow case file. The hooker still hadn't called. Her John and his rental car were a big zero. And other than knowing that my victim once worked for a defunct distribution company, I had nothing on him, either. *Shit!*

Staring back at me was the disk containing hours of grainy black and white images of an empty street. It was all I had left, and I knew right then that I'd be spending the rest of the night in front of my computer.

After so many hours, my eyes were tired of staring at the gray screen; sidewalk, back end of a parked car, base of a street sign, and about half of a traffic lane. Flashes of headlights, passing pedestrians, and vehicle traffic became less frequent as the timestamp ticked into the early morning hours.

When the digital display got to 3 a.m., I slowed the advancing frames to look for anything different occurring around the estimated time of death. Nothing happened until about 3:20 a.m., when a blurred figure passed through the field of view from top to bottom. It appeared as if the person had crossed the street from the park to the near sidewalk. The next frame, which would have been 30 seconds later, showed a black car pulling away from the curb—the same car that had been parked there since the disk began to play.

Probably nothing, I thought. The car would have to have been there since at least 10:47 p.m. when the camera was turned on. According to the medical examiner's computations, that's about 4½ hours before the victim was shot. I added a new sheet in my file—an information log titled *Security Video – 1658 Oak.*

I was just about to shut down my computer when a thought occurred to me. Backing the disk to an hour or so earlier, I searched for a shot where passing headlights reflected off the parked black car. It took a while to locate a frame taken at exactly the right moment, and after slowly advancing the film I found a single frame of the rear license plate—blurred, but illuminated by pair of passing headlights. The numbers weren't readable, but I hoped the quality could be enhanced by our video forensics people.

21

Sometime during the night, the MS Versand had moved from its anchorage in the bay to an offloading terminal at the Port of Oakland.

Crossing the bridge ahead of the morning commute, Tam mulled over the recent information about a second Customs inspection site. To make certain he wouldn't miss the stolen containers meant that he would have to make the 10-minute drive back and forth several times between the two inspection locations. Of course, there was also the chance that the liquor cargo had evaded detection by CBP, in which case it would continue on its way to the San Francisco warehouse.

From a vacant lot on Mitchell Avenue in Alameda, Tam was able to view the entire back side of the second inspection facility. He peered through the binoculars each time a trailered container backed up to the loading bay. But by midday, none matched those that had gone missing.

The setting sun reflected harshly off of the clapboard buildings, and it frustrated Tam that he had spent the entire day relying on little more than a hunch. Had the so-called *federal agent* been more helpful, Tam could have saved time by focusing on the correct location. Instead, the lunatic woman had threatened him with a gun and then refused to disclose any information about the cargo ship.

They had parted amicably enough, but Tam was still bothered by her evasiveness and that she hadn't provided him with so much as a business card.

Despite the obstacles, Tam's patience finally paid off. Just before 5 p.m., two 40-foot FEU containers were trailered onto the Customs grounds—both of them bearing Boaz Integrated Shipping Services logos. Tam couldn't know for certain from this distance, but odds were very high that these were the same containers stolen from Sergei Petrenko.

His plan was to wait until someone came to claim the cargo and then follow the containers to their destination. Whether that turned out to be the warehouse on Russ Street or not, this stroke of luck represented the first decent break in the case for Tam.

Suddenly a small passenger vehicle sped past him and swung around the corner heading toward the security gate. A minute later Tam watched it race up to the far end of the loading dock. The little Kia Soul looked grossly out of place against the backdrop of hulking tractor-trailer rigs.

Tam brought the binoculars to his eyes, somehow already sensing what he was about to see. Springing from the cream-colored car was the agent who had confronted him two nights prior.

At least it answers one of Tam's questions. Only if she was a CBP agent could she have entered the facility so quickly. But he still wondered why she was there. He continued watching as a couple of uniformed CBP agents made their way over to the two Petrenko containers sitting side-by-side at the south end of the raised loading dock.

The back ends of the trailers faced into the building, away from Tam, so he was unable to see whether or not they were being searched by the agents.

After four and a half hours, Tam felt that he had waited long enough. He drove around to the entry gate, which was now bathed in large overhead lights. Tam tried talking his way in, but like the other inspection facility, the security guard would not allow him to enter.

While arguing with the guard, Tam failed to notice the tiny glow of the Kia's interior light. Sarah Brooks had started her car and was heading back toward the gate. Tam glanced up, too late to avoid her. Brooks's car slowed to cross the road spikes on the exit side of the security kiosk, as Tam sat motionless on the entry side. They were suddenly staring at each other, the clueless guard standing in the booth between them.

Brooks's eyes narrowed at the recognition of Tam, and he could only gaze back with equal curiosity. This time the woman did not draw her weapon, though her expression exuded molten distrust.

The little Kia lurched forward, crossed the roadway directly behind Tam, and stopped there. Almost as if Brooks was cutting off any potential avenue of escape.

The woman jumped from the car, her tongue pressing the inside of her cheek. "Okay Mr. Private Eye, you want to tell me what in the hell you're doing here?"

"I suppose I could ask you the same question," said Tam. "I'm not following you, if that's what you're thinking. Like I tried to tell you the other night, I'm investigating some missing cargo containers."

Brooks stood toward the back of Tam's car, forcing him to turn awkwardly in his seat in order to see her. He slowly got out to face Brooks, as the guard stood listening from inside his kiosk.

"Go on," Brooks said.

Tam decided that it was time to capitulate, at least a little. "Two shipments of liquor—both just offloaded from the MS Versand."

Her eyes flickered for a fraction of a second, yet it was enough for Tam to see the recognition in them. She was there for the same reason. She made an effort to play it off and appear unmoved, but Tam pressured her with his stare.

Eventually, Sarah nodded. "What, exactly, is your interest in these containers? Who are you working for?"

Tam shook his head. "An employer who demands anonymity. But I can tell you that these aren't the first to go missing."

"Missing?"

He nodded. "I'm tracking another container stolen a month ago. And there have been twenty-one others before that—all with the same cargo."

The guard looked like he wanted to say something, but neither investigator acknowledged him.

Tam leaned against his car and lit a cigarette. "Now can I ask why you are here?"

Brooks weighed her response. The original liquor shipment had seemed like a low priority; in fact, she had yet to even follow up on it. But if what this investigator was saying was accurate, she may have misjudged its importance. Not only would the case involve international cargo theft, but possibly a string of them.

"I was notified about these same two containers," she said. "And I had already been looking into the one you mentioned, taken a month ago. That's why I'm here."

"So, you guys knew about that one too?" Tam reached into the car and pulled out his notes. "If CBP flagged the stolen container, how come the cargo wasn't seized?"

"Well, obviously, we had no idea that it was stolen cargo." Brooks sounded flustered and defensive, which signaled that she wasn't sure how it happened. Taking the case file from her car, her eyebrows came together as she read the case summary. "Says here that the recipient signed for it and the cargo was released."

73

The two were silent for a few seconds, thinking. Then the security guard spoke up. "Diplomatic immunity."

Brooks and Tam stared at him.

"Yeah," he continued. "I was working when that container was released. The trailering rig showed up along with three guys in a black Lincoln."

"What makes you think the guys were diplomats?" asked Sarah.

"License plates," he said. "They were OFM." The guard gazed back and forth at Brooks and Tam. "Office of Foreign Missions. But don't ask me where from, because I couldn't read it."

Sarah quickly thumbed through the file. "There's nothing in here about any of that."

The guard shrugged. "Irregardless, that's what happened. They flashed some government paperwork at me and the CBP bigwigs inside, and that were all she wrote. Off they went with the container, as if it was never here.

22

138 Ryan Avenue
Mill Valley

I had spent all day Saturday in the office, following leads and doing internet research on my case. I wanted to enjoy a football Sunday that was free from wife and work, but the Forty-niners were losing to the Seahawks and my mind kept drifting to other things.

Doris and Bridge returned late in the afternoon, which forced me to face the inevitable. I googled *How to talk to your teenager about drinking.*

I got up and poured myself a drink, then started down the hall for Bridget's room. She opened the door when I knocked, and then flopped back down on her bed with some sort of teen magazine.

"Bridge?" I said. "We need to talk about what happened at your grandmother's. Your mom said you were drinking alcohol with some friends. I don't know what you're thinking." I paused for a second to consult the website I'd saved on my phone. "Teenage liquor consumption often leads to alcohol-related fatalities, sexual activity, poor academics, alcoholism, gang involvement and violent crime."

She hadn't even acknowledged me, so I decided to shit-can the online coach. "Hanging out and getting hammered with a bunch of your loser friends is not only dangerous, but at your age it's also illegal. Where the hell is your common sense?"

Bridget pulled her earbuds out and looked at me quizzically. "Did you say something, Dad?"

The blood rushed to my head and I felt my lips tighten around my teeth. Stepping all the way into her room, I was ready to ground her for life, banish her from the family, send her on a volunteer mission to India.

Just then my cell phone buzzed in my pocket. "Hold on a minute," I glanced down to shut it off, but saw that the caller was Calandra Moore, the grandmother of my prostitute witness. Perhaps it was a call from Sha Nay Nay herself.

"McKenna," I said, holding the phone to my ear. And though I motioned for Bridget to wait, she only rolled her eyes and plugged the earbuds back in.

My wife stood in the hallway as I grabbed my jacket and started for the door. The expression on her face told me that she'd heard my underage drinking speech. Though she withheld her review of it, Doris watched me slide my gun and holster onto my belt and scoop my car keys off the table.

With sheer hate in her eyes, she said, "So that's it? That's the best you can come up with?"

I held up a hand to say *not now*, but Doris nodded with mock appreciation. "I see how it works: When the going gets tough, Danny McKenna gets going."

I stopped, ready to defend myself. It was my job, for Chrissake. My murder investigation. It wasn't like I was leaving to play golf or join a game of cards with the guys. It was work! What choice did I have?

23

2 New Montgomery Street

The Pied Piper Bar & Grill is a cozy spot at the Palace Hotel on Market Street. Known as a popular after work spot for drinks on weekdays, it tends to draw more of a tourist crowd on the weekends. At a table in the back near the fireplace this Sunday night, were a couple that were neither office workers nor tourists—an Asian man wearing a white cotton dress shirt and black slacks; and a Caucasian woman in a light blue jersey blouse, pressed Levis and white tennis shoes.

After two stilted encounters, it had become apparent that the two investigators were both working on the same case. Brooks and Tam had agreed to the détente meeting at the hotel bar in the hope of exchanging information.

Sarah took the seat against the back wall facing the door, and ordered a draft beer. Curtis selected a Chardonnay from the wine list.

"We could have met in your office," said Tam. "You didn't have to come all the way into San Francisco."

Not wanting to get into her suspended status, Brooks said that she was supposed to be at home recuperating from an on-duty injury.

Tam snapped his finger. "You're the agent who was shot," he said. "I read about it in the paper."

"Shot *at*," she immediately corrected. "This little neck thing was just an unlucky piece of shrapnel. I'm all good now."

Her hyper-paranoia now made more sense to Tam.

Sarah asked again about Tam's employer, and again he balked.

They paused the conversation for a young woman who asked if she could take one of the unused chairs at their table. Tam waited as the girl squeezed the chair behind Sarah and rejoined her foursome. Once she was out of hearing range, he continued. "This person I'm working for is a high profile individual who does not want notoriety, especially in regards to this case." Tam sighed. "Which is why I'm forced to conduct the investigation alone. The fewer people who even know I'm here, the better."

Tam described the investigative steps he'd taken to that point, including the cargo tracking devices, his surveillance of the Russ Street warehouse, and the shooting he had witnessed in the park.

As he talked, Sarah tried to fit together how the stolen cargo could have been released by her own people, even if a diplomatic embassy were involved. She wondered if someone on the inside was a traitor to her own agency.

So absorbed in thought, she nearly missed something Tam said as he described his encounter with the men in front of the warehouse.

"Hold on," she said. "What did you just say?"

"What, inside the warehouse?" Tam tilted his head. "I said there was a container that matched--"

"Not that," the other thing—about a van."

He nodded, now putting it together for himself. "A van was parked just inside the roll-up doors. It was white, a Ford, I think."

Until that point, neither of them had imagined that a single cargo container of stolen vodka could be related to the murder of Rhonda Pitts, who had rented the warehouse; the killing of a man in Golden Gate Park; and now, the attempted murder of a federal agent.

"It's all connected," Brooks said quietly, almost to herself. "I've been barking up the wrong fucking tree. This has nothing to do with goddamn shark fins or computer programmers from Bangalore. It's all about stolen liquor."

"Probably a power shift within the organization," said Tam. "It's got to be about the money."

Sarah nodded. "Somebody got greedy."

"Now that you know where your van is stashed, it'll be easy for you to get a search warrant for the place."

Sarah bristled. "Not quite that easy."

She opened up about her reputation as an aggressive agent, even describing the internal affairs investigation that had resulted in her transfer to a tiny office at the Port of Oakland. "It's actually pretty humiliating," Sarah said. "I'm now *persona non grata* in my own agency. Can't even go into the CBP office."

Now he also understood why she had been so evasive that night in her office parking lot. "So, you're a little overzealous," he finally said. "I've never known a good investigator to be *under*-zealous."

Brushing off the compliment, Brooks asked, "What about the diplomatic thing? How do you think that figures in? It might explain how CBP let the container go; the whole foreign government issue makes bureaucrats shit their pants. But, I have to wonder just who these people are." Sarah paused in thought. "Was there anything about this Rhonda Pitts victim to indicate she had diplomatic status?"

"Not that I saw. But the guy who confronted me in front of the Russ Street warehouse had an Eastern European accent. Was there any mention of a foreign government in your paperwork?"

Brooks shook her head. "Who knows if that's even good info. The security guard could just be talking out of his ass."

"What about the two containers seized today?" Tam asked.

"Same as the first one; 40-foot intermodal, 100 pallets, 56 bottles of vodka on each. And don't worry, this time we won't be releasing them. The enforcement team supervisor said he'd call me on the sly if anyone shows up to claim them."

"Good." Tam thought for a second. "Maybe your guys actually should release them. Once we identify the recipients, we could follow them and the cargo."

Sarah nodded. "Assuming that after all the shootings of late, they'll still show up to claim it. Anyway, the case summary doesn't have much else. The listed shipping address is your warehouse at 168 Russ Street, and there's a receipt signed by the person who picked up that original container. But there's not much I can do with just a name without access to the CBP database."

Sarah set the receipt on the table next to the dish of peanuts, and they both tilted their heads to view the signature line.

Elvis Lang.

24

5411 3rd Street
San Francisco

It was a Sunday night, and knowing that Cassidy was already tucked in with his bottle, I figured I'd have to fudge a little on SFPD's rule that prohibits meeting alone with an informant.

The drive into the city took me over an hour in the rain. I parked in front of the Hunter's Point McDonald's, and saw Sha Nay Nay through the window. Sitting in a corner booth, she was curled up beneath a thin hoodie that clung to her like residue on a crack pipe.

I nodded to her as I walked in, but she just watched me through dark, distrustful eyes.

"Danny McKenna," I offered my hand, then regretted it when she leaned back. "Can I get you something to eat?" I asked.

"How 'bout you tell me what you want, first." She crossed her arms the way I've seen my daughter do a hundred times.

Ignoring her question for the moment, I asked, "Do you remember me? I patrolled your neighborhood back when I worked the street."

"I remember." She cocked her head, taking in what she could see of me. "You got fat."

Unconsciously, I sucked in my stomach. She was right, I had put on a few extra pounds. I'm a pretty big guy, and I had hoped that I was carrying it well. Clearing my throat, I finally let my gut back out to where it was.

A trace of a smile showed on her face. "Double cheese."

"What's that?" I glanced down at my beltline.

"Double cheese burger and large fries," she said. "That's what you can get me."

I wanted to order something for myself as well, but decided against it after her crack about my weight. When I returned with her food, I saw that she had dropped her hood—maybe a sign she was relaxing.

"I didn't think you'd call me," I said.

"Wouldn't have." She flipped back the paper wrapping on her burger and took a mammoth bite. "I been try'n to straighten things out. Don't need no more po-lice shit in my life."

I watched her take another chomp and wash it down with a fistful of fries. Her table manners aside, she wasn't an ugly girl. Her skin was still okay, not sucked in like it used to be in her rock cocaine days. A splash of freckles across her nose was barely visible against her brown face, but gave her an innocent look that I imagined her Johns liked.

"So, why *did* you call me back?" I asked.

"If I got a warrant out on me, ya might as well take my ass to jail now. Like I already told you, I need to clean up whatever shit I done wrong."

"It's nothing like that." I shook my head. "I've got a report here, an arrest from last April..." Watching her eyes for a reaction, I saw none. "You were arrested with some guy in a car parked on Natoma, south of Market."

Still no acknowledgement.

"And?" She polished off the rest of her fries and wiped her greasy hands against the pocket of her hoodie. "What about it? They dropped the case."

"You remember the guy?" I intentionally didn't call him a John, even though I was sure that's what he was. She stared back at me, eyes flat lined. It had been an easy question—either no or yes.

"Nope." She looked away and I saw the lie.

"I know that the cops tried to get a statement, right?"

She didn't answer.

"They wanted to put a b-case on you?"

The penal code section for prostitution is 647(b)—which is often shortened in police jargon. Most hookers are familiar with the term.

"If I didn't snitch to the cops back then, why do you think I'm gonna snitch now?"

I stroked my face from forehead to chin. "Okay, look Sha Nay Nay, I'm a homicide inspector, not a patrolman. I don't give a husky shit what you and Elvis Lang were doing in that car. I just need to find him."

Her eyes flashed when I said his name, and I was sure she knew him. It would be unusual for a street hooker to know her John's real name, so I was thinking that maybe the guy was a regular. Or maybe he was her dope connection, and she paid him with sex. Or maybe there was something more that I hadn't yet figured out.

81

The girl glanced around the empty McDonald's for a second, then out the window to the parking lot. "Two things," she finally said. "One, don't be calling me Sha Nay Nay anymore. Now I just go by Shanay."

I nodded. "Okay. What's the other thing?"

She paused, then glanced out the window again. "You drive a tan Crown Vic?"

"Yeah, why?"

"You 'bout to get towed away."

I turned toward the parking lot and saw the flashing yellow lights backing up to my sedan. "Son-of-a-bitch!"

As I slid out of the booth and started for the door, I saw that wisp of a grin again on her face. Dashing into the lot, I nearly wrenched my bad knee.

In my haste to park close to the door, I must have blocked a fire hydrant. Badging the parking enforcement guy and the tow truck driver, I waved them off before starting back for the restaurant.

Shanay stood watching the encounter from under an awning near the door, which is when I noticed the small curve beneath her sweatshirt. It wasn't much, maybe only a few months' worth, but against the backdrop of her bony frame it was unmistakable.

"Get in," I said. "I'll give you a ride back up the hill."

Shanay was quiet during the ride to her grandmother's place on Reardon Road. When we got to the mouth of the complex, I turned into a roundabout and shut off my car.

"Are you ever going to tell me the second thing?" I asked. "And don't say that it was my car being towed."

She let out a sigh. "Okay, I know who you're talking about... The Russian dude I got busted with."

"Elvis Lang." I nodded.

"Yeah, whatever." She bit the nail of her little finger. "I gotta think about it for a minute."

I sat impatiently waiting while she thought about it, wondering why she had referred to Lang as a "Russian dude." Remembering his ruddy-faced photo, I supposed he could pass for Russian.

Tapping the steering wheel like a ticking clock, I stared at *Shanay*. She rolled her eyes—just like my daughter does—and with a bit of irritation, said, "A *minute*. Like, later, like, not now?"

"Oh." It sort of pissed me off. Partly because I needed to get moving on my case, and partly because I had stumbled over this new generation's use of the word, *minute*. Apparently it no longer meant sixty-seconds. "Fine. Then, can I get your phone number in case something else comes up about this guy?"

She started to tell me the number, and then frowned as I pulled out a pen and began writing on a napkin. "Don't you know how to put in a number? L'me see your phone, McKenna."

Within seconds she had programmed in her cell number. She handed it back, shaking her head. "Dude, you gotta get with the times."

As she opened the car door to leave, I reached into my wallet and pulled out a twenty to give her. It crossed my mind that she probably makes that much for a blow-job, so I handed her another twenty. I wasn't sure exactly why, but in a way it made me feel like I was helping her and the kid.

Shanay paused halfway out of the car, seemed as if she was about to thank me, and then looked right at my eyes and nodded. It seemed to mean something, a connection maybe, or trust. At least I hoped it did. Then I wondered if she'd buy some rock and just smoke up the whole forty bucks as soon as I left.

The detail was as quiet as a tomb when I got back to type up the notes of my meeting with the new and improved Shanay. It wasn't until my phone began to vibrate that I noticed how late it was.

"McKenna," I answered.

"This is Captain Dowd." His voice was serious, like he was giving a briefing or something. "Lou Cassidy's wife just called to tell me that he's been taken to the hospital. They think he had a heart attack."

I got a few more particulars from the captain and thanked him for letting me know.

"And another thing, McKenna." Dowd stopped to clear what sounded like a nasty hunk of phlegm from his throat. "We're gonna have to do something with your case. Get with Mendoza and Taylor in the morning, and--"

"Hold on, Captain. We agreed that I'd have until Wednesday to make some headway on it."

"That was when we thought your partner was coming back. It's only three more days, and I highly doubt you'll miraculously come up with a suspect by then."

"In fact, I've already developed a lead."

"What's that?"

"A lead? It's sort of like a clue to solving the case."

Dowd was quiet on the other end of the line, and I imagined him hacking up another wad. "Not funny. What is the fucking lead, McKenna?"

83

I was pushing it with the humor angle, especially since I'd already stretched the truth by calling it a lead. This was either going to be an outright lie or an admission that my case was so flimsy and speculative that I might as well hand it over to someone else. "Uh, vehicle descript." I said. "Possible license plate. Came up with it on a security camera across the street. I'm still here, working on it as we speak."

"You're at the office now?" He sounded surprised, and I sensed that I might have bought myself more time. "Well... I'm reassigning someone to partner with you. You're not going to run with this thing alone."

"Why?" My mind was ticking through the list of inspectors—all of them already in pairs. "There's nobody to team up with," I said. "Who are you giving me?"

"Linh Phú."

Now I was the one choking on phlegm. "Who is he? I've never even heard of the guy."

"Linh is a woman, McKenna."

I felt the Irish boiling up inside me as I hung up the phone. Not only was I worried about Lou, but I was angry over Dowd's decision to sideline me with a new inspector. The bottle in Cassidy's desk drawer wasn't going to see any action for a while, so I decided to go to work on it.

As I sat drinking in the empty office, the more pissed off I got. I'd gone to Dowd with my concerns over Lou's health, and the son-of-a-bitch blew me off. He had done everything in his power to screw with my first big investigation. Whether or not he was the mole in the homicide detail, his flagrant manipulation of my case made him a suspect in my mind. I made the decision right then and there to report my suspicions about the captain to Chief Fahey.

It was after midnight. I took the chief's card from my wallet, assuring myself that he would want to know. After all, he said that I could call him day or night.

The chief didn't answer.

Another couple of slugs from Cassidy's bottle helped to clarify the importance of the situation.

I need to drive to the chief's house tonight and tell him what's going on.

25

Bay Bridge

Sarah hadn't felt totally comfortable including the foreign private eye in her off-the-books activities but had acquiesced after talking with him over drinks.

Tam followed Sarah's Kia out of the parking garage across from the hotel, down Stevenson toward First Street. From there it was only a few blocks south to the bridge approach toward Oakland.

As soon as they turned out of the garage, Curtis noticed a man on a motorcycle pull away from the curb behind him. Tam watched in the mirror as the bike maintained an even distance, keeping to the same lane as Tam and Brooks. Every turn they made was mimicked by the motorcyclist.

The traffic light at First and Howard turned yellow just as Sarah entered the intersection, and Tam had to speed up to make it through. Glancing in the mirror, Tam watched the motorcycle zip around stopped cars and speed through the intersection against the red light. Recognizing the tail with a near certainty now, Tam guessed that Brooks, and not he, was the subject of it.

By the time they hit the freeway on-ramp, there was no doubt left in Tam's mind. They drove onto the bridge's lower deck, which carries only eastbound traffic.

Tam called Sarah's cell and told her what he was seeing; describing the driver as unknown gender or race, wearing Levis, a black leather jacket and black, full-face helmet. Sarah quickly came up with a plan to find out which of them was being followed, and also how to lose the tail.

She accelerated into the fast lane while Tam maintained an even speed. The motorcycle immediately sped up and moved into the fast lane, confirming that Sarah was the focus. As the motorcyclist tried to pass Tam, he gently eased over in front of it as if he simply wasn't paying attention. The bike quickly swung back to go around Tam on the other side. Again, Tam drifted in front of the motorcycle.

Backing off before his interference appeared intentional, Tam watched the bike speed by. As it passed, Tam noticed its fork stem held a mounted cell phone—which Tam realized had a Bluetooth connection into the guy's helmet. The driver was more than likely coordinating with others as he drove.

Thankfully, the private detective had impeded the motorcyclist enough to give Brooks a comfortable lead. She discreetly took the Treasure Island exit midway across the bridge. The motorcyclist raced past the exit, still straining to spot Sarah's Kia ahead of him.

At some point, the pursuer realized she had given him the slip. Tam saw the bike decelerate suddenly as the driver glanced back. Unfortunately for him, he was well past the off-ramp and in the middle of traffic by that point.

Though impossible for the biker to back up on the one-way bridge deck, Tam realized that he might be directing an accomplice to take the exit he had missed.

Following Sarah's route, Tam exited the bridge and continued onto the island's defunct Naval Station. He found Sarah in front of the old administration building, leaning against her car.

Sarah cautiously led Tam the remaining three miles across the bridge to a parking garage at Jack London Square. Seeing no further sign of the motorcyclist, she parked her Kia there and the two drove the rest of the way to her office in Tam's rental car.

The office building and adjoining parking lot were empty, so Sarah coded her way inside and again pulled the blinds to block the light. Tam slid a folding metal chair over to Sarah's desk as she logged into her computer.

At first, Elvis Lang's name search revealed only a driver's license with a listed address at 168 Turk Street in San Francisco. A GPS map search showed no residential building, only a narrow lot used for parking.

"No great surprise there," said Brooks. "I'll try running the guy on our USCIS ELIS system. If he's a foreigner, this program will out him."

A few seconds later, Brooks straightened in her seat and began typing furiously. "No wonder there isn't much on this guy," she said. "Lang is a bullshit alias." Sarah punched a few more keys. "His real name is Elvis Lugailo."

"What kind of name is that?"

"Latvian, apparently." Sarah read from the monitor. "Says he's been here on a work visa for the past two years."

"What kind of work?"

"Security guard." She squinted into the flickering screen, "At the Latvian Consulate in San Francisco."

"Might explain the diplomatic angle."

"A security guard?" Sarah frowned. "I'm not seeing it. They're not even on the food chain."

She printed a copy of Lugailo's Latvian passport photo, and they both sat studying his ruddy face and puffy eyes.

"That's one of the guys," said Tam. "He spoke to me in front of the warehouse and then went inside with another guy. I followed them to Golden Gate Park later that night, and one of them was killed. I'm sure of it. Either he or his companion were shot by a third man."

With Tam watching, Sarah spent the next few hours searching various federal data bases. They found nothing more on the Latvian, whose bogus signature had authorized the release of the stolen cargo container over a month prior.

She looked at the clock. "Shit, we need to shake a leg."

Tam's puzzled expression made Sarah laugh. "It means we gotta get the hell out of here before my boss shows up for work."

She shut down the computer and turned out the lights before moving through the dark office to the front door. The black outline of the East Bay hills was tinged with blue, signaling the approaching daylight.

"Stop," whispered Tam. "Behind those trailers across the street."

They paused a few seconds to let their eyes acclimate to the dark. Slowly, the profiles of several figures on motorcycles emerged out of the shadows.

"I count four," Sarah said. "You?"

"Four." Tam stepped back into the office, allowing Sarah to ease the door closed. "Identical to the guy I saw following you across the bridge."

"But we lost the tail," Sarah said. "There's no way we were followed here."

"Unless they already knew where you work."

She waved a dismissive hand. "What about a bug? Could they have put a tracker on my car?" Sarah shook her head as soon as she said it. "Never mind. I forgot that we left my car in the parking garage."

A still silence descended over them, as they stared at each other through the darkness.

"Your handbag," said Tam.

Sarah's eyebrows pinched together. "That girl in the bar, the one who borrowed our chair."

Rifling through her shoulder bag, Sarah tossed keys, pens, phone chargers and chewing gum into the air. With her purse nearly purged, her fingers finally grasped an unfamiliar object. Tam used the light from his phone to illuminate the tiny GPS tracker that had been secreted at the bottom of her handbag.

"Son-of-a-bitch." In her fury, Sarah reared back, ready to smash it against the doorframe.

"Wait!" Tam held a hand in the air. "It might be useful to us."

Gathering her cluttered effects from the floor, Sarah stuffed the tracking device back into her purse.

Tam cracked the door again and saw that the sky had lightened considerably. "They're still out there," he said. "All four of them."

Sarah glanced at the clock. "It's six-thirty, and Tim will be here any minute. We've got to get our asses out of here, and I mean now!"

26

**25 San Benito Way
San Francisco**

"So this is how the other half lives."

It was 1 a.m. when I turned off Portola onto the wide, tree-lined streets of St. Francis Wood. Something was different about the neighborhood, but I couldn't put my finger on it at first. Then it came to me. No power poles or overhead wires like the rest of the city.

The chief's house was perched on an upward sloping plot on the east side of the street. It was a narrow, Tudor style home with two floors of living space and a below grade single car garage. Fancy, in an old San Francisco sort of way.

A small lamp was visible through the louvered blinds in the downstairs window. That, and the fact that the trash bins had been set out by the curb, convinced me that the chief was home.

I parked under a streetlight to check my phone messages. No callback from the chief, and nothing from Nay Nay, or Shaday, or whatever the hell she changed her name to. I'd missed a couple of calls from Doris, but I wasn't about to call her back. Dialing the chief's personal number again, I still got no answer. Suddenly, I wasn't so sure that pounding on his door in the middle of the night was such a good idea.

But as I mulled over the facts again, my courage slowly returned. It was at Chief Fahey's direction that I was investigating this corruption thing to begin with. And, according to the chief, it was important enough to keep the investigation just between the two of us. My job was to find out who was steering a big murder investigation in the wrong direction, and for my money, that person was Captain Greg Dowd.

Springing from my seat and closing the car door with gusto, I felt I had found my huevos again. Presenting my case against Dowd to the chief was the right thing to do.

I hit the remote lock out of habit. The car chirped and a dog barked somewhere down the street. A neighbor's light came on and I quickly hustled up the walkway and into the shadow of a tree. Stupid move, I thought. I'd have probably been quieter had I not taken a few snorts. Then, worrying that Chief Fahey would smell it on my breath, I returned to the car for some gum. This time I used my key instead of the remote.

The lamp in the living room was still on when I got to the stone landing at the top of his front steps. Through the slanting louvered blinds, I saw no one in the living room.

I tapped lightly on the front door, waited a second, then moved back to the window. No sound from inside and no movement.

A walkway led around to the left side the house, so I descended the steps and followed the flagstone path toward the back. Feeling my way in the dark, I had made it to a small wooden gate when a sensor tripped and a blinding light came on.

"Shit!" I ran my hand along the inside of the gate until I felt the latch, then flipped it open and slipped quietly into the back yard. Leaning back against the house for what seemed like several minutes, I waited for the sensor to shut off.

As I stood in the shadows, I wondered if I had attracted the attention of some nosy, pretentious neighbor. I remembered reading that the residents were an uptight bunch. In fact, St. Francis Wood did not even allow minority residents when it was originally built. It had actually been written into their bylaws, and wasn't until 1960 that the first minority family moved in.

The sensor lights finally went off and I made my way to the back patio. The rear-facing rooms were dark, and the drapes were all closed. Spotting an open upstairs window, I called up toward it in a loud whisper. "Chief! Psssst! Chief Fahey!"

Still nothing. I'd started to worry that the old chief was sick, or maybe he had fallen.

I tried a couple of doors, but they were locked. One of them had some sort of pet access door, and I suddenly panicked at the thought of a dog. I've had a fear of them since a beagle named Sydney bit me on the ass when I was a kid.

Crouching down in a kind of push-up position, I struggled to keep the knees of my slacks from touching the damp concrete. Then, poking my head through the swinging pet door, I saw that it was a laundry room. On my right were a washer and dryer, and there was a wash basin on the opposite side. The room opened to a kitchen at the far end, but it was dark and I couldn't see into it. I listened for a few seconds and the house was quiet.

Not wanting to get myself wedged in the narrow opening, I began to back my head out. Suddenly, I heard an odd sound—like the groan of our ice maker just before it ejects a new load of ice into the tray. I glanced back into the laundry room, and I heard it again. This time it sounded more like a growl.

I craned my neck and suddenly saw the owner of the doggie door. Not Sydney, thankfully, but a gray schnauzer who looked as ancient as the chief. He offered a halfhearted *woof*, and then sat staring at me from the far doorway.

Realizing that my aching knees had succumbed to the wet patio, I pulled my head out of the opening and stood up. I hoisted my pant leg over my knee brace and tried to wipe the mud off my new slacks.

I'd sobered up a bit, and the impulse to report my suspicions had waned. In fact, bothering the old chief in the dead of night now seemed like a stupid idea. I decided that I had better get out of the neighborhood before someone called the cops.

How could I explain why I was rooting around the chief's house in the dead of night, especially to Dowd once he caught wind of it?

"Well, Captain, I've been on a secret mission for the chief to find a saboteur in our unit. And, with all due respect, I went to the chief's house to tell him that I think it's you."

27

2812 Kelsey Street, Berkeley

"I need to change that damn ringtone." Sarah, groped the top of the nightstand until she found her phone. "Brooks."

"Agent Brooks?" The voice was matter-of-fact. "Paul Bise down at MET. Wouldn't have bothered you at home, but I knew you'd want to hear."

She felt as if she had just gotten into bed, saw the harsh glint of sunlight through her window and asked, "What time is it?"

"Eight o'clock in the morning." The customs enforcement team supervisor paused. "Your manifest hold on the two containers from the MS Versand? Someone's here to claim them. Says he'll have two transport rigs here within the hour."

"Negative." Sarah sprung from her bed. "Do not let anyone touch those trailers. Hold on to whoever else shows up to claim them, and I'll deal with the son-of-a-bitch you've got once I get there."

The CBP inspection warehouse was less than eight miles from Sarah's cottage in the hills of Berkeley, but Monday morning traffic was already thickening. As she jockeyed back and forth between lanes, passing cars on the right and speeding through yellow lights, it occurred to Sarah that she had no official standing at the present time. Sure, she might still be able to talk her way out of a speeding ticket, but what was she going to do when she got to the CBP inspection station? Her enforcement team buddy could only cover for her so far.

Only a few hours earlier, Sarah had narrowly escaped four motorcycle riders who had tracked her to her office. She'd placed an anonymous call to the police, and several City of Oakland and Port Security officers responded to intercept the suspicious bikers. As the motorcyclists fled, the cops pursued them. It was then that Brooks and Tam had been able to slip out.

On her way home, Sarah had tossed the tracking device into the back of a garbage truck, figuring that would keep the motorcyclists busy for a while. She knew that she and Tam had been lucky to slip away, and she hoped her luck would continue today.

Getting to Alameda in under twenty minutes, she found the formless facility nearly blending into the cloudy sky. Turning into the gated grounds and quickly flashing her badge at the security kiosk, Sarah spotted two empty CBP emergency vehicles—their rotating lights reflecting off of the puddled blacktop. They were stopped midway along the row of trailers backed against the building.

A couple of uniformed officers stepped down from the loading dock, a handcuffed man gripped tightly between them. He wore a black cap, sweatshirt and Levis.

Sarah thought it best to park away from the action in case CBP bigwigs happened to show up. In that case, she'd make a hasty exit before being seen.

She stepped from her car to get a better look at the man being detained. Suddenly, the crack of a gunshot sent her diving onto the pavement. She had reacted before her mind even comprehended what was happening. It was like a slow motion rewind of her shooting in Oakland only twelve days earlier.

But no pain, no blood, no broken glass. Sarah realized she hadn't been hit, nor had her beloved Kia. The gunshot had echoed around the courtyard of trucks and buildings, making it impossible to know where it had originated. Scrambling on her hands and knees to the front of her car, she poked her head around the fender, trying to spot the muzzle flash of the next shot. But there was none.

A commotion and frantic yelling drew her attention farther down the loading dock, where she saw the two arresting officers scrambling for cover. The prisoner, who seconds earlier had been held between them, was now crumpled on the ground—his knit cap laying several feet away and the right side of his head completely gone. All that remained was a fibrous mass of tissue oozing over a jutting jawbone onto the pavement beneath the man.

As the officers screamed into their radios, Sarah saw her friend, Bise, spring from the back of the warehouse and bound down the steps. With his handgun at a low ready position, he tried to acquire a target while diving behind a stack of pallets. She heard him ask the officers if they'd been hit. Neither of them had. But Sarah knew they'd been close enough to have been splattered with bone, blood and brain matter.

It wasn't me, she suddenly realized. *This was a sniper attack, and it wasn't aimed at me. The shooter hit his intended target—the detained suspect. They could have shot me, or they could have shot either of the enforcement officers, if that's who they'd been after. But someone had intentionally taken out the guy who had showed up to claim the stolen containers.*

Sarah jumped to her feet and scanned southward—the most likely place from which to have taken the shot. A weed covered mound about the height of a two story building stood on the other side of a chain-link and barbed wire fence. It was, maybe, 200 feet away. Add to that another 100 feet in the opposite direction to where the body fell. The shooter definitely had some training.

A flicker of movement on the crest of the hill caught her eye. Sarah couldn't be certain if it was the shooter, but whatever action she would take, she knew it had to be taken quickly. The incident had been called in by now—a shooting at the CBP facility, one fatality, two federal officers nearly hit, and a sniper on the loose. The cavalry would be rolling toward the scene, and there was no time to spare. Not if Sarah wanted to keep her name out of it.

The Kia whined as it sped past the block-long fence on Mitchell Avenue. Halfway down, a gate stood partially open with its padlock dangling from a severed security chain. She turned through the opening and into the vacant lot, then bounded up a rutted incline. The tires spun, then caught, then spun again. Finally gaining traction, the car made it to the top of the mound where it continued along the ridgeline. At the far end of the hill, the terrain dipped back down to another chain-link fence separating the lot from the waterway.

The sniper's outline was now visible against the backdrop of the murky bay water. He moved quickly toward the fence, a scoped rifle and mounted tripod slung over his shoulder. This guy knew what he was doing, except that he was heading toward the fence—a dead end with only the estuary on the other side. There was nowhere to run.

Sarah slammed her Kia into park and jumped out, taking a covered position behind the wedge of the door. "Stop right there or I'll shoot." She instinctively reached for her duty weapon, but there was no holster and no firearm. Realizing it had been seized by the Oakland PD, Sarah dove back into the car for her shoulder bag. When she emerged with her personal .380, the man had already made it to the top of the fence.

The suspect—dressed all in black—continued over the top. Sarah started to repeat her order to stop, but abandoned it when she saw that the sniper's shoulder strap hung up on the barbed wire. It was her only chance to get off a clean shot.

At the exact second that she fired, the man dropped to the ground on the far side of the fence. He rolled over the edge toward the estuary, out of Sarah's sight. She assumed he had dropped into the murky waters of the shipping channel.

A few tense seconds passed as Sarah advanced on the suspect's last position—her handgun raised and extended in front of her. Fully expecting the sniper to pop up from the rocky shoal and return fire, Sarah was confused by the sudden sound of a motor kicking into gear.

Rushing to the fence, she saw a sleek speedboat accelerating away from the shore. Two black-clad figures—a man and a woman—had hoisted the suspect over the gunwale, while another man in black clothing drove the boat.

At full-throttle, the boat sent a rooster tail of spray into the air as it zig-zagged across the estuary and disappeared into the cool gray fog of the bay.

Sarah stared out at the gray water, quiet and still, as if everything that just happened had been a dream.

Glancing down through the fence, Sarah's gaze suddenly seized. A blot of blood, smeared among the trampled grasses, trailed away over the edge of the embankment toward the water.

Immediately, wailing sirens pierced the morning air from all directions. Sarah had only minutes to decide her next move before a parade of police agencies saturated the entire area.

28

The General

Monday morning was gray and windy. I stopped by San Francisco General on the way into work, hoping they'd let me in to visit Lou.

I'd called the cardiac care unit on the way across the bridge and learned a few things. First, that my partner was still alive; second, that he was in serious but stable condition; and third, that the hospital was now officially, Zuckerberg San Francisco General Hospital. I'm not sure why, but of all the problems that had come my way in the last couple of weeks, the hospital's name change bugged me the most.

Cassidy looked even worse than when I'd seen him last. Glancing at the poor guy, I doubted that he'd ever make it back to the detail.

He was sleeping when I walked in, and his wife was in a chair next to the bed. She looked almost as bad as Lou. I hugged her, told her that her husband would be okay, and I said that I'd be there for her—whatever she needed. She gave my hand a *thank you* squeeze, but I saw in her eyes that my promise of help lacked credibility. I wondered if she had been talking to Doris.

"Here," she said, forcing a cellphone into the palm of my hand. "Lou's phone hasn't stopped buzzing since he got in here."

Slipping it into my coat pocket, I realized that everyone in the detail was on a group text and Cassidy's phone was still receiving Captain Dowd's latest diatribes.

"Lou doesn't need the stress of work calls right now," she said.

I just nodded. "All that stuff can wait until he gets back."

Mrs. Cassidy frowned. My effort to look at a glass half full had fallen flat. The woman had seen her husband through enough in his career, and now she just wanted him to get well enough to retire.

A small TV murmured at low volume from a hinged arm hanging over Lou's bed. A breaking news story flashed on the screen, reporting a shooting at a Customs inspection facility in Alameda. But rather than upset Mrs. Cassidy further by turning up the sound, I gave her husband a pat on the shoulder and left.

As I got off the elevator on the first floor, I spotted Sha Nay Nay Moore walking down a corridor leading away from the lobby. She hadn't seen me, so I followed her to the parking lot on the west side of the main hospital building. She was halfway across the lot, headed toward the bus stop on 23rd Street when I called out to her.

"Nay Nay..." *What is it that I'm supposed to call her?*

She turned. "You stalking me, McKenna?"

"What? No." I caught up to her. "How come you never called me back?"

"I did."

"No." I pulled out my phone as proof, but it was off. Or, the ringer was off. I had turned something off after reading the warnings posted in the ICU: NO CELLULAR PHONES ALLOWED. The signs were all over the place, and I thought the radio waves might interfere with the equipment or something. Anyway, I didn't want to be responsible for killing my own partner.

My informant watched impatiently as I fiddled with the phone. I had missed a text from Doris—something about an appointment with a marriage counselor; several missed calls from Captain Dowd; and a phone message from Sha Nay Nay.

"You don't need to listen to it," she said. "I just didn't want you to think I was bump'n you off."

"*Bump'n me off?*"

She shook her head as if I were a newcomer to the planet Earth. "So, you need to talk to me or what?" She motioned to a button on the side of my phone, which I flipped, and saw that I had volume again. "You really need to get with the times, McKenna."

"Yeah, I know. Anyway, I need to know everything about your *friend*. Elvis."

She scanned the parking lot. "Not here."

I walked her to my car and we drove onto Potrero. "Okay, now can you tell me how you know the guy?"

She smirked. "How you think I know him?"

"Well, yeah, I understand that. But why would you remember him? I mean, do you work for him? Does he sell you dope?"

The girl leaned back and rubbed a hand over her closed eyes. I must have a way of frustrating people, because I've gotten that same reaction before.

"I saw him a lot," she finally said. "Like, he was a regular. Back in the day. Know what I'm say'n?"

"Are you telling me that you don't work the streets anymore?" I must have had a smile, because she pulled up her hood and sat there with her arms crossed.

"No! and I don't use no more, neither." She glared at me. "Like I told you, McKenna. I'm work'n on straighten'n my shit out."

She sat there as I tried my best to visualize Sha Nay Nay Moore going straight.

"Sorry," I said after a bit. "You're going to have a baby, right?"

She nodded.

"Is that why you were at the hospital?"

She nodded again.

"Is everything going all right? I mean, with the pregnancy?"

Another nod. She dropped her hood. "Why were *you* there?"

I took a breath and let it out. "My partner had a heart attack."

She looked away, out the side window. "That sucks. He gonna be okay?"

"I hope."

A minute passed. "Go that way," she said, pointing toward 9th Street.

We drove several blocks up 9th and she pointed down Natoma. "This is where Elvis used to meet me. Just a few blocks down, at the corner of 6th."

It made sense. Natoma was the narrow alley where the two of them had been arrested. The area used to be a cesspool of whores, drugs and parolees. But since the push to gentrify SOMO, the place had become halfway decent. Which made me wonder why they would pick that spot for a car date.

Nay answered without me even asking. "We mostly went to the Beverly on 6th, but Elvis didn't have time that day. So the asshole parked the car right on the street, and then the cops came. That's about all I can tell you about the dude."

The east end of Natoma terminated where it ran into 6th. Directly across the street was a little rat-hole called Hotel Beverly. Apparently, the redevelopment efforts hadn't made it to that side of the street.

"He didn't have time," I laughed. "Classy guy."

Sha Nay Nay shrugged. "I guess he couldn't get away from work for too long or something."

I stopped the car. "What do you mean? He works around here?"

"Yeah, I guess." She twisted in her seat. "Somewhere back there." she motioned in the direction we had just come.

"Show me!" I backed the car up the alley, which is one-way.

She shrugged again. "I guess cops can drive any way they want, huh?"

When we got to the corner of Russ Street, she told me to stop. "There," she said, pointing to the south curb. "We were in the car right there when the cops came up on us."

"You say he works around here?" I threw the car into park.

"Close-by, I think."

"Do you know what he does?" I scanned the buildings. "What kind of job?"

She shook her head.

"Stay here." I got out and walked up Russ. The two-block-long street was a weird mix of fenced lots and old warehouses, with a few homes and apartment houses sandwiched between them. Other than an Italian cookie company, none of the buildings had any signage.

I made a few notes in my case file, then drove Sha Nay Nay back to her grandmother's apartment before finally heading into work.

As I rode the elevator up to the 5th floor, a question crept into my mind: *Why was Sha Nay Nay Moore helping me?*

29

933 Folsom Street
San Francisco

Curtis was up early and out in the foggy San Francisco morning. Armed with the new information about Elvis Lugailo's menial job at the Latvian Consulate, he decided to focus his attention there. He'd phoned Sarah to let her know what he was up to, but she did not pick up. And though he had agreed to share information with her, he left no message.

The consulate building was a shiny steel and glass structure on the south side of the street. A flagpole bearing the Latvian flag extended from a portico-covered stairway, and the country's coat of arms sat inside a plexiglass shadowbox next to the entrance. In front of the building, the one-way section of Folsom Street was congested with eastbound traffic. It offered the private eye limited spots from which he could discreetly conduct surveillance.

Tam settled for street parking, directly across from the consulate. Not the most subtle location, but better than nothing. As he sat there watching—for what, he wasn't sure—Tam considered the events of the previous day; the fact that he and Sarah had somehow been located and followed, and the people who did it had managed to slip a tracking transmitter into Sarah's purse. He wondered how they could have known where to find them, and why they would want to monitor Sarah's whereabouts?

It dawned on Tam that whoever they were, they were not the same people who had shot at Brooks. Instead of following her through the city and across the bridge, they would have simply shot her at the bar if that was their goal.

Just then, Sarah's number displayed on his vibrating cell phone.

"Where are you?" she asked, before he could say hello.

"Uh, in San Francisco, across the street from the consulate."

"See anything?" Brooks sounded out of breath.

"You mean like the security guard, Elvis what's his name? No, not outside anyway." Tam took a sip of coffee. "Coincidentally, this place is on Folsom, only a few blocks from the Russ Street warehouse where our other container is stashed."

"Really..."

"And I've been thinking, these guys put the tracker in your purse for a reason. I think they're hoping you'll lead them to someone."

Sarah was silent.

Tam asked, "Did something happen?"

"I'll tell you about it when I get there."

Tam had just gotten back into his car after smoking a cigarette and stretching his legs when Sarah tapped on his passenger window. She slid into the seat next to him.

"Any change?" she asked.

"No, nothing."

Tam told Sarah that the more he thought about it, the more he was convinced that the guys on the motorcycle had used him to find her. It was the only way he could reason that they were at the Pied Piper Bar at the same time as he and Sarah.

"I called my tech guys in Hong Kong," he said. "Turns out that my bank card company registered two intrusions in the past week, but since no charges were made to my account, they never alerted me."

"Which means what?" Sarah asked.

"It means they hacked my bank's database and found out that I had made charges at the Palace Hotel. That's how they found us."

Again, Sarah was silent—contemplating the suspects' motives and the actions they took after locating her and Tam in the hotel's bar.

Tam continued, "That's why I'm pretty sure they're following you in order to get to someone else."

After a long pause, Sarah said, "And I led them right to him."

"Right to who?"

She explained the series of events of that morning, beginning with her wakeup call from the enforcement team supervisor. She told Tam about the man who had shown up to claim the two containers, of his arrest, and described how a sniper had killed the guy before she'd even had a chance to interview him. "Worse yet," she said, "the suspect had no identification on him. So until the Alameda County Coroner's Bureau can roll a set of prints and run them through the state database, we won't know who he is... was."

"What do you think?" said Tam. "Did his face look like the photo of our guy?"

"It looked like a goddamn bowl of spaghetti."

They sat there in silence, trying to compute the depth of the case they had toppled into: international transportation, stolen cargo, murder, and possibly the involvement of foreign governments. And the worst part was that neither of them could take any official action; Tam, because of his client's need for absolute secrecy, and Brooks, owing to her suspension of law enforcement powers. For two entirely different reasons, whatever actions they took from this point forward had to be unrecognizable to the rest of the world.

Tam gazed across the table at her. "Do you think your shot hit him?"

Sarah nodded.

"So, how did you get away?"

"The locals were looking for a rooftop sniper or someone trying to leave on foot. It was too foggy for a helicopter to get in the air, so I was able to drive past the first police units before they could set up a perimeter."

He nodded to himself then looked across at the consulate. "Let's go inside."

Sarah straightened in her seat.

"Why not?" he said. "We're just spinning our wheels sitting out here. Who knows if this Elvis character even works there anymore?"

After coming up with a plan, the two crossed Folsom and entered the building.

As it turned out, the consulate occupied only the third floor. Off of the main hallway, they entered through a door marked PASSPORTS AND VISAS. Rows of folding chairs took up the right side of the room, and on the left snaked a line of people waiting behind roped stanchions. It looked like a TSA checkpoint.

Tam and Brooks took their places in the line, awaiting their turn at the window in front.

"Hello," said Sarah. "My husband and I are traveling to Latvia next month. What do we need to know?" It seemed a logical segue to the topic she really wanted to talk about.

The woman wore a tight smile as she began a scripted response. "U.S. citizens may enter the Republic of Latvia with only a passport. No tourist visa is required, as long as your visit is no longer than ninety days."

"And if we plan to stay longer?" asked Tam.

"In that case, you would need to apply for temporary residence. The application process includes fingerprinting and an FBI criminal background check."

Sarah held up a finger. "Now, we were told something different the last time we were in here."

"Oh?" The woman's waxy smile melted.

"Yes," continued Sarah. "In fact, we spoke with another of your employees who told us that--"

"Elvis," said Tam. "I remember his name was Elvis, dear."

Sarah nodded and turned back to the woman behind the counter. "Elvis, that's right. Perhaps if we spoke with him..."

The woman tossed her head back. "I can assure you that my information is accurate. And Elvis Lugailo, the employee you spoke with, is merely a security guard. He wouldn't be familiar with the administrative policies. In any case, he did not show up for work today."

Sarah eyed Tam—both of them wondering if Elvis Lugailo and the man shot by the sniper were one and the same.

"Now, if you'd like me to check the validity of your passports," the woman continued, "I'd be happy to take a look at them."

Tam patted his breast pocket. "I must have forgotten to bring it with me. We'll have to drop by tomorrow."

The woman shook her head. "The office will be closed in the morning, but we'll be open between 2 and 5 p.m."

They turned to leave, but Sarah suddenly turned back. "Why?"

"Excuse me?" said the woman.

Sarah stepped back up to the counter. "Why are you closed tomorrow morning?"

Awkwardness edged into the woman's expression. "If you must know, some of us will be attending a funeral—a family member of a consulate employee."

"Can you tell us where?" asked Tam. "My wife and I would like to pay our respects."

"No, I'm sorry. It's a private service."

30

The Bullpen

"Where in the hell have you been, McKenna?"

I had just walked in, had barely made it through the door and into the detail's bullpen—an open area behind Mrs. Ocampo, where Captain Dowd holds his weekly meetings. It's close to the coffee pot and far enough away from our desks that the inspectors aren't tempted by emails and phone calls. Anyway, the boss didn't seem to mind dressing me down right there in front of the other inspectors. And though I wasn't about to get baited into a fight I couldn't win, I did want to make him feel like shit.

"I stopped by the hospital to check on my partner, sir."

A few groans floated from the desks around me, and I could tell that the guilt angle had struck pay dirt.

"And by the way Captain Dowd, Lou sends his best to you. And to the rest of the guys, too." I turned with an arm-sweep around the whole room. "He says thanks for all the prayers and good thoughts."

The group was all smiles and nods. Moretti called out, "God bless him!" And one of the others raised his hands above his head for a slow, reverent applause.

Dowd's eyes burned into me. "Glad to hear it," he snapped. "But we've got bigger things to worry about here. Chief Fahey died last night."

I wheeled around toward him. "Wait, what?" My head started to wobble and then caught fire. Steadying myself, I groped my way over to a chair, then sat down and took some deep breaths. "Died? Chief F-Fa-Fah...?"

"What the hell's the matter with you?" Dowd said as he started around a list of assignments. "Anyway, everything else goes on hold for now. We're putting all of our resources into the Fahey death investigation."

One of the inspectors asked, "Any idea how he died?"

Dowd shook his head. "Nothing obvious, yet. Doesn't appear to have been a struggle. Doors were locked. But the killer could have had a key or found one open and then locked up when he left."

I wanted to yell out: *They were all locked!*

How could this be happening. I was just there...

My first thought was that the chief had slipped, and then I figured no, he probably had a heart attack, or maybe choked to death on a sandwich. But it took me a few more seconds before I realized that the chief hadn't died of natural causes; he had been murdered.

My head went crazy with ideas; some left wing organization was responsible. Muslim extremists. No, a conspiracy inside City Hall, or worse, within the department. Then I glanced up at the captain and I knew. Dowd had somehow figured out that I was about to finger him as the mole. It was Dowd who killed the chief.

There were puzzled expressions around the room. "No point of entry or signs of struggle," echoed Moretti. "He probably passed from natural causes. So why the full investigation?"

"He was the chief of police, for Christ's sake!" Dowd moved on to the briefing sheet in his hand. "Here's what we know: First off, we got a 9-1-1 call at zero-eight-hundred this morning from Fahey's gardener, a Mr. Tito Provencal. He says he found the side gate open, which leads to the back yard patio. The chief's driver, Police Officer Donnie Tye, showed up thirteen minutes later to take the chief to a meeting at City Hall. When Tye couldn't get an answer at the door, he forced entry and found Fahey on the living room floor. He'd been dead for at least five or six hours, we think."

Counting backwards in my head, I realized that the chief was probably killed shortly before or after I went to his house.

"The initial responding units found wet footprints on the patio, yet both Provencal and the driver swear they hadn't set foot back there. Anyway, the gardener checks out okay, and, of course, the driver is SFPD.

At that point the meeting broke up pretty quickly. Dowd ordered most of the detail to the chief's house in St. Francis Wood. A couple of guys were sent to re-interview Provencal, and I was told to stay put in the office.

My brain throbbed in my head as my thoughts swam laps. What would I do now that the chief was dead? Who could I go to with evidence of my secret corruption investigation? For whatever strange reason, I wanted to get back out to the chief's house to see him for myself. But Dowd didn't want me there—which only made me more suspicious of him.

I drifted listlessly back to my desk, only to find my new partner sitting in a stiff chair that we usually use for interviewing witnesses. She had an open laptop balanced on her knees and a paper cup with a teabag hanging out of it on the floor next to her.

She set the computer aside and stood up to greet me. "Linh Phú," she said, her tiny hand extended. "I've heard a great deal about you, Inspector McKenna. So sorry to hear about your partner."

"Likewise." I shook her hand and then unburdened myself of my file, my coat, my hand-held radio, and my car keys. I tossed Lou's phone into my desk drawer. "Guess you can sit over there," I told her, motioning toward Cassidy's train wreck of a desk. "At least until he gets back." I shoved some old newspapers aside, helping clear a spot for her laptop and tea.

"I understand you are currently investigating a homicide that occurred in the Park District."

"Yep." I patted the case file in front of me. "I've already developed several solid leads."

I then told Phú about the case, showing her a few things out of the file—the pathology report, the video disc, and the arrest photo of the possible witness, Elvis Lang.

You could tell right away that she was no dummy; took a lot of notes and asked decent questions. But Phú was a little wisp of a thing, five-one or two at the most. Looked like she'd blow away in a good wind.

"May I view the video evidence?" She asked.

I showed her how to insert the disc into the laptop, and she waited patiently as I demonstrated how to use the mouse clicker to advance the images. After a minute or so she tapped something onto her keyboard and was moving through the frames lickety-split.

"McKenna!" Captain Dowd bellowed across the office. Plowing through the maze of desks, he stopped when he was nearly on top of me. "Lou Cassidy never said any of the things you said! I just talked to the hospital and he's been in a coma since they brought him in last night."

I did my best to excuse it as a misunderstanding. Told Dowd that I knew, intuitively, how my old partner felt, and that he would have been thankful for the good thoughts. I fumbled an apology, telling him that I was still a little distraught about Lou's illness, and I was also overtired from putting in so many hours on my homicide case.

"Yeah, about your case," said Dowd. "Time's up, I'm reassigning it." He gazed around the bullpen, looking for any inspector who hadn't yet left the office.

"Wait, Captain." I flipped open the file. "I've got an informant who knows a person of interest, Elvis Lang."

"Your snitch is named Elvis Lang?"

I shook my head. "She's a hooker out in the Bayview."

"There's a hooker named Elvis Lang?"

"No," I said. "The snitch. Her name is Sha Nay Nay Moore."

The captain closed his eyes as if he were praying for patience. "The story was better when her name was Elvis."

"Anyway, Lang's rental car was abandoned at the scene near my homicide victim, and he's got a criminal record."

"Your victim has a criminal record?"

"No, Elvis Lang does." I took a breath. "He may have been with my victim at the time of the shooting, and may even be a suspect." I was trying to get everything in, probably too rapidly. "And there's another car—the one I told you about, on the security camera video."

"You said you have a photo of the license."

I swallowed hard, knowing how far I had already stretched the truth.

"Show me." Dowd wasn't backing down. He was serious about this, and there was no way for me to get out of it. I had climbed to the end of the limb, and now I was about to saw it off.

Leaning over Linh Phú, I felt Dowd leaning over me. "Go to 3:20 a.m.," I said.

Linh typed in a code that advanced the tape to the exact spot. I swallowed again, realizing that there was nothing but a blurred rectangle at the back end of a dark car.

"What's that?" said the captain, almost shouting. "It's shit, that's what it is. I can't see a damn thing. You can't even tell if it's a license plate. For all I know, it's a block of fucking cheese stuck to his bumper!"

Linh banged out a few more keystrokes and the frame widened and refocused on just the plate.

"How did you do that?" I asked.

"Zoom-in feature," she said, almost whispering. "Command, shift, six, then toggle the arrow keys. If you hit the alt and the up arrow, the system performs a process called interpolation, which scales algorithms and adds pixels into the blank spaces." She looked back at us with a self-conscious smile. "It overlays a program that uses a fractal-based resizing tool to smooth out the image, so you'll be able to see fine details."

And here's me, showing her how to load the damn disc.

The enlarged image of the back end of the car came into better clarity, but the license number was still difficult to read. At least now you could tell that it wasn't a block of cheese. In truth though, it was still shit. The plate was mostly a white rectangle, but the numbers were undistinguishable.

Captain Dowd backed up a step and looked at his watch. "I've got a commander meeting upstairs. Fine, okay then. You two can stay on it a while longer, and let me know what you come up with." Then he leaned close to me and whispered into my ear, "I don't like you, McKenna. Never have. You don't make something happen soon, I'll not only pull you off the case but I'll bounce your silly ass right out of the bureau."

He left, and I pulled my chair around next to Linh.

"I'm so sorry," she said. "I didn't mean to speak out of turn."

"You kidd'n? What you said saved my ass." I slid my chair closer. "Now let's try to zoom-in tighter on that license plate."

But it was as tight as she could make it, and the clarity was still only marginal. The plate appeared mostly white, with some red and blue, and the letters Q and P preceding a series of numbers. Clearly, the formatting was all wrong for a California license plate.

I found a website showing photos of every state's license plates, and with Linh watching over my shoulder, I was able to narrow it down to twelve—the state of Maryland being the closest in appearance.

As part of my new mentoring and training role, I delegated the rest of the license plate research to Phú. She began a telephone search while I started working on a court order for Elvis Lang's credit information. He had used a Visa card when he rented the Ford Focus at the Oakland airport, and I wanted to know if they had a better address for him.

A half hour into it, my new partner advised that the Maryland Department of Motor Vehicles had ten different styles of license plates—from the Chesapeake Bay plate to the amateur radio operator plate. And none of them began with the letters QP.

"Eleven more to go," I said to Linh. "Keep checking."

Mrs. Ocampo had clipped a note to my desk phone saying that the ME had called with the information I had requested about Gustavs Berzins's remains. My homicide victim's body had been released to the Latvian Lutheran Church on Hoffman Avenue.

Hoffman Avenue was the same street where Lam and Moretti's victim was found. I wondered what the chances were that out of over five thousand roadways in the City, my victim's body ends up in a church two blocks from where Rhonda Pitts, was murdered.

Random carjacking. Right.

Somebody was definitely covering something up. With the squad all out of the office, I thought it was a good time to snoop around their desks and figure out who. I owed it to Chief Fahey to find the dirty dog in the unit.

Thus far, I knew that Dowd had manipulated my case. And to the extent that he could, he had blocked my every attempt at finding Gustavs Berzins's killer. But I had to stay objective and keep an open mind. Moretti and Lam had been investigating the Pitts woman who had been shot dead in her car, and those two seemed entirely too comfortable calling it a random carjacking. Maybe one of them is the crooked cop. In any event, I was now convinced that my case and theirs were connected.

I found Rhonda Pitts's evidence folder on Alan Lam's desk, and opened it to a plastic zippered envelope in the back labeled PERSONAL EFFECTS. Inside were a ring of keys, her driver's license, credit cards, some makeup, and a pair of sunglasses.

I had to wonder about the keyring, since her car keys were never found at the scene. Checking them again, I realized that none fit a Toyota. *So, what did these keys go to?* It also seemed to me that someone should have run a history on her credit card charges. My first thought was that the investigators were so certain of the random nature of the crime, they weren't interested in diving deeper into it. Or, maybe they actually had looked into all of this, and I was just being overly suspicious. I put everything back, undisturbed.

Monday afternoon was spent typing up the court order for Elvis Lang's credit card information. With the exception of the car rental and what Sha Nay Nay had told me about where they met for their dates, I still had only scant info about the guy. It was late afternoon when the judge signed the order, but daylight had gotten away from me. Visa's legal department was already closed, and serving the court order would have to wait until the following day.

My Tuesday was quickly starting to fill up. Besides the funeral service for my victim and the court order for the credit card company, I knew the captain would be barking up my ass about the case. I hoped he'd be so busy in meetings about Chief Fahey's death and the pending funeral, that our paths wouldn't have time to cross.

Before heading home, I made a call to the church on Hoffman. Speaking to a guy who identified himself as the evangelical minister, I learned that a service for Gustavs Berzins was to be held the following morning at 10 a.m.

109

It's not unusual for a witness or even a murder suspect to attend the victim's funeral services. According to my promotional study guide, a good investigator should consider the attendees as potential witnesses. And as the lead investigator on this case, I planned to be at the church in the morning.

31

Latvian Lutheran Church
425 Hoffman Avenue

The little church looked more like a house. Its double doors led directly into a compact sanctuary framed with sixties-era mahogany paneling. A quaint little place with a stained glass window and a small raised area at the front. The main sanctuary was only six pews deep, which left no room for Curtis Tam and Sarah Brooks to blend in.

Instead, the two sat in Tam's car across the street and down the hill, watching the small group of mourners as they entered the church. Since the woman who had assisted them at the consulate might be one of them, they kept their distance.

Passing Tam's binoculars back and forth, they watched for anybody who matched the passport photo or general description of Elvis Lugailo. Neither had paid a lot of attention to the young woman at the Pied Piper Bar who had dropped the tracking device into Sarah's purse, but they were alert for anyone who looked like her as well. For that matter, they also kept an eye out for four mourners on motorcycles.

"Way too soon to bury the guy I saw get whacked yesterday," Brooks said. "They probably haven't even done his autopsy yet."

"Seems too coincidental not to be connected."

Sarah shrugged. "Who the hell knows anymore? This service could be for an employee's grandmother who slipped on a bar of soap in the shower."

Only five people had entered the church—a man and four women. None looked familiar to Tam and Brooks. One of the women wore black, and was escorted, or propped up, by the other three women. The two investigators assumed her to be a close relative, spouse, or perhaps the employee who had lost the family member.

The man with them was tall, and wore a black hat and long coat. He had gotten out of a black Lincoln Town Car bearing diplomatic license plates.

At the conclusion of the ceremony, they all left the church. The young woman in black and the three other girls got into one car, and the tall man drove off in the Lincoln. Once they had all left the area, Brooks and Tam entered the church.

A man dressed in a white robe and green vestment knelt at the front of the room, then stood and began picking up flower petals from the copper colored carpet. He straightened when they walked in.

"Can I help you?"

Brooks quickly flashed her federal badge then tucked it back into her purse. "My partner and I are here about the death."

"And to pay our deepest respects," added Tam.

Brooks rolled her eyes. "And that, too. Anyway, what can you tell us about the family?"

"So sad," said the minister. "No real family to speak of, at least not here in the states. Just a sister, I believe."

Tam leaned casually toward the open casket, and then nodded to Sarah.

"Anything else you can tell us about him?"

"No, I'm afraid not." The minister put the dead petals into the pocket of his robe. "Gustavs was not a regular here at the church. I did not know him at all."

"His sister?" asked Sarah.

The man shook his head. "Only that she works at the consulate."

The investigators thanked him, and Tam grabbed a memorial card from a low table near the door. When they got outside, the two stood on the sidewalk and studied it in the daylight: Gustavs Bērziņš, born August 1, 1985.

Motioning back toward the church, Tam said, "The deceased was definitely one of the men I followed from the Russ Street warehouse. He must have been the shooting victim from the other night in the park."

A few seconds later the low rumble of a car engine sounded, growing louder as it drew nearer. They both glanced to their right, down Hoffman Avenue, then Tam put a hand on Brooks's shoulder and hustled her across the street.

32

Golden Gate Bridge

Monday night had been pretty quiet around my house; Bridget stayed in her room and Doris ignored me. I think she was expecting me to finish what I had started on Sunday—lecturing Bridge about the drinking. But the Colts and the Panthers were playing in the Monday night game, and I just figured I'd deal with my daughter once the game was over. The score was close and it went longer than I expected. Anyway, one thing led to another and I never got around to my fatherly talk.

A pillow and blanket had been left on the futon in the den, and the savvy detective in me saw it as a clue. I poured myself a drink and then slept alone. Again.

I showered and left the house before Doris or Bridge were awake. A terse note had been left on the kitchen counter next to my keys: MARRIAGE COUNSELOR TONIGHT – 7 P.M.

I drove over the Golden Gate, deep in thought about my work, my marriage, and, really, about the direction of my life.

The office was empty when I arrived. I'd even beat Mrs. Ocampo, so I went ahead and put on the coffee. A light in Dowd's office made me wonder if he had even made it out of the building last night. Besides overseeing the chief's death investigation, I figured he'd probably been up all night plotting how next to screw me over.

One by one the rest of the detail came in, hung their coats, poured their coffees, checked their messages, and read their emails. When Dowd came out of his office and took a seat on the corner of Mrs. Ocampo's desk, we all started migrating toward the bullpen—a herd of wildebeests heading to the waterhole.

"Where are we with the Chief Fahey investigation?" Dowd started right off, as if there were no other cases to discuss. "Crime scene, first."

Frankie Moretti pulled out a small notepad. "Alarm system in the house hadn't been turned on. Doors were locked from the inside and all the windows were secured." He flipped a page. "But we're pretty sure someone else had been there."

"Inside the house?" asked Dowd.

"Not sure yet," said Moretti. "Looks like whoever it was may have tried to get into the laundry room through some kind of pet access door."

I felt a shudder go through my body. Swallowing the last mouthful of my coffee, I just stared down into my empty mug.

"Fabric impressions on the muddy concrete patio near the door, maybe a knee. And forensics collected a hair from the pet door hinge. Could be from the dog, but hopefully it belongs to the perp."

Unconsciously, I think I rubbed the back of my head.

"Anything else?"

"Couple of shoe prints in the soft dirt along the side of the house," Moretti said. "And apparently the dumbass stepped in a pile of dog shit."

Everyone laughed except me.

"Found traces of it all the way out to the street."

"Witness attempts," said Dowd, turning to Mendoza and Taylor.

"Only one," said Mendoza. "Guy across the street says he heard a car door slam and then the chirp of the door lock. Best he could recall, it was between one-thirty and two o'clock in the morning."

"Your witness see anybody?" asked Dowd.

I closed my eyes, not wanting to hear this.

"Not until the shit heel stepped in front of the sensor light." Taylor was talking now. "A walkway on the north side of the house, partially obscured by trees, but the witness got a glimpse of him." Taylor glanced at his notes. "White, maybe thirties or forties, husky."

"Vehicle?"

"Sedan," Mendoza said. "Maybe a Ford. It was parked on the street, right in front of the house. Oh yeah, and forensics collected a wad of chewing gum from the lawn. If it was his, they'll be able to get his DNA."

"We need a suspect to compare it with, gentlemen." Dowd flashed a glance at Phú before adding, "and ladies." He quickly turned to another pair of investigators. "ME's report."

Someone in the back of the room began talking. "Cause of death unknown at this point, but they're not ruling out asphyxiation or poisoning. Even something weird like electrocution. Lots of labs need to be done, and that'll take a while."

114

I sort of zoned out at that point. My head was buzzing and I felt like I was going to throw up. I'd have been a lot more careful had I known Chief Fahey was dead. Never considered that I was leaving evidence all over a damn homicide scene. This is so screwed up, I thought. They're going to think I killed him.

The meeting dragged on and on. It was getting close to ten, and I wanted to make my victim's funeral across town. My new partner was sitting in back of the group taking notes, and I was pretty sure she'd be able to fill me in when I got back. But when I slyly eased my way toward the door, Dowd called me out.

"Where the hell do you think you're going, McKenna?"

Everyone turned to look at me. I suddenly felt exposed, as if back in the glare of Chief Fahey's sensor light. Imagining a trail of dog shit on the bullpen floor behind me, I quickly answered, "An appointment with a witness in the--"

"Sit down," said Dowd. "You think you're the only one with a case? What part of 'put everything else on hold' didn't you understand?"

When the briefing finally broke up, it was nearly ten forty-five. I slipped on my coat and grabbed my keys.

"A word," said Dowd. "My office."

I looked at the clock again. Whatever he wanted, probably an ass chewing, was certain to take longer than *a word*. I also knew that I'd never be able to make it to the funeral on time to get a look at the attendees.

Hanging my coat back on my chair as if I were staying, I poked my head through the doorway of Dowd's office. "Got to take a quick leak," I said. "Be back in two shakes."

Then, I took the elevator down to the parking garage, got into the car and drove out. As I headed across town toward the Latvian church, I wondered if there would still be a desk waiting for me when I returned.

An earlier accident was still tying up 101, so I took Bryant to 24th. Moving through traffic as fast as possible, I checked my watch and realized that I would probably be too late. Stepping hard on the accelerator, I took the turn onto Hoffmann and gunned it up the hill.

The doors of the church were propped open, but I couldn't see anyone around the entrance. I parked in front, got out, and something caught my eye across the street. Two people—a man and a woman—standing next to a dark gray Toyota 4Runner. It was parked slightly down the hill, and I couldn't tell for sure if they were attendees of the service.

About to turn back toward the church, something made me stop and eyeball these two. I'd seen the man before. Asian, nicely dressed and physically fit. Like déjà vu, I could almost picture him standing on the opposite side of the street, but where? It wasn't coming to me.

I couldn't tell whether he'd also recognized me, but he quickly avoided my gaze and ducked into the 4Runner. Already several paces from my car, I saw that the woman had gotten into his car with him and they were about to drive away. I had only a second to weigh the importance of getting a look at those still inside the church, or trying to go after the Asian guy. In the end, I think I made the wrong decision. Standing fast in front of the church, I watched the Toyota drive off.

Turns out that the service had already ended and the sanctuary was empty. All except for a lone priest.

I flashed my star and asked how long since all of the people left.

"Just a few minutes," he said. "And there weren't many. It was a small gathering--"

I interrupted. "Is there a sign-in book?"

He shook his head. "Like I said, only a handful in attendance."

I walked up to the casket and glanced down at my victim. They had him dressed all in white. Other than that, he looked pretty much the same as the morning I found him in the park; black hair combed back, angular facial features—sans the mask, of course.

Sadly, I was no closer to catching whoever killed him than I had been on that first day.

"Like I told your partners," said the priest. "It wasn't a traditional funeral."

"My partners?"

"Yes," he said. "The young man and woman who just left."

I ran back outside, just in time to see the back end of their car as they made the corner onto 24th.

33

2901 Peralta Oaks Court
Oakland

The Coroner's Bureau is located on a peaceful, tree-lined parcel in the hills above the 580 freeway. In addition to conducting post-mortem examinations for all of Alameda County, the building also houses the county's forensic crime laboratory.

Neither Tam nor Brooks had gotten much sleep in the past few days, yet they had driven back to the East Bay for this surreptitious meeting with Sarah's enforcement team friend, Agent Bise. He had texted that the autopsy of her sniper victim was underway, and that Bise would meet her in the lot as soon as it was over.

Sarah had fallen asleep waiting in her car, which was parked in a shaded spot at the back of the building. Twenty feet away stood Tam, leaning against a cement retaining wall as he waited for Sergei Petrenko's personal secretary to put his call through.

"It's been over a week, Tam." Petrenko sounded a little anxious. "Thought you'd fallen off the edge of the earth. What's going on over there across the pond?"

Curtis wanted to update his client on the events of the past eight days, without disclosing that he had joined forces with the Customs investigator.

"The two most recent stolen containers have been recovered," Tam said. "And two of the suspects have been identified."

The information had an immediate calming effect on Petrenko. "That's great news. Excellent work, Tam. What can you tell me about the two scoundrels?"

"One of them is Elvis Lugailo," said Tam. "The other is Gustavs Berzins—both apparently of Latvian descent."

"Latvians, you say..."

"Mmm. The latter, Berzins, is dead. He was the man shot down in the park a week ago."

"And the other *хуесóс?*"

"It's still undetermined whether Elvis Lugailo is dead or alive." Tam glanced around the lot to make sure nobody else was listening. "A third shooting occurred yesterday at the Customs cargo inspection facility; a man who arrived to sign for the containers. We're waiting for the autopsy results as we speak, to find out his identity."

Petrenko was silent for a long while. "You're still working alone I trust?"

"Of course," said Tam.

"I could have sworn you just said 'we' are waiting for the autopsy results."

Tam closed his eyes, cringing at the stupid mistake. "No, Mr. Petrenko. It's only me."

Another pause followed, though not as long. "Well, you've done good," said Petrenko. "Accomplished everything we could hope for. Whether this other fellow is dead or not, it seems you've disrupted their little gang of thieves."

Tam saw where his client was heading. "There is more to this theft ring," he said. "I'm convinced there are others involved, perhaps even someone in the Latvian Consulate."

"Intriguing, no doubt about it." But Petrenko hadn't become one of the wealthiest men in the world by being stupid. He had put his need for anonymity above seeing the investigation to fruition. "Our work in America is complete," he said. "Time to wrap things up and head home."

It was late afternoon when the Customs supervisor finally emerged from the building. Tam was outside smoking a cigarette, still angry at himself for spooking his client.

Brooks got out and introduced Tam, who Bise eyed while shaking his hand.

"Thought you were operating alone," Bise said to Sarah. "Off the grid and all that."

"I am," said Sarah. "Mr. Tam is not with CBP. He represents foreign interests."

Bise nodded. "We don't have an ID on your dead guy yet, but the coroner has wired his prints to DOJ."

Sarah showed Bise a photo of Elvis Lugailo. "Best guess, could it be this guy?"

"No way." He shook his head. "The sniper made a mess of his face, but the body has darker skin and he's wearing a lot of ink; Latino prison stuff—Norteño, as far as I could tell."

Tam said, "Doesn't really fit with the people we've been dealing with."

"No, it doesn't." Sarah turned back to Bise. "It means our guy Elvis is still out there somewhere. And that means that without an ID on the dude in there, our leads are quickly drying up."

"Maybe these will help," said Bise. He handed her a ring with two keys on it. "They were in the victim's pants pocket. One key goes to his rig, which has already been towed and impounded, but we have no idea what the other key goes to. The keyring is supposed to be entered into evidence, but I figure a couple of days in your custody won't matter."

Sarah lit up as she eyed the keys. Her first thought was the Russ Street warehouse where Tam had spotted the first stolen container.

"Be careful," Bise said. "Your boss was here for the postmortem."

"Sanchez?" She scanned the lot.

"Relax," said Bise. "He parked out front, and I waited until he was gone before coming out to meet you. But these shootings have got him rattled, and it won't end well for you if he finds out what you're up to."

"No shit." She slapped Bise on the shoulder, then grabbed the keyring from him as she got into the car. "Text me with the stiff's ID when you get it, will you?"

Tam offered a penitent smile. "Good to meet you, Paul."

The evening commute was in full swing when they merged onto the bridge approach. Turning to Sarah, Tam said, "You thinking the same thing I am about that key?"

"Russ Street." Sarah nodded. "So, it sounds like your boss wants you done with the case. That's like eating half of an ice cream cone. What the hell do you do with the other half?"

"I would agree; leaving so many loose ends feels incomplete, almost as if I shouldn't accept payment for the job."

Sarah lifted an eyebrow. "Don't go nutso on me, Tam. All I'm saying is that I, myself, need to see this thing through. That means, I gotta get over to that warehouse and see if this key works."

"Tonight?" Tam's head spun toward her.

She nodded. "Tonight... Like, right now. You in or you out?"

34

Café Roma
885 Bryant Street

It was almost noon when I called Linh and asked her to come downstairs to meet me across from the Hall of Justice.

Dowd would be livid by now, and I knew there was no sense in going back inside and trying to explain. What would I say? Sorry to keep you waiting for two hours, but my bathroom break went longer than planned? Besides, by that time I was convinced that my captain was the mole that Chief Fahey had assigned me to uncover.

The Visa card headquarters is in Foster City—thirty-minutes down the peninsula. Linh offered to drive, and I hesitated before telling her that I'd rather she didn't. I didn't want her to take it as racist or sexist, but 101 can be a real bitch of a drive—especially if you don't know your way around. She didn't say anything, but I felt her eyes on me.

Flashing my star, I served the court order on the small Indian man behind the customer service counter. With a pungent waft of biryani, he told me that it would take a few hours for the account records to be released.

I argued that in this age of technology, all he had to do was press a button and print out Elvis Lang's past statements. But the guy insisted that their legal department had to "look over" the document before honoring it. I told him that they had no choice but to honor it; the order had been signed by a judge. Unfortunately, they had me over a bureaucratic barrel and so I decided not to press the issue.

We started back to the city empty handed.

"You married, Linh?"

"Yes, my husband is a software engineer in Palo Alto. We actually live down here in Foster City."

"Uh-huh, any kids?"

"No, not yet."

I glanced over at her, sitting there in her tiny pantsuit and wearing studious glasses that were too big for her face. She looked like a kid, herself. "You speak fluent Chinese, Linh?"

She frowned. "No, do you?"

"Well, no. I just thought that since you--"

"Phú is a Vietnamese name."

"Oh."

The car was quiet during the rest of the ride.

Traffic was a mess, and we didn't get back into the City until dark. Dropping Linh in front of the Hall, I decided that rather than go in I'd just take the work car home. Why not? I was in enough trouble with Dowd already.

As I started for the bridge, I checked my watch and saw that I had given myself plenty of time to make it home for Doris and my big counseling session. And maybe even in time to have a father-daughter talk with Bridget.

I pulled into my driveway and listened to my messages before going into the house. No calls from Sha Nay Nay, but a few missed calls from Captain Dowd—no surprise there. I went to grab my suit jacket, and then realized that I'd left it hanging on the back of my office chair.

Doris looked surprised that I'd actually made it home in time. She told me that Bridge was at a friend's house, which meant that I could postpone my talk with her a little longer. It gave me just enough time to pour a drink for myself and shower before the appointment.

"You're having a drink?" asked Doris, her words dripping with judgement.

I sighed. "Yeah, I'm having a drink."

"Is it too much to ask that you keep a clear head for one night?" Then, wedging herself between me and my little tray of bottles that serves as a bar, she said, "This is our first session, Danny. And you're not going in there to meet her with a bunch of booze on your breath."

"It's not a *bunch* of booze, it's just one... Wait a minute. Her? You never told me we were seeing a female counselor."

"First of all, you haven't been around enough for us to even talk. And secondly, why does it matter that she's a woman?"

"You know, she's probably just going to side with you." As soon as I said it, I knew it was a mistake. And Doris's tight jaw only confirmed that she was too frustrated to speak. I had also wanted to ask how much these counseling sessions were costing me, but at that point I figured that I'd already stepped on my scrotum enough for one night.

"For your information," said Doris. "Ellen is her name, and she seems very nice. Gets good reviews on Yelp.

"Is she a lesbian?"

"What?"

I wasn't sure where the question had come from, it was something that had gone through my mind and just sort of popped out. "I, I, just mean, you know, is she going to be against me already?"

"Damn you, Danny." Doris threw her arms up and let them fall to her sides with a thud. "Do you even care about us? Do you even want to make this marriage work?"

"Yeah," I told her. "Of course I do. Why do you think I'm home so early? I was just... Never mind. I told you I'd go with you, and I'll go."

I'd never been to counseling, but it wasn't as bad as I had thought. Ellen Frohman turned out to be pleasant enough. She had curly brown hair and a round, smiling face that didn't seem as menacing as the therapist in my mind. Part of me wished I could plead my side of the marital situation; form a good impression by making her feel sorry for me. But I figured that complaining about Doris would make me look like too much of an asshole. But the woman seemed objective, and if she had already heard all about what a shitty husband and father I was, she didn't show it. Just smiled.

Instead of trashing Doris, I stuck to telling Ellen about the job. She seemed interested in the mechanics of the work—the long hours, tedious investigations, and being on-call all the time. She recoiled at the vividness of my crime scene descriptions.

I thought it was going pretty well, and Doris hadn't said a whole lot, yet. I was actually proud of how much I was participating. Then Frohman took a left turn down the *you're an injured bird* path.

"Have you ever been treated for post-traumatic stress syndrome?" she asked. "A lot of police officers tend to drink liquor and find other destructive forms of self-medication in order to cope."

And a lot of men drink liquor because their wives nag at them, and manipulate them into buying homes they can't even afford. Luckily, it was one of the few times that I was able to put a clamp on it before the words came out. And before I had time to put together an actual response, my cell phone began to vibrate in my pocket.

They both heard the low buzzing sound, and their expressions were nearly identical.

"Sorry, I have to take this." I stepped out of the room, not caring at that point if it was a wrong number or a telemarketer.

I didn't recognize the caller's number, but answered it anyway.

"Inspector McKenna?" The voice sounded high and soft and vaguely familiar. "It's me, Officer Phú."

"Yeah, hey Linh." I waited, but all I heard was the hollow echo of a speaker phone and ambient traffic noises on the other end of the line. "What's up?"

"Sorry to trouble you," she said. "I have something to report. Well, two things, actually. Both bad and good."

I sighed, not really wanting to do this back and forth thing.

"Yes, so, I struck out on the vehicle license plate. None of the states we narrowed it down to have the type of letter and number sequence matching the one on our video frame."

"I'm hoping that was the bad news."

"It was." I could hear the sound of shuffling papers and hoped she wasn't trying to read and drive at the same time. "The credit card company called to say that the results of your court order were ready to be picked up. And since I was leaving for the day and I live close to the credit card offices, I thought I should retrieve the records for you."

"You have them?"

"Yes." I could hear her tearing into the envelope. "Russ Street," she said. "Elvis Lang's Visa bills are sent to 168 Russ Street in San Francisco."

"Good, okay, yes!" I shielded the phone and lowered my voice. "That fits. He was arrested with my informant a few months back, in a car that was parked at the corner of Russ and Natoma. And she said he worked somewhere close to there."

"This is good news then?"

"Yes, Linh. This is good news."

35

Russ Street Warehouse

In case anyone had followed them, installed another bug, or might otherwise recognize his car, Tam parked around the corner on Howard Street. They both had a lot to lose—each defying their bosses, hoping that the end result would somehow justify the means.

Russ Street was in one of the City's half-finished redevelopment districts. It was two-and-a-half blocks, hopscotched with light industrial buildings, remodeled apartment houses, and a smattering of trendy live/work lofts. About halfway down on the right stood the lifeless gray warehouse, a dead tooth in the middle of a hopeful grin. There was no signage outside, only the numbers 168 painted on the stucco above the door. A row of dark windows on the second floor gave it an abandoned look. No cars were parked in front.

Tam and Brooks made a casual pass on the opposite side of the street, then slowly doubled back. Vehicle traffic was thick on the two streets that bookended Russ, but the street itself was quiet.

Once comfortable that they hadn't been followed, Tam acted as a lookout while Brooks slipped the sniper victim's key into the front door lock. It clicked open and Tam quickly followed her inside. Standing motionless in the dark, they listened. Aside from the normal creaks and cracks of old industrial buildings, it was quiet.

Sarah turned on a compact flashlight, and moved directly toward the white Ford van parked inside. Tam used the light from his cell phone to navigate his way past her, over to the long brown cargo container. He walked around the far side and saw the GPS tracker he had affixed—its battery long since dead from the lack of solar energy. Roughly half of the cargo had been offloaded onto the raised dock, and the rest remained inside the container.

"Everything looks the same as when I saw it nine days ago," whispered Tam. "I don't think anyone's been here since."

Sarah's attention was focused on the van. "Look at this," she said, examining the interior of the side doors. "Does this look like powder burn to you?"

Tam leaned into the Ford, his eyes following her beam to the ribbed metal next to the door frame. On the white paint, a slight discoloration emanated outward from the frame like half of an exploding star. "Could be."

Sarah rolled her eyes. "It is," she said. "I know it is. And I know this is the van that those assholes were driving when they tried to--"

A series of banging noises sounded, stopping Sarah mid-sentence. They stood motionless, listening. Then she said, "I think it came from out front."

Tam held a finger to his lips. "Did you hear that? It sounded like a mobile phone ringing."

A man's voice was speaking low and serious, but they couldn't make out the words. Sarah moved quietly toward the roll-up door and put her ear up to it. A minute later she hurried back over and grabbed Tam's arm.

"C'mon. It sounds like he's coming closer."

They doused their lights and felt their way around the backside of the van.

"Who is it?" Tam whispered.

"How the hell should I know? It's my first time here." Sarah continued pulling Tam until they were behind the cargo container.

Tam said, "I meant, what was he saying on the phone?"

"Couldn't hear all of it." She leaned in close to him. "Something about a marriage counselor."

Tam frowned and Sarah shrugged.

A loud click echoed through the warehouse as the bolt on the front door turned. The two trespassers squeezed into a narrow space between the container and the loading dock. The spot was barely shoulder width, concealed only partially by the open cargo container door.

A gust of cool air was followed by the front door squeaking closed and the latch locking again. The two investigators assumed that the man was doing as they had—standing still in the dark, listening for movement. Frozen in fear, they didn't move or take a breath.

All at once the walls were awash in light. A strong flashlight beam bounced and reflected in the cavernous warehouse like a light show. It was impossible to tell where the beam originated, but it grew brighter as it came closer to them.

Tam realized the tactical error they had made by hiding near the crates of liquor. The stolen cargo was the most likely reason for someone to be there, and it was the most obvious place in the entire building for the person to go.

Sarah could only think that no matter how this played out, she wouldn't be able to keep it from her CBP bosses. Seconds away from taking action, she carried a badge that had no authority and a gun she was no longer authorized to carry.

The slow shuffle of big feet and the sound of heavy breathing grew louder. The light beam continued to spread as it moved closer and closer.

36

398 7ᵗʰ Street
San Francisco

Do you really want to do this? I had asked myself the question as I sipped my drink.

Leaving in the middle of a counseling appointment had probably sealed the fate of my failing marriage. I'd driven back into the City still chewing on the thought that I was missing something.

The only viable lead on my homicide case was that a possible witness was having his credit card bills mailed to an address on Russ Street. So what? Elvis Lang, wasn't even a suspect. His name had only come up in a rental car parked near the scene. Hardly *viable*.

But by the time I made it across the bridge, I'd become harassed by the notion that my homicide and the murder of Rhonda Pitts were connected. As my mind worked to construct that puzzle, it settled on the piece that had eluded me: actual evidence that could link the two investigations.

Stopping into the office, I poked my head into the empty room to make sure that Dowd wasn't around. I then walked straight to Alan Lam's desk where I found the Pitts file right where I'd left it. In the back was the plastic zippered evidence envelope that held a ring of keys.

It was a hunch that I figured was a long shot hunch at best.

The office door abruptly swung open, startling me. In walked Taylor and Mendoza, two fellow inspectors who were working the night shift rotation. I nodded to them as nonchalantly as possible, then quickly palmed the keys and slipped them into my pocket.

"What are you doing here so late?" Mendoza asked. "Dowd's been looking for you all day."

I had spotted my suitcoat still hanging on the back of my chair. "Forgot my jacket," I said, ignoring the mention of Dowd. "Catch you guys tomorrow."

"Another scotch?" asked the bartender, as I pondered whether or not I really wanted to do this.

It was just past eight o'clock, and Rumors was filling up with its usual weeknight crowd. I sat at the bar, hunched over my tumbler, trying to drink my nerves into submission.

I nodded. "Put it in a coffee cup, and I'll take it with me."

Stepping out of the stuffy bar and into the breezy San Francisco night, I weighed the pros and cons of what I had decided to do.

Past the park, I walked across Folsom considering the risks of breaking into the Russ Street warehouse. The place could be alarmed, and if the cops showed up I'd have to talk my way out of it. Not a problem, unless it got back to the captain—which it would.

Or, I could encounter a suspect there and I'd be forced to take action. That, in and of itself, wouldn't be a problem. Until it got back to Dowd. In either situation, I would be hard pressed to explain why I took evidence from Lam's case file and then illegally entered and searched a location that I couldn't really even tie to my investigation.

The building was dark, cinderblock gray in color, with a corrugated roll-up door in front. The few windows on the second floor were cracked and stained with age, too obscured to see into, even if lights had shone from them. Number 168—identified only by numbers painted above a security door—melded anonymously into the urban backdrop.

I knocked a couple of times just for kicks, but it seemed unlikely anyone was around. I took a sip from my paper cup as I slowly scanned up and down Russ Street. Then, just as I was reaching into my pocket for the keys, my phone rang.

"Yes," I whispered, knowing it was Doris.

"Where are you?"

"Hey Doris," I said, like I was right in the middle of something important and hadn't expected to hear from her. "What's up?"

"What's up? Our meeting with the counselor is what's up. Where in the hell did you run off to?"

I sighed. "I got an important call about my case. It's kind of an emergency, and you know that Lou Cassidy is out with a heart--"

"I'm not hearing it, Danny." She yelled into the phone, "You just walk out in the middle of our session? Who even does that?"

I couldn't really blame her for being pissed off. On the other hand, I'm sure my leaving gave her and Dr. Ellen plenty to talk about. "Yeah, sorry about that," I said. And I really was. "I'll make the next counseling appointment, I promise."

Doris abruptly hung up.

I knocked back the last of my scotch and tossed the cup into the street. Angry with her and angry with myself, Doris's phone call evaporated any reservations I still had about entering the warehouse. It was almost as if I wanted to make walking out of the session worth it.

I tried a couple of the keys with no luck, and then the third one worked. Closing the door behind me, I stood in the dark trying to digest what this meant. For one thing, it proved that I was right—the two cases were connected. Why else would *their* victim, Rhonda Pitts, have a key to a warehouse where my suspect, Elvis Lang, gets his mail delivered? It also meant that I was right about Lang; the rental car he had abandoned at the scene wasn't just a long shot hunch. The guy was involved.

The warehouse was quiet. I felt around next to the door for the light switch but couldn't find it in the dark. I flipped on my flashlight, illuminating a Ford van. Beyond it, a cargo container sat against a raised loading dock. Cases of liquor were stacked on wooden pallets atop the dock.

I walked over and glanced into the container. At least fifty more pallets were still inside—each stacked six cases high.

"Hands where I can see them," blasted a woman's voice behind me. "And I'd think twice about making any quick movements."

The shock of it caused me to stiffen, wrenching my knee. Pissed off about that, I was also humiliated that I'd allowed a suspect to get the drop on me. My mind raced to remember the gun takeaway moves we had practiced thirteen years ago in the police academy, but in the end I did as she told me.

Turning slowly, I saw there were two of them—a well-dressed Asian man of about forty years, and a thirty-something Caucasian woman, who I might have, under different circumstances, found attractive. Besides the gun, she also held some kind of badge—which she stashed in her purse before I could catch the agency. It definitely wasn't one of ours.

Relaxing a little now that I was relatively sure these two weren't suspects, I lowered my hands slightly. "SFPD," I said. "My star is clipped to my belt."

"Are you armed?" she asked.

"Yeah, I have a handgun."

"Name?"

"Smith and Wesson." I smirked.

"Your name, idiot."

She had apparently gone to the Greg Dowd school of humor. "McKenna... Inspector, Homicide. Now, how about putting down your little pistol and playing nice?"

The woman swept my coat back with her hand, and unclipped the star holder from my belt. She seemed convinced after examining it, because she finally lowered her weapon. "What are you doing here?" she asked.

"What the hell are *you* doing here?" I fired back. "You got a good reason to be in *my* crime scene? What agency are you with, anyway?"

She didn't answer, and her expression tipped me off that there was something wrong. Something she was trying to hide.

"Hey," she said, putting away her gun. "I think you and I got off on the wrong foot. Maybe we can just take it down a notch."

"Ya think?" I snatched my star out of her hand and clipped it back onto my belt. "Nobody likes having a gun stuck in their face."

The man gave me a slight smile, and then spoke for the first time. "It must be her way of making new friends."

"We're looking into a string of stolen containers," the woman said. "This is one of them." She motioned to the stack of cargo behind her.

I shined my light on the big rust-colored box.

Then she said, "So, if you don't mind my asking... Why are you here without backup? Don't you guys all work with partners?"

Now I was stumped. "It's a long story," I finally said. "My partner is off work with a heart attack." It was true, and it definitely curtailed the questions. But they both seemed to know enough about tactics and police procedures that they weren't buying it.

Turns out she was a fed—U.S. Customs, to be exact. The Asian guy's role in all this was unclear at the time, and though neither of them actually said it, I had the impression that he was some type of government contractor. They had gotten a head start on me, and seemed to have a fairly good handle on who all the players were. He was working on the cargo theft angle, but the main thrust of her involvement was a shooting over in Oakland, in which she had been the target. I vaguely recalled reading about it, but I doubted that it had anything to do with my case, and she offered no evidence of such.

My primary interest was to solve the Gustavs Berzins murder. It was still my investigation, and would be my best bet for justifying my presence at the warehouse.

"Have you two come across anything on my Golden Gate Park shooting?" I asked. "Guy named Berzins was shot to death just over a week ago." I showed them his facial photo.

They both shrugged.

"That's a load of bullshit," I said. "I saw you both at the guy's funeral this morning. Want to try again?"

"How about *you* come clean with us?" spat the woman, her face morphing into my wife's. "You've got no partner, no backup, and I sure as hell don't see a search warrant."

It was the proverbial Mexican standoff.

"It seems each of us has an interest in the outcome of this case," said the man in a quiet but even voice. "And perhaps with our own personal motivations as well."

The tension visibly melted.

"Certainly," he continued, "we are all positioned to help one another."

I eventually located the warehouse lights near the loading dock, but left them off as we continued up a narrow staircase to a second floor. Turning on the upstairs lights, I found a small breakroom with a vintage laminated eating table and four rigid metal chairs. We sat there, talking late into the evening. Each of us took notes and asked questions of the others, and though we didn't cover everything, after a couple of hours I found myself with a half-dozen pages of notes that pertained to my investigation.

Most significant among the newly discovered facts was that this man, a private detective named Curtis Tam, had actually witnessed the Berzins shooting. The downside was that he vehemently refused to be identified in my report or be called to testify as a witness.

In any other situation I would have simply served the man with a subpoena or detained him as a material witness. But this was not any other situation. I did not have the backing of my own department, and he would have likely just fled the country. It didn't matter that much anyway, as he wasn't able to identify the shooter and he offered no new details—except for narrowing down the time of the shooting for me. He had described one of the men as having carried a daypack, which was never recovered at the scene. We all assumed that it left with either the shooter or the partner who ran off—the partner who I was now convinced was Elvis Lang.

The woman, Sarah Brooks, urged me to write a search warrant for the warehouse—specifically for the seizure of the white Econoline van, which she insisted had been used in the attack on her. Because of her injury status, Brooks was unable to prepare the search warrant herself, or so she claimed. I sensed there was more to her situation than she was letting on, but then again she could probably have said the same about me.

It seemed as though we were on the cusp of breaking up an international smuggling ring, collectively solving three separate homicides and possibly the attempted murder of a federal agent. Except that none of us had the backing, support, or official authority to do it legally. On top of which, I was still operating under the secret mandate by the now dead chief of police to find the rogue cop within the homicide detail. And the only person who could legitimize my investigation was the person I suspected as being the mole, Captain Gregory Dowd.

It was late, and I knew I'd have to face him in the morning. Wrapping it up for the night, we gave assurances of non-disclosure and agreements to keep the information between the three of us for now. Standing outside in the dark, we exchanged contact information and cell phone numbers.

I was about to lock up when something trickled through my mind. Something I hadn't thought to ask. Turning to Brooks and Tam, I said, "What led you here in the first place?"

"The container inside," said Tam. "It has a GPS transmitter on it, and I tracked it to the warehouse."

I turned questioningly to Brooks.

"The container had been pulled for inspection," she said. "And the release receipt listed the 168 Russ Street address."

"Who signed for it?" I asked.

"A guy by the name of Lugailo," she said. Supposedly worked as a security guard at the Latvian Consulate."

I shrugged. The name Lugailo meant nothing to me. I locked the door and I walked off in one direction as they headed in the other. Suddenly, I said, "Hold on a minute." I stopped, turned back around. "What's his first name?"

"Elvis," said Brooks. "Also goes by Elvis Lang."

37

500 block
Bayview Avenue
Millbrae, CA

I had been sleeping—if you could call it that—on a fold-out futon in the den the past few nights. Still awake at 4 a.m. and feeling the weight of my investigation, I was convinced more than ever that the captain was the dirty bird in the unit. But he was not only my boss, but a senior member of the department. So I would need a hell of a lot more than a gut feeling. I'd need to be sure. That's when I made the decision to tail my captain.

I'd taken my work car home, which was problematic since it looked exactly like his—an SFPD unmarked unit. Because it screamed *undercover cop,* I knew that I wouldn't be able to follow as closely as I would have liked.

It was still dark when I parked on Lomita Avenue, directly across the intersection from the home of Captain Greg Dowd. It appeared there was an unfinished second floor remodel going on, which I attributed to illicit income from his corrupt activities.

Around 7 a.m., Dowd came out the front door and down the steps to his car. I followed him through Millbrae, onto the 280 freeway and then onto 101 where the congestion forced me to drop back a few more cars. As we approached downtown, Dowd took the Seventh Street off-ramp. But instead of continuing up Bryant to the Hall of Justice, he went left, under the freeway onto Seventh. I had to quickly merge over to stay behind him.

It suddenly struck me that we were only a couple of blocks from the Russ Street warehouse. By chance, or bad luck, the cars between us turned off, and I ended up right behind Dowd's car. He was glancing around, and I knew that my surveillance would be blown if he spotted me in his mirror.

He made a right turn onto Howard, and I realized that we were now only a block from the warehouse. Dowd was heading straight for it—no wonder he was looking around. There was no way I could continue following him into the narrow, lightly traveled, Russ Street neighborhood. He would notice me for sure.

I kept going down Seventh, instead. Trying to quickly loop back around on Natoma, traffic in front of me was suddenly stopped by a construction flagman. I cursed and hit the dashboard as I watched a cement truck driver slowly negotiate an unimpressive backing maneuver. They had me wedged in, and it took several minutes to get free. By the time I made it back to Russ Street, Dowd's car was gone.

Scenarios spun in my head like a runaway film reel. I now saw my boss not only as the mole in the detail, but also part of the stolen cargo ring. Suspecting that Dowd had actually gone into the warehouse, I assumed that he had stashed his car inside as well.

I considered using the key to go in and confront him, but then thought better of it. Waiting there for over an hour without any sign of him, I began second-guessing myself. I wondered if it was possible that I'd presumed too much, added the facts wrongly and come up with an erroneous conclusion.

So after making a couple of laps around the block, I made a final pass of the dark warehouse and called off my surveillance.

When I got to the office, Phú was at Cassidy's desk working on her laptop. "Any luck with the license plate?" I asked.

She told me she had checked every state license plate with a white background, and none began with the QP prefix.

But since my late night meeting at the warehouse, I now knew Elvis's real name and the fact that he worked at the Latvian Consulate.

On a hunch, I asked Linh to check for diplomatic plates. Within a minute, she had it.

"Well done, Inspector," she said. "The State Department's Office of Foreign Missions issues diplomatic license plates that have a blue and red border against a white background." She turned her computer screen to show me. "And the designation QP is unique to the Republic of Latvia."

I slapped my hands together and pulled a chair up next to her. Just then Captain Dowd came strolling in. He slowed to glimpse back at Mrs. Ocampo's empty desk, and then shot a glare across the room in my direction. I wondered if he had spotted my surveillance, or if he had somehow found out that I had been in the warehouse last night. I didn't care if he had. In fact, I almost wanted him to say something, now that I'd followed him to the warehouse. Instead, he went into his office without a word and closed the door.

I moved my chair even closer to Linh and brought my voice down to a whisper. "Okay, now here's what we're going to do. We're going to prepare a search warrant affidavit."

"For what location?" she asked.

"It's a warehouse at 168 Russ Street. But for reasons I can't explain right now, this has to stay just between us. No one else in the detail can know about it. Not the other inspectors, and especially not the captain."

Her surprised expression slowly turned to apprehension. Linh's eyes darted toward the captain's office and then back. "I'll assume you have good reason to handle it this way," she said. "So, as far as anyone is concerned I will just be the uninformed apprentice."

My new partner was really starting to grow on me.

It took me a couple of hours to get it all down on paper: Elvis's rental car abandoned at the scene of the Berzins murder, his use of an alias, and that he received mail at the warehouse. I had also added the fact that a key to the same building was found in the possession of Rhonda Pitts, another murder victim.

The last part of the affidavit turned out to be a little tricky. I knew that I had to be specific about what evidence I expected to find in the warehouse, and why I believed it would be there. I'd be signing my oath, swearing to it in front of the judge. So, I based my justification on the fact that Tam had seen my victim and Elvis together at the warehouse on the night my victim was killed, and that Brooks had seen the stolen cargo container inside the building. But since I promised them both that I wouldn't use their names, I had to list them in the affidavit as *confidential citizen informants*—identifying them only as 'X' and 'Y'.

I intentionally omitted the fact that I'd taken the key from another inspector's case file and used it to enter the warehouse—essentially searching the place already. These were desperate investigative steps that were, well, *technically* illegal.

Another point that I sort of fudged on, although for a completely different reason, was failing to mention the Ford van parked inside. Rather than complicate the affidavit by bringing up the possible connection to the Sarah Brooks's shooting—which still sounded a little iffy to me anyway—I left out that information as well.

Lastly, I made no mention of the possible Latvian Consulate connection—which also seemed a tad farfetched. In the world of San Francisco politics, it would have puckered every asshole from the Hall of Justice to the mayor's office—including that of the judge I'd be asking to sign off on it.

Around noon, Phú and I brought the paperwork over to the DA's office. It's SFPD policy that a deputy district attorney reviews a search warrant prior to it being presented to the judge. But the deputy assigned to the police department was about to eat her lunch, so she asked us to leave the affidavit with her.

With at least a couple of hours to kill, I thought it might be worth paying a visit to the consulate.

Maybe Phú and I would get lucky and find Elvis Lugailo there.

38

Latvian Consulate
Folsom Street, San Francisco

Parking in the red zone out front, I slipped my business card onto the dashboard and hung my radio microphone over the rearview mirror.

My partner and I walked in, noting that there was no security guard out front. We found the consulate on the third floor, and, after avoiding a sizable line in the visa and passport section, entered a room marked: CONSULAR SERVICES.

A young lady seated at a desk smiled as we entered. Behind her were a series of modular office cubicles, the occupants of which were hidden from our view.

"I'd like to speak to the ambassador," I said, extending my police star toward the woman. "Please tell him that Inspectors McKenna and Phú need a few minutes of his time."

"The ambassador does not work in the consulate building," she said. "His Excellency, Mr. Teikmanis has an office in the embassy."

"Can you give me that address?" I took out a notepad and pen.

"Yes, sir." The woman's warm blue eyes smiled along with her angelic face. "Our embassy is located at 2306 Massachusetts Avenue Northwest, Washington, D.C."

I stashed my pad and pen, and stared at her flatly. But her expression told me that she wasn't being sarcastic. She really thought I needed the D.C. address.

"Who can I talk to *here*, in this building?" I asked. "The person in charge?"

"That would be Leo Krumins, but he's gone for the remainder of the day. I'm so sorry." She smiled again. "Is there something for which I can help?"

I asked about the security guard, Elvis Lugailo, and right away her face registered surprise, or worry, or possibly anger. Glancing over at Linh, I saw that she had noticed it, too.

"Where can we find Mr. Lugailo?" asked Linh, stepping up to the desk in a more officious manner than I'd seen.

The consulate woman's powdery face flushed pink. "I, I'm afraid that our security guard does not show up to work for over one week." She glanced back at the cubicles as if she was hoping to be rescued. Lowering her voice, she said, "I think Mr. Lugailo maybe is not any longer a consulate employee."

"Why would he leave so suddenly?" Linh asked.

The woman was an easy read; her innocent face was like a human polygraph needle.

"Why? Uh, I, I haven't any idea," she answered. "Again, I'm so sorry that I can't be more helpful. You'll really need to talk with Mr. Krumins."

I took out my notebook again. "And can I get your name, ma'am?"

Again she flushed. "It's Inga." She wiped her dark hair away with the back of her hand. "Inga Berzina."

The woman's last name sounded a lot like my victim's, Gustavs *Berzins*, but I figured that Latvians probably have common or similar sounding surnames—like *Kim* in Korea, or *Patel* in India.

Ms. Berzina was obviously upset by the exchange though, and it was clear she was holding back. The male in me wanted to calm her, reassure her that I was someone she could trust.

Phú, on the other hand, saw that same weakness as something to exploit. To intimidate the woman into telling us what she knew about Elvis Lugailo. I guess I would have done the same thing if Inga had been a man.

Before Linh was able to take another crack at her, Inga answered her desk phone. Speaking only a few quiet words in what I assumed was her native tongue, she mostly nodded as if the person on the other end could see her. When the call ended, the woman was quick to end our conversation as well.

Inga stood and motioned toward the door. "There is some urgent work I must tend to, but thank you for coming in."

It was a nervous brush off, but I had one more question for her before we left. "Does the name Gustavs Berzins mean anything to you?"

A glint of terror swept across her face, though only for a second. Unconsciously, she glanced over my head to the corner of the room and then back at me. "No, I'm sorry."

When my partner and I turned to leave, I looked up, following Inga's line of sight to a tiny CCTV camera in the corner over the door.

Interesting.

As we stood in the hallway waiting for the elevator, the office door swung open. Out came Inga, moving quickly and looking back over her shoulder. In a voice that was barely audible she said, "In case I remember something, is it possible that I may have your business card, Inspector?"

I handed her my card and she scurried back into the office. Linh looked as surprised as I was. The itch to go after her was almost more than my impatient nature could bear, but I looked at my watch, saw that it was nearly three o'clock, and stepped into the elevator.

We had a search warrant to execute.

39

Hall of Justice
3rd floor

Deputy District Attorney Katie Nelson glanced over the top of her reading glasses when we walked in to her office. My warrant was laid out on the desk in front of her, and I had no doubt she'd been heavily scrutinizing the supporting facts of the affidavit.

"It's not bad, Inspector." She removed her glasses and motioned for us to sit. "My only concern is the reliability of your X and Y informants, the two people you didn't name. I'll be honest with you; judges around here don't trust cops. And depending on which magistrate you go to, he or she may suspect that these informants are fictitious. That you made them up."

I shook my head. "They're real."

"I have no doubt," she said. "But will they be available to testify when and if this case goes to trial?"

"Sure, of course." My lie sounded almost forced. Too certain to be believable. Brooks was working off the books and Tam was about to beat feet back to China.

Ms. Nelson glanced at my partner.

"I'm new," said Linh. "Just learning what I can from Inspector McKenna."

I saw the DA's jaw flinch, then she leaned back and took a breath. "Okay," she said. "Go see Judge Rosenberg in department twenty-one."

I gathered the paperwork from her desk and slipped it into my folder.

"One more thing, McKenna." Nelson leaned forward in her seat. "You had better give your captain a call."

My head snapped around like someone had slapped me. "What?"

"Greg Dowd," she said. "I ran into him during a lunch meeting at the probation department and happened to mention your warrant."

I suddenly felt like my clothes were on fire.

"He seemed annoyed or something," she said. "Don't know what's up between you and him, but don't put this office in the middle of it."

I glanced at my cell phone. Dowd had called several times and left one message. We hustled down the hall and had a bailiff take us back to the judge's private chambers. Rosenberg signed the warrant without questions or hesitation. My first bit of good luck in a while.

I listened to Dowd's message when we got down to the garage, and it was definitely not a friendly *how-do-you-do*.

"McKenna! You better have a damn good reason for not taking my calls. And what was that little stunt yesterday, skipping out on me when you knew damn well I wanted to talk to you? As a matter of fact, I was going to tell you that the Berzins homicide is no longer your case. I've given it to Mendoza and Taylor. So, whatever's up with this supposed search warrant of yours, forget it. You are not to do anything more with regard to that investigation, or any other investigation, for that matter. Now, get your ass back to the detail and into my office, posthaste!"

Linh asked if everything was all right.

Everything certainly wasn't *all right*, but I didn't want to tell her that. "Don't ask," I said. "It's called plausible deniability."

"Then where to, now?"

"Russ Street," I said. "We're going to serve our search warrant."

Linh smiled. "Like I said, I'm just the uninformed apprentice." But just beneath it was a hint of worry.

I could hardly blame her.

40

5 Embarcadero Center
San Francisco

After having been followed by the four motorcyclists, Curtis Tam had heightened his security measures. Abruptly checking out of the Palace Hotel, he used a spurious ID and cash to secure a room at the Embarcadero Hyatt Regency. It would no longer be possible for someone to monitor his whereabouts via credit card.

Taking the glass elevator down to the hotel's atrium, Tam considered McKenna's invitation for he and Sarah Brooks to come along on the warehouse search warrant. Having her own reasons for wanting to be there, Brooks had agreed to go. Tam had been less enthusiastic. As much as he wanted to see his case to fruition, his Russian client would be furious that Tam was now working with others—even if he hadn't named his client.

The waiter brought Tam's order of clam chowder and a glass of wine. Dipping the French bread into the bowl, Tam thought about how he might be able to justify his continued involvement in the case. It was 6:15 p.m., which meant it was 4:15 a.m. in Riga, Latvia. Too early to call Petrenko.

His phone suddenly buzzed and the screen flashed *Sergei Petrenko*.

"Mr. Petrenko," he said. "I had just thought about calling you."

Petrenko was on his private jet, heading from the company headquarters in Luxembourg to his Scottish Highlands estate. "Wanted to let you know that I just received a call from my shipping broker, and both of the seized containers have been released by U.S. Customs. The consignee agrees that the boxes would cost more to ship back than they're worth, so we're done with it."

"They'll probably be sold off by a government auction house," said Tam.

I don't care what they do with them at this point. And since we're done in America, you'll be heading back then."

"Again, sir, some of the suspects are still outstanding and others have yet to be identified."

Petrenko brushed off the line of logic. "Three dead and two containers recovered. I am satisfied enough with those results. Besides, Tam, when you scratch the wound a little bit, the scab falls off and healing begins. But when you dig too much, you end up with a festering, infected abscess." Petrenko let out a sigh. He knew his metaphor wasn't enough to convince the private detective of his real rationale for letting it go. "Look, Tam, I have my reasons."

"I understand, Mr. Petrenko." Tam regretted the overstep. "I work for you."

Another sigh issued from the other end of the phone and then a pause. "I just don't want to shove this stick too far into the Russian hornet nest."

It wasn't the first time Petrenko had mentioned the Russian government. Tam stayed silent, waiting for his client to elaborate.

"Our...disagreements go back to '91—perestroika and the fall of the Soviet Union," said Petrenko. "Within a few years, the idiots had run the new federation into ruin. We were on the brink of financial collapse. In order to keep the lights on, they put all the nationalist corporations on the open market. Everything was getting privatized—sold to the highest bidder."

"And you were one of them," said Tam.

"Indeed. I bought their beggarly vodka company for a pittance. Improved marketing and distribution, and grew my fortune fiftyfold."

Curtis hadn't been aware of the corporation's background. "It all sounds fairly amicable," he said.

"It was, until the Kremlin saw what their former companies were worth now that they were managed efficiently. First Yeltsin and then Putin; they've been coming after me ever since. Lawsuits over trademarks and production rights, claims that I threatened officials. Putin's goons went so far as to search my headquarters, which were in Moscow at that time. They even issued a warrant for my arrest," he said. "Can you believe that, Tam? That is why I haven't allowed you to work with anyone else on this, and it's why I've been steadfastly averse to my name being connected in any way to your investigation."

Curtis quietly took it in, comparing the facts as Petrenko told them with what he already knew about the case. They still didn't fit with the stolen containers; nothing had come up Russian, only Latvian—which according to everything Tam had read, was a former Soviet state, now with their own strained relations with the Kremlin.

"So you see, Mr. Tam, whether or not the Russian government is involved in all of this, I know enough to quit while I'm ahead. We've gotten what we've come for. Now we cash in our chips and go home."

"I understand, Mr. Petrenko."

"I'm assuming you are at the airport?" Petrenko said. "I would like to sit down with you as soon as you get back."

Tam grimaced. "I haven't left yet, sir. I've paid for my hotel room in advance, through Friday. So I thought I'd take tomorrow and rest up, see the sights, maybe take in a show before heading back. At my own expense, of course."

Petrenko grunted. Not about the day of recreation, he knew Tam was a dedicated investigator and deserved it. But the shrewd business tycoon had picked up on a couple of faux pas in the last couple of conversations with Tam, and they had nagged him with worry ever since. To ensure that his company's investigation on American soil remained clandestine, Petrenko insisted that Tam get out of San Francisco and out of the United States without further delay.

Sarah had walked into the hotel lobby while Tam was on the phone. She spotted Tam and took a padded, high-back chair in a booth directly behind him. Tam couldn't see Sarah and didn't know she was there, but she was listening to every word.

Tapping the name *Petrenko* into her phone's search app, Brooks read about Tam's mysterious client. She waved a waiter over and ordered a beer. When it came, she walked around to face Tam and then took a seat across from him as he ended the call.

"I was just on the phone with my wife," said Tam.

"Sergei Petrenko?" she said with a knowing smirk. "So, what does one of the world's wealthiest men have to be so worried about?"

Curtis frowned. "How long have you been listening?"

"My intention wasn't to eavesdrop," she said. "I was actually trying to give you some privacy while you were talking. Couldn't help hearing at least some of it."

Not that it mattered any longer, Tam sensed that his boss already suspected as much. Besides, Tam trusted Brooks and felt that he owed her the truth. Explaining the specifics of his association with Sergi Petrenko, Tam also told Brooks about the billionaire's adversarial relationship with the Kremlin.

Like Tam, Sarah also attempted to knit the pieces of information together with what she already knew. But nothing fit. She didn't doubt the veracity of Petrenko's history, but that was there and then and this was here and now. The whole Russian thing sounded like a conspiracy theorist's fantasy.

"Now that you've heard my secrets, what are yours?" Tam asked. "Why are *you* sneaking around behind your boss's back?"

Sarah didn't like talking about her personal life, in fact, she didn't even like to think about it. It was too cumbersome, too muddled with childhood anguish.

Brooks took a breath and let it out slowly. "I've been told that I'm overly aggressive. Too confrontational."

Tam suppressed a grin.

"Shocker, right?" She forced a smile. "It's been in my nature since as long as I can remember. You know, Army brat, moved around a lot, always the new kid. I think I struggled so much at being accepted that I just gave up somewhere along the way."

"You've been in trouble recently because of this?"

She nodded. "So far it's cost me a marriage—which was only partly my fault—and a *reassignment*, which is CBP jargon for a disciplinary demotion. They haven't found a way to blame me for getting shot at a couple of weeks ago, but believe me, they would if they could."

"Let me guess," said Tam. "This mandatory recuperation after the shooting was non-negotiable."

"Worse than that," said Sarah. "I've had my police powers taken away, and I'm an ass hair away from being out of a job."

She didn't want to get into the topic of her brooding, drunk, Vietnam veteran father or her passive, codependent mother. She had already shared more with Tam than she cared to.

Tam said nothing, and Sarah thought he might be stalled back on the *ass hair* analogy. "Anyway," she said, swatting the air between them. "I never knew you were married."

He nodded. "To a beautiful lady. She's a history professor at the University of Hong Kong."

"Wow, beautiful and smart."

They sat quietly for a minute, Tam finishing his soup and Sarah sipping the last of her beer. Both of them were thinking about their respective investigations. Finally, Tam hailed the waiter and paid his tab.

"Let's get ourselves out to the warehouse," he said, "and see what McKenna's search warrant comes up with."

41

Russ Street Warehouse

Six of us were there, staged in front of the building; me, Linh Phú, Sarah Brooks, and Curtis Tam. I had also asked Teddy Muniz and his partner, Larry Vargas, to accompany us. Not only was it protocol to have uniformed officers present during a search, but Muniz was the Southern Station cop who had arrested Elvis Lugailo (aka: Lang) and my informant half naked in the minivan. In the event that we ran into the guy at the warehouse, I wanted Muniz there to positively ID him.

Tam would be able to recognize the stolen cargo, and Brooks could identify the van used in her attack—although Tam and Brooks wouldn't be mentioned in my warrant service after-action report.

Everything was covered, or so I hoped. My only worry was what to do about Captain Dowd. I'd have to claim that I hadn't heard his phone message until *after* I had already executed the search warrant. And if I recovered the evidence I hoped was there, and was able to solve these cases, which I was sort of banking on, it would all be moot anyway.

It was 8 p.m. and the warehouse was dark. I banged on the door with a balled fist. "San Francisco Police! Search warrant! Demand immediate entry!"

I felt ridiculous yelling at an empty building, but I'd remembered reading about the *knock and notice* requirement when I was studying for the inspector's exam.

The keys were already in my hand, and I fingered through them to find the one that opened the door. The two uniforms stepped in just behind me, both unclasping their holsters and resting their hands on their pistols. Phú followed next, and then Brooks and Tam.

I couldn't find a switch near the door, then remembered it was across the warehouse near a stairway. I flipped on the overhead lights and the first thing I noticed was the empty spot where the shipping container had been.

Son of a bitch!

The next thing I noticed were the missing pallets of stolen cargo—gone as well. A deflating sputter came from behind me, and I could only imagine Tam's disappointment at having to tell his client: *Hey, you know that cargo I recovered? Well, it's missing again.*

The white Ford van was still there though, which, for me, meant very little—since I still had my doubts about its relevance.

Other than the van, the rest of the warehouse had been cleaned out; no records, no stolen cargo, and no Elvis Lugailo.

I released the two uniforms to resume their patrol duties, and then called for a tow company to impound the van. It was the least I could do for Brooks, who was still convinced it was the same vehicle the gunmen used during the attack on her.

Tam stayed pretty quiet, and I found myself apologizing to him as if it was my fault his cargo had been stolen for the second time. In my own mind, I blamed Dowd. I kept replaying the route he took when I followed him that morning. I had lost him near the warehouse, and then there was his phone message pulling me off the case. He had to be the one behind this.

"I appreciate all you've done." Tam sounded defeated. "I suppose I'll be heading back to Hong Kong now. Nothing more I can do to help anybody here."

Struggling to find words, I resorted to a silent handshake. It was good timing that Brooks came over just then.

"How are we going to explain seizing the van?" she asked. "I mean, if I'm not even supposed to be here, and nothing in your entire investigation suggests a connection to my shooting..." Her words trailed off.

"I don't know," I said. "I guess I'll just have to call the Oakland investigators and tell them I have a hunch that this is their suspect vehicle."

Brooks rolled her eyes. "They'll think you're a lunatic."

I nodded. "Maybe I'll have our crime scene people go over it first. If we find anything, then I'll notify Oakland." It sounded like a better plan, but it was the least of my worries. All I could hear was the angry voicemail Dowd had left me.

I'm so totally screwed.

42

The McKenna Home

My wife hadn't spoken to me in days. The futon in the guestroom was like sleeping on a bucket of bolts, and my whole body ached.

Limping down the hall in my boxers and knee brace, I was in no hurry to get into work. Dowd already had me in his crosshairs. And now that I had defied his order, and then come up empty on my search, he was sure to drop the hammer.

I gimped past Doris to the coffee pot, watching her in my periphery as I poured a cup. She was doing her best to ignore me.

"Still pissed?" I asked in a croaky morning voice.

She groaned under the weight of my presence, then turned toward the window.

During my nights in the guestroom, I'd found myself thinking of the woman from the consulate—her soft, accented voice and her sparkling blue eyes. Her talcum skin. And unlike the way Doris looked at me, the young Latvian saw me as someone important. Her eyes shimmered with admiration. At least that's what I imagined.

To act on it would undoubtedly complicate my life even more, making things at home worse than they already were. Still, the fantasy was a pleasurable respite that made me feel a few years younger and a few pounds lighter.

I sipped my coffee. "Doris?"

She was all dressed up for work, still not moving, just gazing into the yard.

My wife is attractive, don't get me wrong. Maybe 5-foot-6 or 7, and a figure that, despite being a 36-year-old mother of a teenager, hasn't gotten away from her.

Anyway, I found myself wondering why she was wearing a skirt and heels. I knew it wasn't for me, and I wondered if there could be someone else. My clenched jaw came with the realization that I still cared, at least on some level. Maybe I was projecting the guilt of my own duplicitous thoughts.

"We're really on shaky ground, you know that?" Doris said, turning from the window. "This marriage brings me no happiness anymore. And I can't imagine that it brings you any, either. You've completely undermined our attempt at counseling, and it's obvious that you care more about your job than about our family and our marriage."

"It's not that." I gazed into my mug.

"What's not what?"

"It's not what you said. I do care. I mean, about you and Bridge, I do. It's just that things are happening at work right now that I can't really--"

Doris sighed. "Can't really talk about. Yeah, I know. It's your standard go-to line, Danny. Always an important case or some big arrest. I'm done with it, Dan. Can't do this anymore."

"Whoa!" I lifted my hand, accidentally splashing coffee in the process. Her eyes closed in frustration as I grabbed a dish towel. Then, while I was on my good knee, wiping up the spill, I made my plea. "How about giving me another chance? We've been together for what, fourteen years?"

"Sixteen."

"Right. Isn't that worth another try? If not for me, at least for Bridge. She doesn't need a broken home; she needs two parents."

"Bridget hasn't had *two parents* for a long time."

"I can do better," I pleaded. "C'mon Doris, one more chance."

Her eyes narrowed and her lips tightened. "Okay," she finally said. "Here's your one more chance, Danny. Bridget gets the braces taken off of her teeth today at three o'clock. I've got a meeting at work and there is no way I can drive her into the City."

"So...you...want me to take her?" I pictured Captain Dowd, Elvis Lugailo, the girl at the consulate. I thought of all the things I still needed to do, all that was happening on my homicide case. Well, not exactly *my* case anymore. But I still needed to train Linh Phú, and then there was the whole thing with Chief Fahey's death...

"Danny?" Doris's sharp voice slapped me back to the present. "Your second chance?"

"Sure, yeah." I heard myself agreeing to it. What else could I say? It was either take my daughter to the orthodontist or pack my bags. "Tell Bridge I'll meet her in front of her school at two o'clock."

43

425 Sycamore Avenue
Mill Valley Middle School

Thursday had been unexpectedly pleasant, probably because Captain Dowd was tied up in meetings all morning. I'd been able to finish my final report on the search warrant, which didn't amount to any recovered evidence—only a van, impounded for dubious reasons.

My new partner, Linh Phú, had gotten a call from someone upstairs. A gang fight in Chinatown had left two young men stabbed—one of whom spoke Vietnamese. Phú had been reassigned to Central Station for the rest of the day to help with translation and victim interviews. She had taken our unmarked car, leaving me to pick up Bridget in my own car.

She was in front of the school when I pulled the Jeep Cherokee to the curb. A slight grin crossed her lips when she saw that I had made it on time, but then it dissipated into self-consciousness as she flopped into the car.

"Hey," she grunted.

"Big day, huh? The braces finally come off."

"I guess." Another trace of a smile, and then out came the phone and I had lost her again to various social media apps.

My cell phone vibrated in my pocket when we were halfway across the bridge. I hoped it was Doris, in which case I could gloat about having picked Bridget up on time. But it was a number I didn't recognize, and I let it go to voicemail.

Pulling into the red zone in front of Westfield Orthodontics on Market, we were still a few minutes early for Bridget's appointment. I listened to the message.

"McKenna, it's me," said Shanay Moore, her voice barely above a whisper. "*I'm with Elvis at the motel right now. He in the bathroom, and he fix'n to leave pretty soon. You better move quick if you wanna catch him.*"

"Son of a bitch." Seventeen minutes had already passed since she left the voicemail. I steered the car back onto Market and flipped a U-turn. Tires squealed as I swerved around a muni bus.

"What are you doing, Dad?" Bridget's iPhone and headset had flown off of her lap and lay tangled on the floorboard.

"Not now, okay?" I pleaded. "This is important. It's work." I raced back a block to 6th, leaning on my horn and cutting through a cluster of pedestrians in the crosswalk. They swore and flipped me off as a venti macchiato skittered across the hood of my car.

Bridget slunk down in her seat, as if one of her classmates might have been among them.

Five blocks down I cut across oncoming traffic and onto the sidewalk in front of the Hotel Beverly. There she was, sitting against the painted brick façade, hoodie pulled over her head and a cigarette wedged between her lips.

"Took long enough, McKenna." Sha Nay Nay eyed my daughter as she slid into the backseat. "What's this, bring your kid to work day?"

I turned in my seat. "Where is he?"

She shrugged. "He gone now."

"Who's she, Dad?" Bridget twisted in her seat to take in my informant.

"Which way?" I called over the seatback, my car's tires spinning in reverse across the sidewalk. "How long ago did he leave? In a vehicle or on foot?"

"He walked that way," she said, motioning toward Natoma. "Probably going back to wherever he work at."

The Jeep fishtailed wildly, nearly colliding into a cab. In a cloud of blue gray smoke, we shot across four lanes of traffic onto the narrow one-way street. Heading the wrong way, I edged along looking for Elvis Lugailo.

But my suspect had disappeared.

I pulled to the curb and slammed my fist into the steering wheel. "What did he do, Dad?"

Sha Nay Nay leaned around the headrest. "Killed some dude."

Bridget's face went ashen. "Do you work with my dad?"

"Sort of," said Sha Nay Nay.

Bridget ran her eyes down the girl's ragged clothes, stopping on her pregnant abdomen. "You're a cop?"

Sha Nay Nay shook her head. "Nah, I used to be a drug addict."

Thankfully, she'd left out her *other* vocation.

Then she added, "And I used to be a prostitute, too."

My eyes rolled up into my head. "Never mind all that!"

I considered phoning into dispatch for assistance, but this was no longer my case and I was already on everybody's shit list.

I swung around onto Russ Street and made a couple of passes by the warehouse. Still no sign of him.

"Dad, what about my orthodontist appointment?"

"I know, I know. No worries, we're only five minutes late."

I still had time to drop Bridget off and get back to check the area. Suddenly, I remembered the consulate. Why hadn't it occurred to me sooner? The Latvian Consulate building was only a few blocks south of where we had lost Lugailo.

My Jeep shot forward again, pinning the girls against their seats. Pulling around the corner onto Folsom Street, I spotted the odd looking white and red Latvian flag out front.

Then my heart seized when I saw two men coming out the front door. I caught only a glimpse of the first man—darker and shorter than the other; he had quickly ducked into the car parked at the curb. But the second man stood at the driver's door. Clear as day... Captain Greg Dowd.

My boss had been working with the Latvians all along. Paid off to protect them. He had pulled me off the case because I was getting too close. He was the corrupt cop that Chief Fahey had suspected. And the guy in his passenger seat... He's got to be my suspect, Elvis Lugailo.

As I watched Dowd climb into the car, I shouted, "Hold on girls!"

The captain's Crown Vic pulled into traffic and I floored it, fishtailing away from the curb a half block behind them. I reached for my .38 and slid the holster along my belt so I could get at it quickly.

Bridget's hands gripped the seat, but she said nothing. I saw Sha Nay Nay in the mirror and her face was as terrified as my daughter's.

I worked my way through traffic, neither subtly nor tactfully, until I was right behind them. Without red lights or a siren, all I could do was flash my headlights and lean on my horn.

But instead of pulling over, Dowd sped up and changed lanes. He was making a run for it.

Swerving around a delivery van and into oncoming traffic, I raced alongside the captain's sedan. Cars veered, and all around us tires screeched and horns blared. This was the final showdown, and either way it was going to end here and now.

Dowd's wide eyes glared at me through his window, and I saw fear in them. We both knew he was trapped. Wrenching the wheel, I slammed my Jeep into his front fender. The force and suddenness of it knocked his car sideways, spinning the Crown Vic across the road and into a lamppost at 8th and Folsom.

"Dad!" Bridget screamed.

Then Shanay cried out, "You gonna get us killed, McKenna."

I grabbed my gun and jumped out of the car.

"Hands up!" I yelled as I ran toward my boss and my murder suspect. Using the butt of my firearm, I smashed out the driver's window. Then I plunged the gun barrel right into the side of Dowd's panicked little face.

"One move and I'll blow your fucking head off!"

44

SFO – International Terminal

The status board showed an on-time departure for eight o'clock—still 90 minutes away.

Tam set his carry-on down next to him while ate a dry tuna sandwich and read an online version of the South China Morning Post. He then answered a couple of emails from his Hong Kong office.

After closing his laptop, the PI gazed through a tall bank of windows onto the tarmac. Unable to shake the feeling that he had run an entire marathon only to walk the last fifty yards, Tam still wanted to do more for his high-paying client.

The final rays of daylight glistened on a rooftop several hundred yards to the north, where a field of solar panels covered Terminal 3. Very progressive, he thought.

That's when it struck him.

Quickly logging back into his laptop, Tam brought up the GPS tracking site. The unit on the Russ Street container had lost power sitting in the dark building for so long. But if it had been exposed to sunlight after being moved from the warehouse, Tam realized that it might emit a signal again. He couldn't recall the exact specs, but knew that its battery's deep cell capacity and its ability to hold a charge was one of the device's selling points.

Punching in the code designation for that particular unit, Tam saw that it had transmitted a weak, intermittent signal after leaving the warehouse that morning.

Five minutes later, Tam was in a cab heading east over the Hayward-San Mateo Bridge.

He hurriedly scrolled through his stored numbers, stopping when he got to *Sarah Brooks*. The federal agent answered on the first ring.

"You busy?" Tam asked.

"If watching Judge Judy is busy, then yes."

Tam had no idea who Judge Judy was or why Brooks would be watching her. "Well, I think I might have something. If you can drive to Hayward--"

"I thought you were catching a slow boat to China," she said. "What in the hell are you doing in Hayward?"

Tam shook his head at the misunderstanding. "I decided to forgo my flight. At least for the time being."

"Whaddaya got?"

"Meet me at Arden Road Business Park," he said. "I'll explain when you get here."

It took Sarah nearly an hour to get out to the former salt flats, now an industrial park on the bay. Most of the businesses had closed for the day, and she found Tam standing on a dark corner at Eden Landing and Arden Road near a vacant deli. He was holding a laptop case in one hand and a carry-on bag in the other.

Getting into the passenger seat of Brooks's Kia, Curtis explained the basics of the tracking program. "I've been using GLONASS, which is a global navigation satellite system. It allows me to track containers in transit across the ocean."

"Not that I'm in a hurry, Tam, but fast forward to why I'm here."

He nodded. "The GPS software also has a mapping component for use in urban settings." Tam sensed her impatience. "Bottom line; the solar powered battery went dead in the warehouse, but came back to life when the container was moved. It must have been temporarily exposed to sunlight, because even a little bit can charge the cells—though not for long."

Brooks glanced outside, assuming he had found its location.

"As I was waiting for my flight, I saw that the tracker was emitting a weak signal. I grabbed a screenshot of its position before it died again. This is where it was as of 6:37 p.m."

Tam opened his laptop to show her.

Sarah checked her watch. "That was almost two hours ago. How accurate is this thing?"

"Normally, it's quite accurate," he said. "But the signal becomes degraded as the battery drains, and the mapping coordinates can fluctuate—maybe as much as a quarter mile."

She squinted at the image on his screen. The small red map pin showing the container's location was somewhere on the south side of the street about mid-block.

Putting the car into gear, they gradually made their way along the street past rows of flat industrial offices and warehouses.

155

"This thing could be anywhere, Tam. There must be a hundred cargo bays, just in this one block."

Light drained from the car's interior as Tam closed his laptop. "But in another hour or so this place will be completely deserted. Any activity, any movement at all, and we'll be able to narrow down the container's location right away."

Sarah glanced around again. "No offense Tam, but we've already recovered my van. Finding your container in an industrial building in Hayward seems extraneous at this point."

"What about your positon at U.S. Customs? Isn't this container part of the case that precipitated the assault on you?"

"I'll give you that." Brooks grinned. "If I even have a position at Customs anymore."

The on-duty watch commander in Hayward was a guy named Nakamura. He sat behind his desk with an illegible expression while Sarah explained the course that the stolen container had taken—stolen, recovered, then stolen again.

"Why did Customs release all that liquor to the consulate guy in the first place?" he asked. "Aren't there a bunch of restrictions on liquor imports?"

"It's a loophole in Customs Regulations and Harmonized Tariff Schedules." Brooks grinded out the words through clenched teeth. "The Department of State extends certain duty-free privileges to diplomatic missions, consulates, and for the personal use of families of foreign diplomats residing here."

"Personal use." Nakamura grinned. "A forty-foot container full of booze?"

Brooks shook her head. "Yeah, that would be the loophole."

She and Tam left the police station with a promise of help from the lieutenant, should they come up with anything. But they both knew that spotting the container in the sprawling industrial tract would be nearly impossible.

"Even as remote as the lead is," said Tam, "we should let McKenna know about it. Especially since he was good enough to bring us in on his search warrant."

Sarah nodded her agreement as she dialed her phone. "McKenna, it's Sarah Brooks. I'm with Tam over in Hayward. Call me as soon as you get this message."

45

Office of Risk Management
1245 3rd Street

I sat across the table staring at the two nameplates in front of me. Lieutenant Michael Prowse was the Internal Affairs Lieutenant, and Sheila Young was a sergeant. Next to me was Bill Rampone, my union rep, and at the far end of the table sat a department stenographer.

"Inspector McKenna," said the lieutenant. "We have read over your written statement of what went on today, and we've also had an opportunity to interview your captain, Gregory Dowd. Now, before we go any further, we are obligated to read you your constitutional rights as well as your Garrity warning."

The lieutenant read me my Miranda rights, and then my police officer advisement—which is required during concurrent criminal and administrative interrogations. The whole thing made me feel like I'd done something illegal, which I found hard to believe, since Captain Dowd was the criminal here.

"Having these rights in mind, do you agree to speak with us?" asked Lieutenant Prowse.

"Yes."

Prowse purportedly had some kind of legal degree, which he liked to flaunt, and he had a reputation as a Dowd supporter. Neither of which impressed me, but they had been integral to Prowse's rapid ascent through the ranks.

He asked me to elaborate on why I thought Dowd was involved in criminal activity, and I explained that he had tried to sabotage my investigation from the start—postponing my victim's autopsy until Cassidy got back and then threatening to hand the case over to someone else.

The lieutenant listened patiently, then asked, "Do think it's unreasonable for a captain in his position to want a more tenured inspector leading a high-profile murder investigation?"

"Well," I said. "It was more like..." Prowse's question had made Dowd out to be the good guy. It was obvious this wasn't going to be an objective look at the facts. Without the context of the agreement between me and the former chief, I couldn't even defend myself. "Okay," I finally conceded. "I see what you mean."

Then Prowse asked if I often conducted on-duty surveillances in my personal car, accompanied by my thirteen-year-old daughter and a convicted prostitute.

"Of course not," I fired back at him. "I had to drive my daughter to an orthodontic appointment, and then I got a call--"

The lieutenant cut me off. "Let's move on to your vehicle pursuit on Folsom Street, and your use of force during the detention."

"Use of force?" I asked.

Prowse leaned over his nameplate, staring me in the face. "Unless you feel that running your captain's vehicle off the road and into a pole, smashing out his window, and then thrusting your firearm into his face doesn't constitute a use of force..."

"At the time, I believed that the captain was in the company of my homicide suspect," I said. "Maybe even helping the murderer get away. I was following tactical protocol, since I knew Dowd was armed and I believed that my suspect probably was as well."

"And your murder suspect is?"

"Elvis Lugailo," I said. "He works as a security guard at the--"

"You might find it helpful to know that the passenger in the car with Captain Dowd was not named Elvis Lugailo. In fact, it was the Republic of Latvia Consul in charge of the San Francisco office."

"I didn't know that at the time."

"*Ignorantia juris non excusat*," he said with a condescending grin. "Ignorance does not excuse the action."

I tried to find a comeback. "So, why was Dowd in the car with him then?"

The lieutenant deferred to Sergeant Young, who glanced through her notes and said, "They were going to a meeting at City Hall. Apparently it was a planning session for the Latvian Proclamation Day parade. It's on the eighteenth." She closed her notebook. "The captain had been asked to represent the department at the meeting, in place of Chief Fahey."

Again, Dowd had come off smelling like a rose.

"Proclamation Day parade." I scratched my head, couldn't think of a counterpoint, and just kept scratching. I finally thought of something, and asked, "What about yesterday when I tailed Dowd to the Russ Street warehouse?"

Prowse tilted his head. "You were surveilling your captain?"

"Yes," I said, feeling myself stumbling into another tar pit. "He was on his way to work, and instead of going up Bryant he turned left onto... Look, never mind. I'll withdraw the question."

"No," insisted the lieutenant. "Let's bring him in and ask him. Maybe we can clear this up right now."

Sergeant Young went out and returned a minute later with Dowd. He wore a small bandage on his cheek where I had pressed my gun, but otherwise looked okay. Standing at the end of the table, he glared at me but did not take a seat.

"Captain Dowd," started the lieutenant. "*Acting* Inspector McKenna is under the belief that you visited a warehouse on Russ Street yesterday morning."

"No, I did not."

"He claims to have seen you there," said Prowse.

"I didn't actually see him enter," I interjected. "I had to continue straight when he turned on Howard, and--"

"Now you're following me, too?" Dowd shouted. "I don't even know where your fucking warehouse is. The only stop I made on the way to work yesterday was to pick up my uniform at Celia's Dry Cleaners. It's on Seventh near Howard. Been going there for years. Want to see my damn receipt, McKenna?"

Prowse nodded at me with a belittling, *so there*, smirk. He was clearly posturing to impress the captain.

A tap sounded at the door and a young uniformed officer stuck his head in. "There's a Mrs. McKenna here to pick up her daughter."

"That's my wife," I said. "I'd like to speak with her--"

Prowse ignored me. "They're nearly finished taking the girl's statement. Tell Mrs. McKenna that her daughter will be right out."

"Wait a minute," I said. "You're questioning my daughter?"

"Yes, McKenna." The lieutenant's tone was more patronizing now. "Your daughter was a witness to a possible crime. Taking statements from witnesses is what we do."

"What about my informant? You're not holding her, are you?"

Sergeant Young glanced down at her notes again. "Would that be a Miss Sha Nay Nay Moore?"

Prowse flashed a smug grin, and Dowd shook his head in disgust. That stupid name of hers was making me sound less credible. Then again, I was doing that pretty well on my own.

"Your so-called informant refused to give a statement," said the sergeant. "For some inexplicable reason, the young lady seems to look up to you."

They asked a few more questions, but nothing of any substance. Suddenly, Dowd interjected, "Oh yeah McKenna, and what's up with you ripping off some keys from Lam's desk?" Then, turning to Prowse and Young, he said, "They were physical evidence in someone else's investigation."

"I didn't... No, that's not an accurate--"

"Bullshit, McKenna. The two guys working the night watch saw you at Lam's desk, sniffing through his case file."

I wanted to tell them that there was a lot more to it. Explain about Curtis Tam and the stolen cargo he'd tracked to the warehouse. That a Customs agent named Sarah Brooks had come up with my suspect's true name. And how the now-dead chief had given me a mission. But again, I couldn't prove any of it. So, I remained silent.

Without revealing the identities of Curtis Tam and Sarah Brooks, I had nothing. And to disclose Chief Fahey's classified operation now would only make me look like a delusional liar. There was no way they'd believe it.

"Since you're still technically assigned to Captain Dowd," said Prowse, "he'll have to be the one to make the decision about your work status while this incident is being investigated. I think it's prudent that we be present to witness that conversation, given the fact that you already assaulted him once." Then he turned to Dowd. "Captain?"

What a suckass!

I wanted to get ahead of this and apologize to the captain for misreading the situation. So before Dowd answered, I said, "I'd just like to state for the record, that I was only acting on what I believed to be accurate information. But I understand if you want to take the Berzins homicide away from me. I don't like it, but I'll accept it."

Dowd let out a breathy chuckle, and I saw that he had been waiting for this moment to exact his pound of flesh. "Take the case away?" He grinned so hard it looked like it hurt. "I'm taking your badge and gun away, you jerkoff. As of this second, you are relieved of duty. Suspended! Your status is that you have no status! You're on administrative leave pending the outcome of the internal affairs investigation. Is that clear, McKenna?"

The two IA investigators, my union rep, and the stenographer all turned toward me in unison.

At that moment the uniformed cop opened the door again. "All finished with the girl, sir."

There wasn't much left for me to say to them, and all I really wanted to do was apologize to Bridge and explain the whole thing to Doris.

"I'd like to talk to my wife now," I said.

Prowse sneered. "We're done here."

But as I got up and started for the door, the officer held a cautionary hand toward me. "Just a moment, sir. I'm afraid your wife doesn't want to talk to you. In fact, she asked that we escort her and your daughter out of the building safely before releasing you."

Dowd's little eyes burned into me. "In other words McKenna, you're pretty much screwed all the way around."

46

Homicide Detail

The IA people had relieved me of my duty weapon, my badge, my office key, and my city-issued cell phone. Now I had no way to check messages or call anyone—including my wife. Didn't matter, I guess. She wasn't talking to me anyway.

Dowd would only allow me to retrieve my personal effects from the building as long as I was "under the watchful eye" of a police chaperone. So I got a cardboard box from Maintenance, and under the *watchful eye* of a patrol sergeant, cleared out my things. Thankfully, it was late enough that almost nobody else was in the office; only Mendoza and Taylor, the inspectors my case had been reassigned to.

"Hey, McKenna," said Mendoza. "Tell me that it's true. You really screwed your gun into Dowd's ear?"

My jaw tightened. "Good news travels fast."

"I'd have paid to see that," said Taylor. "For what it's worth, it was good working with you."

I nodded back.

The Gustavs Berzins case file was on my desk. I wanted to slip a few things out of it before my escort noticed, but the guy was on me like jock itch. I handed the folder over to Mendoza and Taylor. The only thing it didn't contain was the van's impound sheet, which was still sitting on my desk. I managed to slide it into my moving box without being noticed.

The top drawer of my desk held a bunch of office supplies that I realized I'd never get to use. And I hadn't been in the detail long enough to fill the rest of the drawers—except for the bottom one, which held Lou's Scotch and his cell phone. The battery had died, and though his stored numbers and fancy apps wouldn't do me any good, at least I'd be able to make calls once I recharged it.

Placing both items into my box, I looked around the office for what I knew might be the last time.

Mendoza and Taylor had picked up the Berzins file and were now heading out of the office. "We're going to check your suspect's address in the Tenderloin," said Taylor.

I'd already written down that it was a bad address. So, either the two inspectors hadn't bothered to read my notes, or thought I didn't know what I was talking about. Either way, it was on them.

I nodded. "Good luck with that."

The last thing I did before leaving was write a note to Linh Phú, asking her to give me a call. I left Cassidy's cell number, hoping that she'd be the first to see the note when she arrived in the morning.

Doris hadn't answered my calls, and I'd begun to wonder if she'd gone to her mother's again. But the lights were on inside my house, so I was pretty sure that she and Bridge were there. I had already put my daughter through enough though, and the fact that she still hadn't gotten her braces off made me feel even worse.

I thought about going inside once they went to bed, and quietly slipping into the den. But if I happened to bump into Doris, I'd be facing the wrath of Lucifer incarnate. So I ended up driving to the Manzanita Park & Ride lot a couple of miles from my house. Only a few cars were there when I arrived, and I backed into a corner spot beneath the Highway 1 overpass.

It was windy and noisy, and the vibration from trucks overhead felt as if the span above me was collapsing. I made one last call to the house, but again, nobody answered. It was almost eleven, and I knew I was in for a miserable night.

Out came Lou's bottle, which I figured for a threefold panacea. First, it would help me to forget the shittiest day on record. Second, the booze would keep me warm. And finally, it would eventually help me to fall asleep in the cramped car.

An hour later, I was still freezing. So I started the car and turned on the heater and the radio. As I began to thaw, I must have dozed off because I woke suddenly to an obnoxious default ringtone. For a few seconds, I had no idea where I was. It was a Scotch and sleep induced disorientation. "Hello?"

"Inspector McKenna, it's me. Linh Phú. I wouldn't have called so late, but I just heard about what happened today."

"No, no, I'm glad you called. You saw my note then?"

"Yes, I've been working with the Asian Gang Task Force all day, and I just got back to the office. I'm about to head home."

I tried not to sound as drunk as I felt. "Just wanted to let you know that I've been suspended from duty, and, well, it was a real pleasure working with you. I mean, even though it was short-lived."

"Thank you, sir." Phú paused a moment. "I'm not sure if you still want to know about...well, since you're no longer..."

"Yes," I told her. "I'm not allowed to actually work on any cases, but I'm not going to give up. If you hear about anything that might help, please let me know."

She paused again. "The woman from the consulate, the one you gave your card to."

"Inga Berzina?"

"She called for you today. Said she did not want to talk with any other inspector. Apparently there is something of importance she wants to pass on."

I thought for a second. "Did the call come through Mrs. Ocampo? Could Captain Dowd have caught wind of it?"

"No," said Phú. "Dowd doesn't know. And Mrs. Ocampo is still off work. Ms. Berzina actually called on your desk phone, and I answered it thinking it may be something important."

"It was. Thank you Linh."

"Speaking of which," she said, "after our earlier call I researched Latvian names. I think that the similarity between that woman's last name and that of your victim may be more than mere coincidence."

"I'm not following you, Phú."

"Surnames within the same Latvian family don't always have the same endings. While male last names will almost always end in the letter *s*, surnames of Latvian women take on the endings of either *a* or *e*. Your victim was a man named Berzins, so his sister would take the surname Berzina."

Now my head was really spinning. "You're telling me that the woman we talked to at the consulate is my victim's sister?"

"I'm telling you that based on what I've read about Latvian language idioms, Inga Berzina may be related to your victim."

I sat there in my Jeep; amazed at what my partner had figured out, curious about why the Latvian woman wanted to talk to me, and worried that I had left my car running too long.

"And just on the off chance you needed it," added Phú, "the woman's address is 680 Steiner, apartment 701."

47

Alamo Square Park
San Francisco

Checking my 360 had become a habit, I guess, especially while parked on a dark street. Although, there wasn't much moving at 1:30 in the morning.

I gazed up at the seven story building across Steiner, took another swig from Lou's bottle, and dialed Inga Berzina's phone number.

After a few rings, a woman answered. She sounded a little groggy, but at the same time tried to come across as alert. I apologized for the late call, explaining that I'd been busy working a serious crime scene and had just now gotten her message."

"Not at all, Inspector," she said. "I was hoping we could talk sometime, but not at the consulate. Perhaps someplace private."

"Of course, yes."

I thought about how best to present the idea to her, not wanting to sound too much like a drunk, disgraced cop, suspended from work and sleeping in his car. "I'm just leaving the office," I said. "If it's not too late... I could..."

"You mean, meet with me tonight?" I heard the frantic rustling of bed sheets. "Okay, uh, sure." More effort in her voice, cleaning and straightening as she spoke. "Now is fine."

I pretended to be talking to someone else, holding the phone away from my mouth. "You fellas go ahead and knock off for the night. But make sure you get those reports to me first thing in the morning." Then I came back, "Okay then, Ms. Berzina, I'll be there in about ten minutes."

The bottle was nearly done, so I finished the last couple of gulps. I shoveled several sticks of gum into my mouth and then walked into Alamo Square Park to take a leak. The cool wind helped clear my head a little, and it refueled my tanks. I wished I'd had time to get some coffee.

A man walking his Beagle on the sidewalk stopped to eye me as I came down the steps on the Hayes Street side of the park. I gave the dog a wide berth.

"You know," said the man as he cleared his throat, "This park closes at midnight. There's a sign." He motioned toward it.

I grunted. "Make sure you pick up your dog's shit; there's a sign about that, too."

The park's incline had irritated my knee, so I did a couple of stretches against the back of my Jeep. Then I grabbed my notebook and crossed the street to the apartment house.

Just my luck—the asshole with the beagle lived in the same building, and I had to share the elevator with them. They got off at the fifth floor and I continued to the seventh.

Inga answered the door in stretchy leggings, sandals and a San Francisco Giants tee shirt. I wondered if she was really a fan, or if it was her attempt to acculturate. In any case, she looked even prettier than she had at the consulate—more fresh and natural. Her blue eyes were still her best feature, but even in the loose top I could tell she was a nicely proportioned young woman.

We made small talk for a few minutes; me apologizing for the late hour and her trying to convince me that she'd been awake reading. "Can I get you anything to drink?" she asked. "Coffee, or..." She paused. "Sparkling water?"

I told her I was fine. Slowly, I eased into the subject of what used to be *my* investigation. "The reason you wanted to talk with me; does it have anything to do with Elvis Lugailo?"

Inga nodded. "He, he is not a good person. I think Elvis is involved with bad people and does bad things."

"Do you know who these people are?"

"Not really," she said.

"Do you know what these *bad things* are that Elvis does?"

"I believe it has to do with stealing liquor." She stared at the floor. "Not little bit, but lots of bottles. Thousands, maybe even millions of them."

"Are you talking about cargo containers?"

She looked up. "Yes, I think, yes."

I asked, "How do you know this?"

Inga looked away again, and tears started down her cheeks. "My brother, Gustavs. He was tricked into helping Elvis. To be honest, I think that he was persuaded by money. But my brother, he was not a bad person. Gustavs was always a good boy."

"And you think Elvis killed him?" I stopped taking notes to study her expression.

She shook her head adamantly. "They were friends, thick-like-thieves. No, someone was after them, wanted them dead."

I began writing again. "And you know this, how?"

"Because they kill Gustavs," she said. "And Rhonda. They kill her, too."

I looked up. "Rhonda Pitts?" It was on my list of questions, but all the better that she'd brought it up on her own.

"I think so, yes. But I only meet her once. She said only that her name was *Rhonda*."

"What was Rhonda's role in all of this?" I asked. "Did you know about the warehouse she rented on Russ Street?"

Inga shook her head. "I don't know about warehouse." Then she let out a long breath. "Rhonda was girlfriend to Elvis. She care about him, let him stay at her apartment and give to him money. But, he was not good to her. He was, how do you say? Showing his dominance of her, and taking advantage."

I nodded. "Why do you think Elvis killed her?"

A bitter look creased her face. "No, no. He would not kill her, either. These people they were mixed up with... I think they shoot poor Rhonda to give Elvis warning."

"What warning?"

"I don't know," she said. "Maybe that they kill him next."

As I sat at the low coffee table writing my notes, Inga got up and went to the kitchen. Then she called out, "I am sorry for rudeness Inspector, but I would like right now to have drink. I am very afraid that they will also come for me. Do you think so, too?"

"No, I don't think--"

She suddenly emerged with a serving tray, and I watched as she set down four small glasses—two containing a dark, syrupy liquid, and two that looked like water.

"Latvians believe it is poor manners to drink alone in presence of guest."

"I'm not fond of traveling, but I think I'd like Latvia." I leaned over the tray to examine the beverages. "Can I ask what it is?"

"This is Black Balsam," said Inga. "It is popular drink of which the exact ingredients are not well known. I'm told that it contains ginger and oak bark and cognac." She smiled, motioning to the other two glasses. "And this, of course, is vodka. We drink them together."

It was already very late, or early, depending on your perspective. As an inspector, being here and drinking with a witness would be a violation of several policies and procedures. Besides which, I was sure that Doris would see it as a monumental matrimonial transgression.

But taking into account that I was no longer a sanctioned police officer, and considering the pulverized state of my marriage, I continued to enjoy the only high point of the past few weeks.

I remember the conversation being buoyant and relaxing, thanks to my new favorite drink, though my recollection gets a little hazy from that point on. I don't think I asked anymore questions or took anymore notes, however.

At some point I tried to get up, and I have a vague memory of tumbling back onto the couch. Inga said something about being unable to drive in my condition, and I seem to recall her getting a blanket and a pillow for me.

I awoke to daylight creeping through the window next to the couch. My head felt like a base drum, and I had to take a leak something awful.

When I came out of the restroom, I found Inga sitting in a chair in the living room with a cup of coffee. She wore the same clothes as the previous night, and other than her hair being a little rumpled, she still looked great.

She had put a mug for me on the table next to where I'd slept. Apologizing profusely for having drunk too much of her Black Balsam, I sipped the coffee. The fog slowly lifted inside my head, and I remembered that I had finished off Cassidy's Scotch before I'd even gotten to Inga's house. It was probably why she looked so much better this morning than I did.

My goodbye was rushed and clumsy as I grabbed my things and then raced across Steiner to my Jeep. As I sat behind the wheel, I suddenly wondered why I was in such a hurry. I couldn't go into work, and I couldn't go home.

The idiot with the dog walked by again, glaring at me as he passed. So I flipped him off.

Then I pulled out Cassidy's phone, supposing it was time to get in touch with my wife to somehow grovel my way back into my house.

I dialed Doris's number at work. "Please, don't hang up!" I yelled. "Just hear me out, Doris."

Going into a fast-talking rant, I tried to explain the situation I'd become embroiled in at work—from Chief Fahey's secret directive to the murders and the international cargo theft ring. When I was done, there was only silence on the line. I worried that she might not believe me, think I was making up the whole thing. On the other hand, it was the first time I had opened up to her since my promotion. She had to at least give me points for that.

"And, please," I said. "Don't tell anyone about any of this." I not only wanted Doris to grasp the confidential nature of the information, but also to feel a sense of companionship or partnership—anything that might shoehorn me back in the door.

I heard Doris breathing on the other end, so I knew she was still on the line. But I didn't push her. I waited patiently as I drove along Richardson Avenue, past the rolling lawns of the Presidio.

Finally, she spoke. "We'll see how it goes, but things are not going to continue the way they've been. I swear to God, Danny, the next time will be the last time."

I let out a sigh—the weight of a thousand sins lifted. "I promise, Doris. I know I've said it before, but this time I mean it."

She moaned, like she was already having second thoughts.

"Is Bridge okay? Has she been asking about me at all?"

Another groan. "Actually, she has. As terrifying for her as that little chase-down episode was, I think she saw a different side of you."

"Not my good side, either."

"She loves you, Danny. And I think she felt sorry for you." Doris was quiet for a minute. "Believe it or not, Bridget now thinks she wants to be a cop."

I chuckled. "Do you think you could deal with two of us?"

"I'm still not sure if I can deal with one."

48

Home Sweet Home
Mill Valley

I got to my house around noon. It felt good to shower, shave and take a nap. I wanted to do something nice for Doris, so I mowed the lawn and did a load of laundry while she was still at work.

Bridge and a couple of her friends showed up as I was vacuuming the living room. I didn't see them come in, but I suddenly noticed my daughter standing there with her mouth open.

"Dad?" she said, as if seeing an apparition. "Does Mom know you're here?"

I told her that we had talked earlier, and that everything was going to be okay. Apologizing again for the wild ride around San Francisco the other day, I also promised that we'd get her braces off soon—come hell or high water.

I found myself still wrestling with a couple of things that, in this new spirit of transparency, I should probably tell Doris. The most pressing was my suspension from duty and the internal affairs investigation against me for violation of department policy—vis-à-vis, running my captain off the road and engaging in a vehicular pursuit in my own car with civilian passengers. The other thing was by comparison, a non-issue. That *non-issue* being the details of where I'd just spent the night. For the time being, I decided to let sleeping dogs lie.

Doris was expected home at six o'clock, and I wanted to have dinner ready, too. I drove down to Lam's Kitchen and picked up all of her favorite dishes. Bridge even came with me and then helped me set the table.

It was like Doris was walking into Operation Shock and Awe. Finessed with an abundance of thoughtful little courtesies, she had no choice but to forgive me.

"I even took out your favorite movie to watch while we're eating." I held up the Jerry Maguire DVD.

Doris still hadn't said much, but her expression was one of pleasant surprise. As I watched her put on a pair of slippers and take a seat at the table, I felt things definitely going my way.

I turned the TV on and set down the movie while I went to find the DVD remote. Behind me, the evening news played on a local network.

"Got it," I said, holding up the remote.

The TV flashed a full screen image of the apartment building at 680 Steiner Street, and I suddenly felt all of my blood coagulate in my veins. The shot panned to police cars and crime scene vans blocking the street, as a flurry of uniformed and plain clothes cops hustled around the apartment building.

One of the reporters began talking—a voiceover of the Steiner Street scene:

"A terrifying discovery this morning in the city's Haight District, where a woman was found brutally murdered in her apartment. Police are not releasing the name of the victim at this time, but our sources tell us that it was this woman."

Just then an inset image appeared, taking up half of the screen. *"Inga Berzina, a twenty-nine-year-old employee of the Latvian Consulate."*

"Put the movie on, Dad." Bridget was talking, but everything was suddenly in slow motion and close-up. I saw her swollen lips moving over her braces, and the spit clinging to the tiny rubber bands inside her mouth.

Doris's enthusiastic face metastasized into rubber before my eyes. "D-a-a-a-n-n-y." Her words burdensome and tangled in half chewed mu shu pork. "T-u-r-n o-n t-h-e m-o-v-i-e."

The remote suddenly left my hand, as Doris stepped in front of me and pointed it at the DVD player. She popped in the disc and went back to the dinner table.

As I sat in front of the opening credits, all I could see was the crime scene image that had already left the screen. I thought I was going to pass out. Sounds around me echoed heavily in my head: Doris reciting Tom Cruise's lines along with him, and Bridget's wisecracks about the dated film.

I had let Inga down. Hadn't taken her situation seriously enough, and now she was another victim. It was all I could do not to jump up from the table and race back into the City. Dowd would have no choice but to listen to me, now that I finally had something concrete.

171

But what did I really have? Inga had provided some details I hadn't known, but now she was dead and couldn't testify. Who was to say that I hadn't made it all up?

"Here it comes," said Doris, her voice moony as she shushed me and Bridge. Then, "*... She had me at hello.*"

It was all I could do to contort my face into a grin without throwing up all over the meal that sat untouched on my plate.

Bridget took three cookies from the take-out bag and passed them around the table. I was still deep in thought when she pulled out my fortune and read it aloud. "*Luck sometimes visits a fool, but it never sits down with him.*" She shrugged. "What the heck does that mean?"

Doing my best to appear engaged and interested during the rest of the night, it felt as if I was keeping the biggest secret known to man. Instead of sleeping comfortably in my own bed, as I had been longing to do, I lay there all night staring at the ceiling, thinking.

Why would somebody want to kill Inga?

The next morning was the first Saturday in a while that felt like I lived in a normal household. Bridge slept late and then stayed in her room texting friends. Doris was enjoying her coffee as I scoured the newspaper. The story of Inga's murder took up a third of the front page, and I couldn't stop reading it, over and over and over.

The article didn't contain any new information, but between the lines I could tell that the department was keeping more tight-lipped than usual. This, I attributed to Inga's having worked at the consulate. Any scandal, particularly a murder, would be a political hemorrhoid for both the city and the Latvian government.

"You still seem distracted," said Doris. "I'd have thought it would feel pretty nice for a change, not having to work today."

I set the paper down, and just looked at her. Doris gazed back at me, taking stock of my expression. Then she set her mug on the table. As she continued to study me, all expression drained from her face until there was only an emotional sink hole.

"I was going to tell you," I said. "I wanted to explain--"

"Dad?" said Bridge, emerging from her room—cell phone in hand. "Ashley says you're on the news."

As I scrambled to find the right remote and turn on the TV, I glanced over at Doris—still slumped in her seat at the table. My hope was that whatever was on the news had something to do with my investigation. If Mendoza and Taylor had managed to find and arrest Elvis Lugailo, I might be mentioned as the original investigator. In which case, my screw-up with Dowd might also be vindicated.

On went the television, and I hurried through the local channels to find it. The story flashed on as a breaking news update. First thing I saw was my departmental photograph—the one taken for my ID card when I was first hired. Dressed in a Class-A jacket, tie and uniform cap, my young smiling face seemed to fill the TV screen.

"Officer Daniel Patrick McKenna, a thirteen-year veteran of the San Francisco Police Department, has been identified as a person-of-interest in the murder of Inga Berzina, found yesterday in her Steiner Street apartment."

I couldn't move and I couldn't look away. Somewhere behind me I heard Bridget gasp. But the news bulletin wasn't over yet.

"Sources within the department have confirmed that Officer McKenna, currently suspended from duty, may have spent the night with the Berzina woman on Thursday evening. She was found dead Friday morning by Leo Krumins of the Latvian Consulate."

I turned around to see Doris, pale as a sheet, her hands steadying herself against the table. Bridget had already turned away. Then, plugging in her earbuds, she walked into her room without a word and slammed the door.

"Doris," I pleaded. "Just let me explain..."

But she stood up as if she couldn't hear or see me, then turned and headed down the hall to our room. I was about to turn off the TV when I saw that my on-screen photo had now shrunk to the corner of the frame. The reporter was now interviewing a resident of the building. I watched only long enough to see that son-of-a-bitch dog walker.

"Me and Tucker actually rode in the elevator with the killer," he said. *"I knew he was up to no good that night, and then I saw him get into his Jeep and take off the next morning, all squirrely, like he just done something."*

I shut it off, unable to listen to my own eulogy any longer. The only thing left for them to do was drop my carcass into the ground and cover it with dirt.

I'd been framed for Inga's murder, which, even though I hadn't committed, I felt responsible for.

Then, through my guilt, bewilderment, and self-pity, it occurred to me that the cops I'd been working with in the homicide detail were either on their way to Mill Valley at that very moment, or had already staked out my house and were waiting for me to step outside so they could arrest me. So, as much as I wanted to sit down with my family and tell them my side of the story, I couldn't. I had to get moving.

Peeking out from behind the drapes, the neighborhood appeared normal. I cautiously stepped onto the porch and eased my way out onto the lawn. Other than a neighbor woman out for a walk, there was no one else in sight. The front door swung open behind me and out came my suitcase and knee brace. Doris called me a few choice names before slamming the door.

Suffice it to say that I was also wrongly accused by her, this time of being an unfaithful husband. With that, I'd been evicted from my own home.

My car keys were still inside the house, so I took Doris's 2004 Honda Civic and drove aimlessly around the North Bay trying to figure out what to do. Only two days ago, my biggest worry was solving the Berzins case. Then yesterday, I thought that keeping my job was my most pressing issue. Now I was a wanted man, on the run for a murder I didn't commit.

I remember thinking at that moment that things couldn't possibly get any worse for me.

49

On The Run

I sat on a bench, looking out at the yacht harbor and imagining myself sailing away on one of the boats. It didn't really matter which one. Anything that could float me out of the mess I'd gotten myself into.

The dream of owning a little skiff dated back to my childhood, when my dad used to take the family sailing. He was an ex-Navy guy— a Vietnam vet. We never had the money to buy a boat of our own, but he somehow managed to scraped together enough to rent one each summer. Seduced by the sun, a spinnaker full of wind and a cooler full of beer, my father seemed at his happiest on the water. I suppose that is why I recall those rare days through the fragile lens of affection. Day-to-day life was less carefree. We all had our struggles; Dad with his depression, my mom with Dad's depression, and us kids with Dad's depression.

Luckily, my size and athleticism earned me an early graduation from high school and a football scholarship at Berkeley. Not that my dad gave a damn, because by then he couldn't see past his own self-pity.

I'd occasionally go home to visit, only to endure his endless griping about the university's liberal agenda, the pot-smoking hippies, or that Charles Manson's disciples were from Berkeley. He even called me *Patty Hearst* when the mood hit him. After my mom died, I never went back to see my dad.

Returning from my trip down memory lane and my improbable fantasy of boat ownership, I plugged back into the here and now. It occurred to me that the SFPD would not have released my name—the identity of their prime suspect—to the press. Especially before inspectors had even tried to arrest me.

So, how did the networks get my name?

I checked Cassidy's phone and saw that the volume was down and I'd missed several calls from Linh Phú.

"Hi Mom," Linh answered when I called back. "I'm walking out to the hallway so I can hear you better." The background noise sounded like the detail's bullpen. After a minute she said in a lowered voice, "I had to pretend to be talking to someone else, Inspector. Are you all right?"

"I've definitely had better days." A short lull followed. "I hope you know I didn't do it, Linh. I swear I didn't--"

"Yes, I know." Phú continued to speak quietly, her mouth close to the phone. "Otherwise, I wouldn't have tipped off the media. When you didn't answer my phone calls, getting your name on the news was the only way to give you a heads-up. Captain Dowd and the rest of the detail were already crossing the bridge with a search warrant. In fact, they're detaining your wife and daughter at your house as we speak."

My eyes rolled back in my head. By now Doris's loathing will have degraded into apathy. She won't care if I live or die.

"Thank you for alerting me, Linh."

"What are you going to do now?" she asked. "Where will you stay?"

"I don't know... Maybe I should just put an end to it."

She was speechless, and right away I wished I hadn't given voice to my rambling thoughts. Not that suicide was a bad idea though.

She said, "I hope you don't mean--"

I let out an annulling chuff. "No, no, I was just making a joke."

"I understand," said Phú, although I don't think she really did. "I'd like to help, but nobody in the detail is telling me anything. I guess I'm still something of an outsider here. But I definitely sense an undercurrent of tension throughout the office."

"Yeah, they're closing ranks," I said. "It's because they don't like having to go after one of their own."

"I'm not so sure that it's only that," said Linh. "I think something else is about to come down. You know how you get that feeling?"

Linh was perceptive, but I wondered what subtleties she could pick up on after only a few days in the detail.

I said, "Let's hope that if something is happening, it turns out to be a good thing. I could use a point in my favor right about now."

"It may have something to do with Chief Fahey's death," she said. "Even though we haven't gotten the lab results yet, many of the inspectors now seem convinced that he was killed."

I wondered if they had found his killer by now, though I didn't have a really good feeling about it.

Linh said, "Regardless of what they're keeping from me, Inspector, I am still committed to helping you."

She was taking a huge risk. It was too much to ask of someone in her position—a trainee whose status was tenuous by nature. Adding to that Phú's gender and ethnicity, the road to becoming an insider was already long enough.

I told Linh not to put herself or her career in jeopardy, at least not any more than she already had. I thanked her and let her know that she could phone me anytime. We ended the call with everything still up in the air. I was no better off than before.

By now the inspectors would know that I was driving Doris's car, and they'd be searching for it. They would be monitoring all of my credit cards in real-time, and staking out my house in case I showed up.

I had $37 in my wallet, and found just under four bucks in change inside Doris's glove box. It wasn't even enough to rent a crappy room for the night.

There was literally nowhere for me to hide.

50

Parking lot C
250 Bon Air Road, Greenbrae

I awoke not knowing where I was, head pounding and hoping that everything I thought was real had just been a bad dream. It was becoming a pattern—both the hangover and the remorse.

Looking around, I realized that I'd spent the night in Doris's car. Crumpled into the backseat, my legs hung awkwardly over the reclined front seats. The booze bottle spurred the memory of the night before when I stopped at a liquor store, and then parked in one of Marin General Hospital's parking lots. I vaguely remembered my reasoning: Hospitals are 24/7 operations with public restrooms, and I doubted that anyone would think to look for me or Doris's car there.

But drinking my meals and living out of a Honda Civic wasn't a viable long range plan. Something was going to give out—either my money, or my luck, or my liver. I was quickly becoming a younger version of Lou Cassidy.

Worse, the notion of *ending it all* was still a background chorus inside my head. I'd once read that suicide happens when a person feels a complete and utter lack of hope, and I was rapidly approaching that point as well. The logical me knew it was a chickenshit way out of my problems. Even so, I decided to leave the idea on the table for now.

Groping the pocket on the car door panel, I desperately searched for anything else that I could either use or sell. I flipped open the center console, rifled through a bunch of Subway napkins and charger cords but couldn't find any items of value. At the bottom was a tiny container of pepper spray that I'd bought for Doris as protection. Barely the size of a pack of gum, I slipped the *Mugger Monkey* into my pocket.

Lou's cell phone showed that I'd slept through another text from Linh Phú. It said: call as soon as u can.

"Inspector." She's answered quickly, without a greeting.

"What's up, Linh?"

"Bad news, I'm afraid." She hesitated. "I overheard a conversation in the office. It seems they're looking at you, uh, that is, you are a suspect in the murder of Chief Fahey."

I sat there stunned for a few seconds. "Oh for God's sake, Phú. Why in the hell would I want to kill the chief?"

She didn't answer. "This changes things a little bit, Inspector."

"So," I said. "You think that I did it and now you're taking back your offer to help?"

"I'm not saying that," Phú's tone was sober and guarded. "You must know that they'll be coming after you with everything they've got. In their minds, this isn't just a *good-cop-gone-bad* situation. The inspectors no longer see you as one of them. To them, you killed their police chief, and that means you are the enemy of every badge-wearing-cop in the Bay Area. They don't want you behind bars, they want you dead."

I knew Linh was right. In one miserable day, my situation had gone from desperate to hopeless. *'A complete and utter lack of hope'*, I think the term was.

"But there are people who know I didn't do it, right? People who can help me prove..." I had to catch my breath. "There's this woman, Linh. An agent who works for Customs and Border Protection at the Port of Oakland. Her name is Sarah Brooks, but since Dowd took my phone I don't have her number." I heard the desperation in my own voice. "Will you try to find her for me? Give her this phone number?"

"Brooks, you said?"

"Yes, and there's this other guy named Tam, I think. Yeah, Curtis Tam. He also knows what's going on. You can find him at the Hyatt Regency on the Embarcadero. He'll vouch for me."

Suddenly a security guard in a powder blue uniform appeared, holding a leather bound ticket book as he walked along checking the row of parked cars. Pausing in front of my space, he eyed me, Doris's car, and then the car's license plate.

"I gotta go, Linh. I'll call you back." Abruptly disconnecting, I fumbled blindly on the floorboard for the car keys. A rap on the window came a second later.

I'd found the keys but was still clam-shelled into the tiny back seat. Motioning with an index finger for him to give me a second, I slowly unfurled my stiff and aching body out the back door. Now we stood face-to-face. The guy was a couple of inches shorter than me, slightly overweight, and wore reflective aviator sunglasses.

Trying not to breathe on him, I smiled politely while smoothing my rumpled hair. He took a half step back, probably smelling the stale booze on me, then glanced into the car where my bottle lay half empty on the seat.

"ID and vehicle registration," he said flatly.

"Look, officer." I'd decided to try the nice guy approach, even though he was the equivalent of a mall cop. "I've been up in the ICU all night with my grandpa." Then, rubbing my eyes as if I were trying to stifle tears, I said, "Poor guy had a tumor the size of my fist removed from his rectum."

The guard winced.

"Anyway, I really need to get back in there." I motioned toward the building. "He's going to need my help getting to the toilet."

The security guard gave me a half nod, so I quickly walked off toward the building. Glancing back, I saw that he was calling in the license plate over his radio. Doris's car had almost certainly been linked to me by now, and had probably been entered into DOJ and NCIC as a wanted vehicle. I'd sort of screwed myself by leaving it parked there, because now I was stuck on foot.

I acted like I was going into the main hospital, then cut through the emergency room lobby and out a side door. Skirting around the north side of the building, I made my way across lawns, through hedges, and into an area of medical offices and clinics.

As I came over a low rise, I saw two police cruisers racing up Bon Air Road—both with red and blue lights flashing. They screeched onto the hospital grounds, heading in the direction of Doris's car.

Ducking back into a grove of eucalyptus trees, I waited until they were well out of sight before continuing.

A Marin Transit bus was pulling out of a bus stop, heading away from the hospital on Bon Air. I had to hustled to intercept it, and wrenched my knee a little bit as I was coming down the hill. Limping into the street, I waved it over.

The rapid thumping of rotor blades sounded in the sky as I quickly stepped into the bus, trying not to look like a killer on the run. Taking a seat, I glanced out the window in time to see a blue and white California Highway Patrol helicopter. It hovered momentarily, then circled the area, obviously searching for a suspect—me—within the perimeter of the hospital. Another police car raced by, and then a couple of Marin Sheriff's cruisers. At that point I realized that leaving the car had saved me from getting caught.

The bus took me to San Rafael, where I transferred to a San Francisco bound Golden Gate Transit bus. For whatever reason, the City was the only place I could think to go.

On the way, I recalled a section in my investigative study guide about common inclinations of a criminal: *The guilty suspect often returns to the scene of the crime.* And although I was innocent, driving back into San Francisco made me feel as if I weren't.

The back of the bus provided a sense of anonymity and gave me time to think. I needed to decide whether to end my life, escape to a remote village in South America, or grow a set of huevos and figure out how to exonerate myself.

We were downtown before I knew it. I peeked out the window, and then up to the sky overhead. No cops on the ground or in the air. At least there was that.

51

United Nations Plaza
San Francisco

It was a nice day in the City, sunshine with just a slight breeze. The UN Plaza and area around Civic Center felt like an ant farm, and luckily for me the ants were too busy to notice one more. But I knew that it would only take one person to recognize my mug, and I'd be done.

Curious to read any updates on Inga Berzina's murder, I made my way to a newsstand on Market and bought the Sunday Chronicle. My operating funds had now dropped to $37.85, and I realized I needed a game plan sooner rather than later. Step one was to get off the streets and out of the public eye.

I set off southbound across Market, and after only a couple of minutes I stumbled into the perfect place where I could blend in without having to answer questions—a homeless encampment. It was around the back side of the Social Security Administration building at the end of a small alley where new construction provided shade, shelter, and several large dumpsters for the half-dozen folks residing there. I joined the small group—five men and a woman—sitting together on strips of flattened cardboard laid out beneath a tattered blue tarpaulin.

Lou's phone rang, and Linh Phú's number stared back at me. Worst case, she was now helping Dowd to set me up. I envisioned the rest of the detail hovering nearby, monitoring her call, recording my every word, and triangulating the cell towers to learn my location. Best case, Phú was really trying to help me.

I had to trust someone.

Unfolding my newspaper as I hit the answer button, I held the phone to my ear. At the same time, I glanced at the paper and was suddenly unable to speak. The only sound to escape my tremoring lips was an excruciating exhale—part groan and part profanity.

"Inspector McKenna?" She asked quietly. "Are you...?"

I stared down at the front page photo of myself. Above it, in huge bold letters, was the headline: DISGRACED COP SUSPECTED IN CHIEF'S KILLING. The subheading was even worse. FUNERAL FOR CHIEF FAHEY MARRED—SUSPECT ONE OF SFPD'S FINEST.

"What in the hell? Linh! Did you see this?"

"I'm not sure what you're..."

"The paper, Linh, the damn Sunday newspaper. They're not just 'looking' at me in Fahey's killing, they've named me, publicly! Can you believe this?" I kept scanning through the article. "They've already got me tried and convicted. "Shit. I'm as good as on death row."

The article characterized me as a *serial killer*, which I suppose made some sense since in their estimation I already had the Inga Berzina murder under my belt.

"They say a neighbor across the street from the chief identified me." I flipped to the third page where the article continued. "It says the guy recognized me after seeing my picture on the news—the story, the incorrect story, about Inga's killing." I read more. "Oh, great, and get this... He reported seeing me '*sneaking*' past the security light on the side of Chief Fahey's house. *Sneaking!* That's inflammatory wording. I'm gonna sue those sons-of-bitches!"

Linh was silent on the other end of the line.

"Figures," I continued my rant. "Dudley Do-Gooder calls in after supposedly recognizing my picture on the news, and that was all Dowd needed for his little vendetta against me."

Phú waited a few beats to make sure I was done. Then she quickly got to the point. "I'm afraid I've been unable to contact your friend, Agent Sarah Brooks. I spoke to her supervisor..." Papers rustled in her hand. "A Mr. Timothy Sanchez. He says that Agent Brooks is off work and unavailable. Wouldn't give me her phone number or home address. The man was nice enough, but adamant. Reading between the lines, it sounds like there's a disciplinary issue going on with her. Anyway, I struck out. Sorry."

"What about Tam?"

Linh sighed. "Again, I apologize. I went to the hotel and spoke to the manager, personally. They went through all of their files, but could find no record of a Curtis Tam staying there in the past few weeks."

I sat against the folded cardboard, numbly rubbing my temples. The private detective was pretty cagy about his business, and it was possible he had registered under an assumed name. Or maybe Tam wasn't his real name to begin with. Either case, I was totally hosed.

"You gonna use that?"

I glanced up into a rotted mouthful of gums. One of the transients was stooped over me, motioning toward my newspaper. "Gonna keep it or can I have it?"

I thought about it for a second. My image was right on the front page, along with the whole disgusting fabrication about me being a serial murderer.

"Doesn't matter anymore," I said, handing him the paper. "You can have it."

Linh was still silent on the other end of the phone. "I feel that I'm obligated to ask you, Inspector. Would you be willing to turn yourself in? I can promise you safety, and a guarantee that you will be treated with fairness and respect."

Phú's conscientiousness might have made me smile under different circumstances. I could hardly blame her for asking me, especially after reading the article. She had stuck her neck out far enough, and was probably trying to balance her loyalty to me with doing the job she was sworn to do. And in her own way, she was trying to keep me alive, too.

I thought about it a minute before responding. "You're obviously questioning whether you should even be talking to me, let alone helping me."

"Unfortunately, Inspector McKenna, there seems to be a sizable amount of evidence being brought against you."

"Such as?"

"Besides a positive identification by the former chief's neighbor," she said, "there were also hair follicles left at the scene—on a pet door hinge, I believe. And a piece of chewed gum on the lawn. Both were collected, and preliminary testing of them seems to match your DNA."

"Humph." Trying to conceal the feeling of utter defeat, I asked, "Is that it? That's all they got?"

"Well, that and the fact that you ran. All due respect, Inspector, it doesn't bode well for you that you've gone into hiding."

I had to admit that the circumstances didn't look good. Worse, the physical evidence mounting against me was catastrophic. Holding the phone to my ear, I wandered to the other side of the street where a sliver of sunlight fell across the sidewalk. I studied my disheveled reflection in a window. I not only looked like a loser, I was a loser. Seeing no way to dig myself out of this hole, I knew it was only a matter of time until they tracked me down or someone recognized me and turned me in. Either way, I was a heartbeat away from prison or the gas chamber.

It suddenly dawned on me that I'd been hoping for my luck to change, for someone to figure out that I was not a killer. That they had the wrong guy. But that wasn't going to happen. The deck was stacked against me at work and at home. Nobody was going to do this for me, and the only way to change my luck was to do it myself.

"Inspector? Are you still there?"

"Yeah, Linh. I'm here." My eyes locked onto my reflection and I felt the anger boiling up inside me. "First of all, I swear that I didn't do any of this. Secondly, I'm not *running* and I'm not *hiding*, but I'm not turning myself in, either."

"Then what are you going to do?" asked Phú.

"I'm going to pull my head out of my ass and start doing what I do best. I need to put a case together that proves my innocence. And there's no way I can do any of it if I'm rotting in a jail cell. But I'll need a little time. A couple of days is all.

"Two days?" she said. "You won't be able to--"

"Leave that to me, Linh." I took in a breath and let it out slowly. "Here's the deal, you give me forty-eight hours to sort this out. If I can't put the pieces together by then, I'll give you my location so you can send in the troops. Fair enough?"

"Yes, Inspector." She hesitated again. "And to answer your earlier question; no, I wasn't taking back my offer to help. I only wanted you to consider another option. It was for your own safety and wellbeing."

"Appreciate it, I do." As much as I wanted to leave Phú out of the whole mess, the fact was that I really needed her. "If you're serious about helping, Linh, you would be saving my life."

"Whatever you need, sir."

"There's one more person you need to call for me—a prostitute by the name of Sha Nay Nay Moore."

Phú was quiet for a second, probably wondering if I was looking to kick up a little dust before heading off to prison. "She's my informant, Linh."

"Of course, Inspector. I was just writing down the name."

"And there's a white Ford van in the police impound yard. It was seized during the warrant service at 168 Russ Street, but the paperwork was kept out of the file. Neither Dowd nor Mendoza and Taylor know anything about it. I need some tech and lab work done on the vehicle, strictly off the radar. Full fingerprinting of the van's interior, and a thorough check for gunshot residue around the inside of the sliding side door."

"Got it. Anything else?"

"I've been thinking... This investigation keeps pointing back to people at the foreign consulate. There has to be a connection we're not seeing. You need to find out if--"

"Uh," she interrupted. "Per Captain Dowd, the consulate is off limits. No investigation, no interviews, no contact, whatsoever. 'Too political', he says. Between your *vehicle intervention* with the Latvian Consul in the car, and the murder of Ms. Berzina..."

"Wait a minute," I said. "The guy in the car with Dowd that day was the Consul?"

"Leo Krumins," she said. "He's the top diplomat in the consulate."

"Hmm." I rubbed my stubbly chin. "And he's the same guy who found Inga dead in her apartment. That's kind of interesting, don't you think?"

"Off limits," she said. "Dowd's been quite clear about that."

"Since you can't, I'll have to work on that angle on my own."

"But the entire SFPD is looking for you. How can you even--?"

"No worries, I'll figure it out." We were about to disconnect. "Oh, one last thing, Linh. As long as I'm technically still on the payroll, can you have Mrs. Ocampo forward my paychecks to my home address?"

"I will," she said. "But it'll have to be when she gets back. Apparently, Mrs. Ocampo's son passed away and she's been out on family leave."

"Hmm." I rubbed my chin again.

Phú suddenly grew quiet, and I could hear people talking in the background. When she spoke again it was in a whisper. "Tomorrow is Chief Fahey's funeral. As you might imagine, everybody will be out of the office attending the services. If you'd like me to stay back and check Inspector Mendoza's case file..."

I told Phú not to put herself or her career at risk any more than she already had. I thanked her and asked that she call me right away if anything changed with regard to the case against me.

The call ended, and I stood warming myself against the building. It felt good, and it reminded me that my fate was not a forgone conclusion—I wasn't in San Quentin just yet. Mindlessly, I thumbed the phone's screen, wondering how I'd be able to move about the city undetected while trying to investigate the case against me.

My eyes, I realized, had stopped on a list of calls Lou had placed from his cell. One number looked familiar to me, but I couldn't pull it out of my gray matter. It was a single call, placed on October 3rd, two days before I was told of my promotion.

And then I flipped to the phone's address book and saw the name programmed next to it: Chief Fahey—Home.

52

179 Sussex Street
San Francisco

I had impatiently decided to make my journey to Glen Park during the day. Standing at the far end of the platform with my eyes cast downward, I'd waited quietly for the J-Church train. Cameras were everywhere, and I hoped that someone wasn't sitting in a control booth somewhere, identifying me through some facial recognition software and recording my every movement.

At Mission and Bosworth, I got off and hurried the few blocks over to Sussex. My knee was still acting up, and by the time I got there I was walking like a stroke victim.

The house was as I remembered, having stopped by only once before when Lou forgot his wallet. A boxy two-story place, mustard yellow with white trim. I could see the form of a woman moving about inside, and imagined Mrs. Cassidy scurrying up and down the stairs, bringing Lou everything from chicken soup to his bookie's phone number.

Hoping she wouldn't freak out when she saw me, I tapped lightly on the door then held my breath. The woman opened it, and just sort of stood there looking me up and down. By now, she, too, must have seen the news. But rather than an expression of shock or fear, Mrs. Cassidy's was one of pity. Like I was a damaged package not even worth refusing.

"Lou's in the bedroom upstairs," she said, stepping back to let me pass. She glanced out to the street before closing the door—perhaps making certain the neighbors weren't watching, or maybe checking to see if I'd been followed.

"Holy mother of the Christ child," Lou yowled as I walked into his bedroom. "When was the last time you slept? Your eyes look like piss holes in the snow."

"And this is me on a good day." I tried to smile.

He was propped up with pillows, a portable TV playing a Sunday night football game at the foot of his bed. He motioned for me to sit on an armchair, which I suspected had doubled as Mrs. Cassidy's bed since Lou's heart attack.

We spent a few minutes talking, mostly about the case and Dowd, and it was obvious to me that Lou was doing his best to ignore the elephant. But it was there, of course. And we both knew it.

I hadn't seen his wife since she let me in the door, and I had a flash of worry that she had already dropped a dime to dispatch. And that my remaining moments of freedom could be clocked with an egg timer.

I finally asked, "Don't you want to know if I did it?"

He laughed, said that I'd already be out of the country if I had. "You wouldn't be here, paying me a social visit."

"A social visit," I repeated. "To be totally honest, it *is* and it *isn't*."

He lifted an eyebrow.

"I need to come right out and ask; why did you phone Chief Fahey's home number?"

Lou's face rumpled. "What are you talking about, kid? The chief is dead. Why in the fuck would I call his house?"

"No," I said. "A month ago. On the third of October."

He closed one eye and squinted at the ceiling with the other, then shook his head. "Shit, McKenna, I can't even remember what I ate for breakfast this morning. But heart attack or not, I'm pretty damn sure I'd remember calling Fahey."

I sighed.

"What the hell are you trying to say, anyway?" Lou pulled himself upright. "You trying to lay Chief Fahey's murder on me? I ought to kick your ass all the way back to--"

"That is quite enough!" yelled the missus from the doorway. "I think you had better leave now."

I took out the phone to show Lou, but his face was red and he had turned away from me. I held it out to his wife, but she just frowned. It hadn't been one of my better interviews, in fact, it was just one more in a series of disasters.

Someone had called the chief from Lou's phone, and the timing was right that it was the call tipping Fahey off to the crooked cop in the detail.

I got downstairs and reached the front door, still studying Lou's phone screen. Suddenly, I stopped and wheeled around toward Mrs. Cassidy who had followed me down. "It was you, wasn't it?"

Her eyes widened.

"You made the call to Fahey."

188

She took a couple of steps backward, stumbled a little, and then steadied herself against the bannister. She didn't admit it, but she sure as hell didn't deny it. Then, after a minute or so of silence, her eyes began to mist over and I knew I had her.

"Yes, it was me who called Chief Fahey," she said quietly, as if she didn't want Lou to hear her confession. "It was tearing Lou apart. I had to do something..."

53

5159 Mission Street

The temperature had dropped considerably by the time I left Lou's house in Glen Park. My knee was still throbbing and I was beginning to think about turning back. But back to where? I still had no place to go and nobody to turn to. In my haste to return to San Francisco, I hadn't considered where I would sleep, or eat, or use the bathroom. Nor the fact that all of the city's 2,600 cops wanted to use me for target practice.

In hindsight, SF was probably the worst place for me to go.

Suddenly, the flashing lights of a fire truck perforated the gray dusk ahead. An ambulance raced by on Alemany, followed by two SFPD patrol cars and a motor cop. I'd worked the Ingleside District for two years, and I still knew a lot of the street cops. Worse, of course, was that they also knew me.

The emergency vehicles were clustered in a knot around the Alemany and Geneva intersection where there appeared to have been a car accident. So, I quickly backed up a block and cut over on Seneca to Mission Street. But more police cars had shown up, and they were fanning out onto the side streets using their side alley lights to search for someone. Knowing the routines, I figured that a suspect had fled from the crash into the surrounding neighborhood.

It was bad timing for me. I wondered if tomorrow's paper would name me as the prime suspect in a hit-and-run.

The military surplus store stood beneath a row of apartments, next door to Lucita's Bar. As I huddled in the doorway waiting for the police activity to die down, I couldn't help but wish I had ducked into Lucita's instead.

"Closing in ten minutes," said the shaved headed guy behind the counter. "Help you find something?"

"I could probably do with a cheap hat and jacket."

The guy fixed me up with a drab sweatshirt and a black knit watch cap. The purchase would help keep me warm, and as an added bonus, would add to my unshaven face as something of a disguise. But it left me with only sixteen cents.

With my head down, I gimped the rest of the way up to the Daly City border. Colder and windier after the sun went down, the entire area was now shrouded in fog. So much so that I had to walk right up to the street signs in order to see where in the hell I was.

Half of the houses on Flournoy are in San Francisco, and the other half are in Daly City. Her house was a faux brick job on the north side of the street, one house outside of the city limits.

I'd always assumed the woman was a spinster. Something about the way she carried herself—as if she'd spent a lifetime alone, just her and her cats, her microwave dinners, her crossword puzzles, and her evening glass of sherry. Probably why I was so shocked when Mrs. Cassidy mentioned her name—the woman Lou had been trying to protect.

A lamp in an upstairs bedroom came on when I rang the bell, and within a minute I found myself illuminated by the porch light.

Marisol Ocampo was the homicide detail's beloved secretary. And even though I hadn't known her as well as the other investigators had, I recognized that the cheerful face she usually wore had recently been transformed to ashen dolor. The kind of look that only children can bring.

Mrs. Ocampo opened the door, almost as if she'd been expecting me. Saying nothing, she turned on an end table lamp and then asked if I'd like some coffee—just as she had many mornings in the detail's bullpen.

I declined the coffee and sat down across from her. The house was warm and smelled of cooking grease and smoke from a wood-burning fireplace. "I'm so sorry for your loss," I said. And although I didn't know this for certain, I had a hunch that the son she'd lost was the suspect whose face had been blown off in front of Sarah Brooks at the CBP inspection facility in Alameda.

"Thank you." Mrs. Ocampo took up a framed photo of a hulking brown man, covered in tattoos and wearing a white tank-top. "Little Ruben was such a good son."

With as sad a face as I could fake, I nodded, certain that the thieving asshole would have stolen the fillings right out of my teeth.

"You didn't kill that woman," she said. "Or Chief Fahey, either." It was more of a statement than a question.

191

"No," I said. "I didn't. But if I could find out who did, I might be able to live the rest of my life outside rather than inside of a prison cell."

"How did you know?" she asked.

"My partner, well, ex-partner, Lou Cassidy," I said. "One of his snitches is an ex-con who did a stretch in Soledad with your son. Little Ruben."

She glanced at the photo with motherly embarrassment.

"Evidently," I continued. "Your son bragged quite a bit. Told this informant, and a lot of other inmates, that his mother worked in the SFPD's Homicide Unit. He made it known that you would be able to get him out of any jam."

"I would never do that," she said. "Yes, I have helped my son with bail money and always gave him a place to stay. I may have even turned a blind eye to his sinful lifestyle. But I've never used my job with the city or my positon in Homicide to help him in that way." Mrs. Ocampo shook her head ruefully. "Little Ruben had a difficult life. I raised him alone after his father died, and he always seemed to find himself in trouble."

"I can appreciate that." I took out my notebook and had to borrow a pen. "Your son," I said. "Do you happen to know what kind of *sinful* things he was into?"

She nodded. "Some stuff they took from ships. Liquor, I'm pretty sure. He was constantly on the internet checking for wholesale prices of vodka. And his friends, the thugs he did the stealing with, they were no good. I told him to stay away from those two."

"Did you know the friends?" I asked.

"I never saw them, but I overheard the names. Elvis was one of them, and Gustavo."

"Gustavs?" I asked. "Could that be it?"

"Might be Gustavs, I'm not sure. But I know someone shot him— this Gustavo. You know this, Inspector, because it was your investigation. I learned this information from Ruben after it happened, and when I returned to work I saw that Captain Dowd had given you the case to investigate. I didn't know you very well, but I could tell that you are a good worker and were determined to find out who did it."

"I wish I could say I was successful, but I still don't know who shot Gustavs. Did Ruben know who did it?"

"The big boss," she said, as if she thought I already knew. "He also killed the young woman. Elvis's girlfriend, Rhonda Pitts."

"Why?" I asked. "Why would their boss come after them?"

She hung her head, lamenting. "The money," she answered. "They were supposed to drive the trucks and sell the liquor to bars and stores. But they kept the profits for themselves. It was probably Elvis's idea, and Little Ruben only went along."

Without my reading glasses, I had to hold the notebook a few inches from my face as I wrote. "And you know this from Ruben?"

She nodded. "And I think that poor girl, Rhonda, was truly a victim too. A message for Elvis and the others to give back the money, or else. I saw that Inspectors Moretti and Lam are investigating her murder."

"Uh huh." I couldn't help wondering about Mrs. Ocampo's claim that she would never use her position to help her delinquent son. She certainly paid enough attention to who was investigating Little Ruben and his friends. And come to think of it, she was in a perfect position to hear all that was happening, the investigative updates, and the weekly debriefs in the bullpen.

"May I ask you a question, Inspector McKenna?" She'd poured a cup of coffee for me, then sat back down. "If Lou Cassidy thought that I was covering for my son, why didn't he just report me?"

I shrugged. "I'm sure he thought about it, but he probably couldn't bring himself to ruin your good reputation—especially if he was wrong about you obstructing an investigation that involved your son. His wife said he struggled with what to do.

"Do you think that worry is what caused Inspector Cassidy's heart attack?"

I'd actually thought of that, though in truth Lou was already a hot mess. He drank like an Irish priest, couldn't focus on his work, and, according to his wife, was having trouble sleeping.

"No," I said. "I'm sure that had nothing to do with it."

But it was enough of a factor for Lou's wife to call the police chief anonymously and tip him off to a traitor in the ranks.

It all finally made sense to me, and I could see the progression of events; how Mrs. Cassidy had provided just enough specifics to worry Chief Fahey, without causing any blowback on her husband. And why Fahey brought an outsider like me into the unit to figure it out.

It was a little after midnight when I stepped out of the Ocampo house and into the misty terrain known as Top of the Hill, Daly City. It was too late to walk all the way back downtown, and for the life of me I couldn't think of any all-night diners in the area. Besides, a guy like me loitering around at that time of night was a sure bet for getting stopped.

"You are going to catch him, right?" came Mrs. Ocampo's voice from the top of the steps. "The person who did this to poor Ruben?"

A dozen tiny details swept through my brain—all of the reasons that would prevent me from catching the person responsible. But rather than explaining that her son had been killed in another city, in another county, and that I was a fugitive wanted for two murders, I simply answered, "Yes."

"If you need a place..." Mrs. Ocampo stepped back, holding the door with one arm. "You may stay the night, here."

54

111 Flournoy Street
Daly City

What I had hoped would be my first restful sleep in a while turned out to be one of the most fitful. I hadn't slept in a twin bed since I was eight years old, and Ruben Ocampo's felt like it still had its original mattress and box springs. Not to mention my finicky hang-ups when it comes to someone else's pillow, pillow case, sheets, and weird odors. The only upside was that the bed of a dead, ex-con son of the detail's secretary wasn't a place where the cops were likely to be looking for me.

Mrs. Ocampo had left a towel and a washcloth in the bathroom across the hall. I showered, forcing myself to use the bar of soap that was already in there. More nastiness. Aside from the image of where it had previously scrubbed, the soap was *Lava* brand—a sandpaper-like cleansing bar, which I'm pretty sure is used for scouring grease off the hands of auto mechanics.

I came out fully exfoliated, finding an entire outfit laid out on the bed. Little Ruben's khaki pants and button up plaid shirt. The dead guy's clothes would normally be the line I could not cross, but my own tee shirt was getting so ripe that it was a tossup. I left Ruben's pants—which were too short anyway—then slipped on my knee brace, my own pants, and Ruben's plaid shirt.

Mrs. Ocampo looked at me approvingly as I came down the stairs. "Ruben would have wanted you to wear them."

That, I heartily doubted.

Thanking my host for her kind generosity, I gathered my meager possessions and left with only a cup of coffee in my tank. Again, as I stepped into the light of day, I had to wonder if I was any closer to salvation than I was last night. The only thing I knew for certain was that I was that much closer to my surrender deadline.

Taking stock of the few new facts I'd learned, I began my long trek back downtown. I had successfully identified the suspected mole in the homicide detail, though it wasn't the cunning double agent that I or Chief Fahey had imagined. But I supposed that I'd at least held up my end of the agreement and done the old chief proud. Additionally, I had linked the crimes that nobody else in the detail thought were connected.

My mind's eye envisioned the players' faces on an analytical chart as I trudged toward downtown. The string that ran between Elvis Lugailo and Gustavs Berzins now extended to Ruben Ocampo. Off to one side ran another string connecting all of them to the liquor container thefts. And from there, another thread led to the Russ Street warehouse.

Also linked to the warehouse and the cargo thieves, was Rhonda Pitts—the shooting victim who naïvely trusted her boyfriend, Elvis Lugailo. Then, off to the other side of the chart was Inga Berzina, and even further over, the federal agent, Sarah Brooks. Four people on the chart had been killed and one had been shot at—nearly killed. The whole thing was overwhelming. What I wouldn't have given for a dry erase board right then.

My head hurt as I tried to keep the image clear in my atrophied mind. I imagined drawing a circle on the upper left side of my link chart, and within it, the Latvian flag symbolizing the consulate. From there, I pinned one end of string to Inga Berzina, and another to Elvis—the erstwhile security guard.

At the very top of the chart was a big question mark. It was the person from which all of the other strings emanated.

I looked away, up into the overcast sky and then tried to step back into my mind. Suddenly realizing that I had veered from Mission Street, I found that I had wandered onto Bernal Cut Path—a raised walkway overlooking San Jose Avenue. It was a quiet little spot where I hoped to focus my thoughts.

Again, I pictured the question mark at the top of my chart. Squeezing my eyes closed, I tried to visualize the connections. I saw the strings leading down to the victims, the cargo thefts. In my head I drew another circle with a dollar symbol in its center. After all, that's what had to be at the root of it all. The final sting led from the unknown person at the top, down to the money.

I kneaded my palms harshly against my closed eyes. I was missing something. There was a piece I wasn't seeing. These damn stings went everywhere. I couldn't keep track in my head. And on top of that, I couldn't concentrate with all this noise. Maybe if I could quiet these kids...

My eyes opened to a couple of swashbuckling six or seven-year-old boys, playing in the bushes along the footpath. Wearing red and black capes, I guessed that their outfits were vestiges of Halloween costumes from a few weeks back. Stretching the kinks from my neck, I paused to watch them. As they swiped and jabbed with plastic swords, I saw that one wore a bandana and the other wore a black eye mask.

I was reminded of my victim, Gustavs Berzins, and the mask he wore when he was killed. It was an odd detail that I had originally chalked up to... I don't know what, maybe that he was coming from a masquerade party? But why in the hell would anyone wear a mask during a dangerous meeting in the middle of the night?

Lou's cell phone rang, jarring me from my thoughts like a stubbed toe. "Yes," I answered.

"Where the hell you been, McKenna?" It was Sha Nay Nay Moore. "Besides waste'n that lady and the police chief, that is."

I started to say something, but she talked over me. "And why'd you change your phone without tell'n me? I been calling you, like, a million times."

"Yeah, I've been a little busy."

"Uh-huh." She coughed out a laugh. "Bad enough, you crash'n your boss into a pole. Now you all over the TV."

"Look, Sha Nay Nay, I'm kind of in the middle of something right now."

She didn't say anything.

"Are you still there?" I asked.

"Yep. Just waiting to hear what you in the middle of. I mean, either you be trying to catch the dude who set you up, or you goin' downtown to turn yourself in."

Now, I was quiet.

"And one more thing, McKenna. I already told you, I be goin' by the name Shanay, now."

"Okay, yeah, sorry...Shanay. By the way, they took my phone, and I had to get another one. So, I wasn't trying to *bump you off*."

"Hmm." There was a clicking sound, like she was picking her teeth. "You wanna know why I been calling you, or what?"

"Okay, why?"

"Your boy, Elvis, be trying to get with me," she said. "Dude keep text'n."

"Why didn't you say so? Where is he?"

"I don't know—somewhere close, I think. He's scared, though. Be acting all paranoid and freaky."

"Like how?"

"Like how?" She thought a minute. "Like, he thinks someone trying to follow him and stuff. Say'n he can't talk on the phone 'cause it's tapped. Stuff like that."

"So, where does Elvis want to meet you? Hotel Beverly?"

"Most likely. He ain't got a car now, so it's gotta be close by."

"Can you call him?"

"Nah," she said. "Blocked number. He's the one who calls me."

I sat down on the curb and stared into the street, thinking.

"You still there, McKenna?"

"Yeah," I answered. "I'm still here. And I have an idea..."

55

Angelo's Alley
San Francisco

It had been a slow and agonizing three miles along Mission, the downhill slope jarring my knee the entire way.

By mid-afternoon, I was back to the encampment on Angelo's Alley where I'd spent part of the previous afternoon. Most of the campers were still reclined on their cardboard strips, though the workweek had increased construction activity on the tiny street.

Unlike the day before, however, I now had a focus and a plan of action. For the first time in a while, I felt hopeful.

I foraged through some dumpsters and came up with a two-by-two piece of relatively clean cardboard. "Does anyone have a pen or pencil I can borrow?" I asked the group of transients.

They exchanged looks of indifference, and then the guy I'd given my newspaper to nodded. Reaching into a trash bag bulging with aluminum cans and various other treasures, my new buddy came out with a brown, felt tipped marker.

Figuring out what clever thing to write turned out to be something of a challenge. I wanted to keep it short enough for a passerby to read at a glance, yet it needed to be different than the thousands of other signs. Believing that honesty is the best policy, I carefully penned my message: KEEP ME OUT OF JAIL.

Panhandling competition around the Civic Center and Powell Street BART stations was fierce, and there were cops on foot patrol everywhere I looked. But it was getting close to the evening commute, and I wanted to capitalize on the office crowd.

Across from the Powell Street cable car turnaround, the Westfield San Francisco Centre took up the entire city block. I noticed that the security people were only monitoring the main entrance on Market Street, so I meandered around the corner to 5th. There were only two others there, an old woman and a war veteran in a wheelchair.

It was a slow process, and most people who walked past didn't even look down. The few who did offer a handout, paid little attention to my sign. It could have said, *I am the police inspector accused of a double murder*, and it wouldn't have garnered me any more or less cash.

By the end of the businesses day, I'd earned enough for the materials needed for my plan, plus a little extra for something to eat. Aside from that, there wasn't much more I could do except try to survive until morning.

I bought some cheap burgers with the extra money, and returned to the encampment. Sharing them with my fellow residents felt good, though I was still an untrusted outsider to them. Maybe they thought I was a social worker, or an undercover cop. Or perhaps they had recognized me from the newspaper photo.

Awhile later, some social outreach people came by in a van. They seemed to know most of the homeless, called a couple by name, and stood around in the glare of their headlights talking with us. They asked me a few questions about my medical history, access to health care, and if I had any social security benefits. I made up a few middle-of-the-road answers, ambiguous enough that they soon lost interest in helping me. In the end, they offered free hypodermic syringes, and condoms in a variety of sizes and colors—none of which I wanted or needed. They were also handing out, at no charge, small personal hygiene kits that included soap, a tooth brush and tooth paste. Those, I did accept.

"Wait a minute," I called out suddenly, just as they were getting back into their van. "I think I can use one of those condoms after all."

"Just one?" the guy asked, holding the little square packet out through the window.

"Yep, just one."

The free gifts notwithstanding, I realized I couldn't spend the rest of the night on the street—too many hazards, and too much potential to be rousted by cops.

It occurred to me that I knew of a relatively safe place to stay, and it wasn't too far away. If I thought I was off the grid at the Ocampo house, this place was even more so. The last place on earth the SFPD would come looking for me.

After a cautious half-mile walk, I arrived at the warehouse on Russ Street.

56

77 6th Street
San Francisco

Who would have thought I'd be able to find a fishing store smack in the middle of downtown? But sure enough, I used Lou's phone to Google it and there it was.

The place was small, but as I peered through the barred windows I saw that it held everything a fisherman could need. And though I wasn't technically going fishing, my methods would be comparable. It would involve luring a prey with bait, setting the hook when he bites, and then, if it all worked as planned, landing the whopper.

I'd spent the night inside the gray cinderblock warehouse at 168 Russ Street, cold and dank as it was. The place felt as barren as the last time I'd seen it—no cars out front, no lights on, and nobody around. And even though it was still vacant, every noise propelled me upright—heart pounding, listening for intruders.

I had considered sleeping in the meeting room upstairs, which was a bit warmer, but there was no other exit up there. I'd have been a sitting duck if someone had come in during the night. So I climbed to the top of a stack of pallets at the far end of the loading bay, and spread a bundle of plastic sheeting over the uneven wooden slats. It kept me hidden from sight and offered an elevated view over the entire first floor of the warehouse. The downside was another cold and uncomfortable night's sleep. Astonishingly, I found myself wishing I was back in Ruben's bed.

By nine o'clock on Tuesday morning, I was on the sidewalk in front of the bait and tackle shop when they opened.

"What can I help you with?" the gruff-voiced owner asked.

"Well..." I scratched my head, looking at hundreds of spools along one entire wall. "I need some strong string."

"Line," he said through pressed lips. "Over here," he motioned toward a case at the far end. "Seventy-pound test will handle anything you'll catch in waters around here."

"And a small hook."

A groove formed across the bridge of his nose. "My lure and flasher combos are down here--"

"No, I just need one of these." I tossed a single cellophane baggie onto the counter.

He held it up and squinted into it. "This tiny hook? With seventy-pound test line? That's like using a sledge hammer for a thumbtack."

"And these, too." I handed him a roll of gray duct tape and a small clip-on bell."

The man stared at the bell in his hand, then back at the heavy line.

I'm no fisherman, but even I know that the little bells are used to alert someone that a fish is on the hook—usually something small, like a lake trout.

The guy just shook his head as he rang up my purchase, then shrugged. "Thirteen eighty-five, altogether."

He put my items in a bag, took my cash, and handed me a couple of bucks in change. It was just enough for a cup of strong coffee, which I was going to need.

I then walked three blocks south on 6th to the Hotel Beverly. Maybe it was my cleanliness and hygiene issues acting up, but I swear the place smelled like semen.

Behind the glass partition sat a robust man of about sixty. His thinning gray hair was raked sideways across his white scalp and his mustache, which was in need of a trim, curled over his upper lip into his mouth.

"How long?" he said, without looking up.

"How long, what?"

He looked up. "How long you want the room for? An hour, two hours, the night, what? No more than two people per room. And no animals, either."

I flipped open my wallet, waving it in front of him as if flashing my credentials. I slapped it closed before he noticed that it only held my driver's license. "SFPD, Vice Squad." I shoved the wallet back into my pocket. "We're investigating reports of illegal activity at this establishment."

The guy's eyes glanced toward the stairway leading up to the rooms. "Like what?"

"Like prostitution, underage minors, drugs, human trafficking. Need I go on?"

I saw the guy's mouth moving—silently repeating my accusations. "Anyway," I continued. "We've got undercover cops watching this place, and unless you want your hotel raided and closed down for good..."

He held up a hand. "I get it. But why are you guys picking on the Beverly? There's plenty of other--"

"We're cracking down on all the pube mills around here," I said. "So pass the word to your partners in the other dumps. I turned to leave—and using the tail of my shirt to protect my hand from the door's push bar, I called over my shoulder, "Just consider this a friendly warning, pal."

On the way back to Russ Street, I phoned Sha Nay... Shanay... Nay, whatever. She told me that she hadn't heard from Elvis yet, but was certain he would call soon. I hoped that my threats to the Beverly manager worked, and that Elvis would be desperate for a place to take Sha Nay Nay.

I was impatient and knew that time was running out for me. I'd told Phú that I would turn myself in if I couldn't figure this thing out within a couple of days. Forty-eight hours, to be exact. That was on Sunday afternoon, which meant that my time was almost up.

Entering the warehouse was always unnerving. There was no way to know if someone had gone in while I was gone. And I had to assume that whoever would be there would also be connected to the cargo theft ring, and would probably be armed.

Stepping into the dark loading bay, I felt around for the light switch. Grimacing, I realized again that it was across the room at the bottom of the stairway.

In the cramped meeting room upstairs, where I had met with Brooks and Tam, I took a metal chair and carried it back downstairs.

It wasn't quite noon, and I knew that Shanay could be calling anytime. I had to work fast, so I quickly set about putting the specifics of my idea in place.

From my pants pocket, I took out the condom I'd been given by the outreach people, and the compact pepper spray I'd taken from Doris's car. Adding them to my bag of fishing tackle, I laid all the instrumentalities of my little plan side-by-side on the warehouse floor.

First, I tore off the wrapper and unrolled the condom—a ribbed purple thing that reminded me of the Barney character. To look down at a purple cartoon seemed counter intuitive to me, and sort of a mood kill. But that wasn't what I needed it for.

I held the prophylactic upside down and shook the pepper spray to get it mixed well. Then, using my hand to cinch the rubber tightly around the head of the atomizer, I discharged all of the pepper spray into the condom. The little Mugger Monkey carried more of the stuff than I expected, filling it until it began to expand. Once the sprayer was empty, I used a piece of the fishing line to knot the top of what now looked like a small eggplant. Using another length of line, I stood on the chair to secure the whole apparatus onto a beam above the light switch.

The fishing hook I had purchased was pretty small, and I hoped that it was sturdy enough to pierce the rubber when the time came. Attaching the hook to a third length of line, I climbed back onto the chair and very carefully taped the hook firmly against the condom— right into the crease where it was tied at the top.

The next item to put in place was the little silver bell, which I gently clipped to the same piece of fishing line that held the hook.

Then I ran the filament line all the way along the back wall to a concealed spot behind the stack of pallets. From there, I could pull on the line without being seen.

I stood in my hiding spot, looking back at the capsicum pepper filled condom dangling at the end of a nearly invisible string—a colorful little piñata filled with a sweet prize.

My phone rang, and I suddenly panicked. I wasn't ready; there was still more that I needed to put in place.

"Sha Nay Nay?"

"No," said the voice. "It's Shanay."

"Did he call?"

"Uh huh. And he wanna get busy w'me, like, right now."

"Where?" I probably sounded scared, or nervous, or out of breath. And I was all of these. The timing of one thing depended on the timing of everything else. The entire plan had to meld precisely. It all had to work, or none of it would work.

"He ain't gonna meet at the Beverly," she said. "The boy got word that Vice Squad is watching the place."

I silently pumped my fist. *Yes!*

"I told you he's paranoid, McKenna."

"So, where is he meeting you?"

"Since he ain't got a car, he said something about taking me to the place where he works."

I looked toward the heavens in thanks. "I think I know where that is," I said. "I'll already be inside waiting when you guys get there."

"But McKenna, how you gonna--"

"Don't worry about me," I told her. "This guy is dangerous, and you are going to have a baby soon. So, listen to me. As soon as Elvis gets inside the place, I want you to turn around and leave. It will be dark, so if you do it quietly, he won't know until it's too late."

"You want me to just leave?" she said. "You know he got him a thumper."

"Thumper?"

"A gun, McKenna. You sure you don't want me to call it in, get you some backup or something?"

"No, but thank you. I don't want you anywhere around, just in case things don't go well."

"Hold on," she said. "Elvis is texting me. The boy's close by, says he on his way right now. You sure you're ready for this, McKenna?"

I thought about everything that had happened to me in the past couple of weeks; of how hard I had tried, and of all the people I had failed. I thought of Chief Fahey who had believed in my character. And of how my reputation had since disintegrated into nothing right before my eyes. And then I pictured my wife, Doris, and my daughter, Bridget, and tried to imagine all of the embarrassment they had endured because of me.

Maybe I hadn't been the best father, or husband, or investigator, but I still cared and I still had my integrity. At that point, dying wouldn't have been the worst thing to contend with. But having lost everything in my life that was important to me was. And I'd be damned if I was going to let Dowd or anyone else get away with taking all that from me without a fight.

"Yes, Shanay. I'm ready to do this."

57

168 Russ Street

I didn't know exactly how much time I'd have until they arrived, but I suspected it wasn't a lot.

Hustling around the warehouse, I tore a dozen or so two-foot strips of duct tape and then hung them on the side of the raised loading dock. I slid the metal chair over next to them, leaving a clear path from the door to the light switch at the foot of the stairway.

Taking up the spool of heavy duty fishing line, I was poised to set the last piece of my trap—a trip line. Using a new length of line, I secured one end to a water pipe near the stairs and ran it tightly across to the roll-up door. I did the same thing, on the other side of the stairway—both lines pulled tightly at a height about a foot off the ground. They ran parallel, like a slice of pie, outlining a clear path from the front door to the light switch at the base of the stairs. And hanging above the switch, of course, was the crown jewel of my contraption.

As I stepped back to admire my handiwork, I recognized right away the flaw in my strategy. The interior of the warehouse had been pitch black at night, but now, the midday light trickled down the staircase from a second floor skylight. The effect was a whisper of luminance across the warehouse floor—enough for the eye to discern the contrasting shape of my piñata trap.

I raced back up the stairs and stood on top of the table, duct taping my newspaper over the skylight. Then, moving faster than I should have, I darted back down the steps and across the warehouse floor. The trip line that I had set for Elvis caught me mid-shin, launching me headlong into the stack of pallets. I swore loudly, using a string of expletives that made no sense, whatsoever.

The top of my head stung from a small cut right in the middle of my hair's thinnest spot. And my knee, which was near useless to begin with, had now ballooned and was throbbing.

My plan had already begun to fall apart. Without my duty weapon, I had intended to use speed, aggression, and the element of surprise to overwhelm Lugailo. Limping badly, with most of my weight on my good leg, I had now lost the advantage of speed.

I stood hunched into a dark corner between the shipping pallets and the loading dock. Balancing on one leg, I reached down for the loose end of the fishing line—the other end still tied to the hook taped to the pepper-filled condom.

Three minutes passed, then five, then ten.

By putting heat on the Hotel Beverly, I had hoped to leave Elvis no other option than to bring Shanay to the warehouse. But what if I was wrong, and by "work" he meant an empty room he had access to at the consulate? Or, maybe he simply decided to go elsewhere. Everything would fall apart at the seams. The efforts I'd made to clear my name would have been a complete waste of time, and I might as well just turn myself over to Phú.

Seconds ticked by.

I looked at my phone and saw that it had been thirty-five minutes since Shanay's last call. After an hour, I realized they weren't coming. Maybe Elvis had found a different hotel—somewhere out of the area. Or perhaps he just got cold feet.

It was time. This simply wasn't going to happen.

Forty-eight hours had passed since I'd made my deal with Linh Phú, and I'd given her my word. A promise was a promise.

I dialed her number.

"Hello, you've reached Officer Linh Phú, acting inspector in the SFPD homicide detail. I'm unavailable at the moment, but please leave your name and a contact number at the tone."

"Linh? It's me, McKenna." I paused, not having had the foresight to think of a message to leave. "Uh, hey, so I guess I thought I'd be able to figure it all out by now. Actually, I pieced some of it together, but obviously not enough. What I've got is mostly secondhand anyway. No real physical evidence or anything... Anyway, Linh, I suppose I'm avoiding the inevitable. When you get this message, you can come get me. I'm at the warehouse at 168 Russ Street. I'll leave the door--"

Like a sudden crack of thunder, the roll-up door vibrated violently and was thrown open. Sinking back, deeper into the dark crevasse next to the pallet stack, I thumbed the phone keys, disconnecting the call to Linh.

Unfortunately, my message to her had already been left.

58

168 Russ Street

It was like staring into the sun. The rollers reversed course almost immediately and the door slammed closed again. I tried to focus my eyes, but they'd been left with ghostly green shapes.

Someone had entered, but I couldn't tell who or how many. The warehouse seemed even darker than it had been before, and I was not only blind, but momentarily stumped. I had expected Elvis to come in through the front door, which was where I'd placed the trip line. Going back over the conversation with Curtis Tam, I now recalled that he had seen Elvis and Gustavs entering through the roll-up. Another stupid oversight on my part.

Listening to echoing footfalls, I tried to sense his whereabouts in relation to mine.

I guessed that it would take no more than four seconds for him to reach the light switch, but I hadn't thought to count, and by the time I realized he was probably there, the fluorescent lamps overhead flickered on.

Yanking hard, I felt the line go taught and heard the tiny fishing bell jingle.

I peeked out from behind the pallets. He was there, standing right where he was supposed to—hand outstretched onto the switch.

Startled by the bell, he jerked his head back and looked up at the dangling condom. The hook had done its job, because at that very moment a wave of burning fluid cascaded straight into his puzzled face. The same face, which I recognized from my photo, as Elvis Lugailo.

His hands sprung upwards, first protecting himself from the shower's impact, and then, almost immediately, grasping and clawing at his searing eyes. He let loose a snot-filled wail that reminded me of an injured animal—low and guttural at first. Then came the full throated high notes of a soprano, and finally, rapid heaving breaths—wet and raspy.

Spinning in a tight pirouette, Elvis's hands worked feverishly to clear the mucous from his eyes and nose. But it was to no avail. His head bucked back and forth as the arc of his spastic dance grew in wider and wider circles. It was like a wildlife documentary.

Another couple of inches, I thought, as I watched the man's feet stumbling toward the trip line. Then, he was there. His foot raised slightly—the tip of his brown oxfords snagged in midstep—and then the twang of a guitar string's sour note as his body pitched awkwardly.

He hit the concrete floor face first, in a collision that sounded like a dropped melon. Beneath him, a momentary metallic glint as his hands fumbled to dislodge a pistol tucked into his belt.

I'd already left my hiding place, stepped three or four feet toward him, and just as he began to lift his head off of the floor, I went airborne.

Driving my shoulder into the middle of his back, I felt that I'd definitely stuck my landing. The sound that followed was something I hadn't heard since my football days at Cal. *Elvis's lungs have left the building!*

Unfortunately, it felt like my knee's meniscus had also left the building.

His handgun skittered across the floor, and it was a race to see who'd come up with it first; Elvis, out of breath and with the sense smacked out of him, or me, one-legged Long John Silver. All I needed was a parrot on my shoulder.

We scrambled and clawed across the concrete, crawling over one another like two boys in a Labor Day picnic sack race.

I grasped the gun only inches ahead of Elvis.

"Enough!" I yelled.

We were laying astride each other, exhausted and breathing hard. It was only a short reach to put the barrel against the center of his forehead.

"Now, get up slowly," I said, "and sit your ass on the chair."

His pudgy face, redder and puffier after his pepper shower, glowered at me in defiance. "You have no idea to whom you are fucking with, my friend."

The man's words were coated with an Eastern Bloc accent, but his message was clear enough. He was hard and unafraid. Still, Elvis lifted himself slowly off of the floor, one knee and one hand at a time, and plopped onto the metal chair.

I immediately secured him in place using the strips of tape that I'd pre-cut. First his wrists to the armrests, and then his ankles to the chair legs—his oozing eye slits glaring the entire time.

Once he was tethered tightly into his seat, I glanced around the room. Shanay had made it out safely after slamming the roll-up door and locking Elvis inside.

The gun I had snatched was a revolver, a Ruger 38 Special. Small, but it would have done a job on me had Elvis gotten to it first. I set it on the loading dock, behind him and out of his view, then covered it with a rag.

My knee was still killing me, but I was riding high on a good dose of testosterone. "Now..." I turned back to my opponent. "Let's knock off all the bullshit."

I caught his smirk as I limped around the chair to face him. "Piss off," he said. "I tell you nothing." Then he hawked a syrupy mess from his throat and spat it in my direction. It landed on the floor, but close enough to provoke me.

Lunging at Elvis, I caught his jaw like a clamp between my thumb and middle finger—the web of my hand directly over his larynx. The force slammed his head backward, driving the chair hard against the concrete loading dock. "Now, let's try again," I said. "Or if you still want to play games--"

He cut me off. "Then you will do what, call police? Go ahead and call, and we both go to jail together." Elvis laughed. "Yes, Mister Inspector McKenna, I see you on news. You do some bad things. Maybe we are cellmates with each other, yes?"

His eyes kept darting toward the door, then back to me.

"Expecting someone?" I said with a splash of knowing arrogance.

"Yes, actually, I do expect someone."

I shook my head. "Not coming. She left after shutting you in here."

Elvis gave me a cocky huff. "I don't give rat's ass about the bitch, McKenna. The man who is coming here, he will have gun. And he don't give rat's ass about you or me."

"Don't bullshit me, Lugailo. I already know about the stolen cargo, and how you skimmed the proceeds. Who did you piss off?"

He glanced at the door again. "You will find out soon."

If he was trying to bait me into looking outside so he could make his move, it wasn't working. I was going to get him to talk one way or another.

Both Inga and Mrs. Ocampo had been adamant that Elvis hadn't killed Rhonda Pitts or Gustavs Berzins, so I decided play it another way. "You did a hell of a number on Rhonda," I said. "Poor girl never even had a chance."

"No!" Elvis screamed, his face looking as if he'd gotten another dose of pepper spray. "Listen to me you fucking mother, it was not me who kill her!"

"Who are you trying to kid?" I said. "I know you smoked Gustavs, too. And he was your friend." Then I gave a demeaning laugh.

His eyes became even smaller, darker slits and I saw his meaty hands retract into red balls beneath the layers of duct tape. I'd struck another nerve.

For a minute it looked as if he was going to dive into me, chair and all. But a second later his fists unclenched and he took a long breath. "This man... He is the person who does these things you accuse of me." His expression was forlorn. "And he also kill little Inga."

One of the missing pieces suddenly fell into place. I'm not sure how I'd missed it. "The mask," I said. "That's why Gustavs wore the mask into the park that night. The man who did all of this is from the consulate."

Elvis scoffed, as if anyone with half a brain would have seen it.

I nodded to myself. "The son-of-a-bitch worked there with Inga, and Gustavs didn't want the guy to see his face. Gustavs was hiding the fact that he was *Little Inga's* brother." I thought for a moment. "So, was Inga involved? Never mind, it doesn't really matter now."

He stayed quiet.

I took Lou's phone out of my pocket. Nothing from Linh yet. Then I scrolled through the icons, searching for the recording app that Lou had bragged about. If I could figure out how to operate it, I'd be able to record Lugailo's confession. Still fiddling with the damn phone, I paused when Elvis spoke again.

"Your police chief," he said. "You did that?"

"No, of course not." I held the phone to my mouth to make sure it recorded my denial. "*No, I did not kill the chief.*"

If Elvis was asking me if I did it, then obviously he hadn't done it either. "What about your guy at the consulate?" I said. "Did he kill the chief?"

Elvis shook his head.

I stepped closer, holding the phone up. "What about your guy at the consulate?" I nodded toward the speaker. "Please give a verbal response."

Elvis looked annoyed. "No."

"Was he the guy driving the black car with diplomatic license plates? The guy who shot Gustavs at the park?"

After a hesitation, Elvis nodded.

"Answer verbally."

"Yes, okay? Yes, it was him."

"I hope this damn thing works." Squinting at the display, I tried listening to what I'd recorded: STOP, <<, PLAY >.

211

Clap! – clap! – clap!

The slow applause echoed mockingly around the room. I turned quickly, looked around, and there he was—the big question mark on my chart—standing behind me near the front door, his hands raised in ovation.

"Bravo! Bravo!"

59

Homicide Detail
Captain's Office

"...and you have the right to a union rep," said Dowd.

Linh Phú declined.

"Funny thing," the captain continued. "McKenna's phone shows a bunch of calls received from your number, going all the way back to Saturday morning. Three missed calls and then a three minute, forty-nine second call that he made to you."

Before Phú could respond, he added, "Next day, a text from your phone to his, telling him to call you right away. That was followed by a four-minute conversation. Another call from you to him late Sunday, this one for over six minutes. Want to explain those, Phú?"

Linh smiled timidly. "I'm sorry, Captain, but I can't explain that. I was under the impression that Inspector McKenna had been relieved of his city issued phone."

"He was," said Dowd. "The calls were placed on Lou Cassidy's phone."

Phú frowned and shook her head. "I've never even used Inspector Cassidy's phone, sir."

"Not you, damn it. McKenna! McKenna's using Cassidy's phone. Lou's wife gave it to him after Lou's heart attack. She expected McKenna to turn it in for her, but instead he kept it while he was on the lam. We just figured out this little phone deception, and now we've got a printout of the numbers called and received. It's only a matter of time until we track his location."

"I see," said Phú.

Dowd's bearing stiffened as he cleared his throat. "So, what I'm telling you, Phú, is if you know something, anything at all..."

She shook her head.

Frank Moretti leaned into the office. "Excuse me, Captain. Phone company just advised of another call made from Lou's cell."

"Probably to that whore again, Shay Shay." Dowd stood up. "Did we get a warrant out for her yet?"

Moretti nodded. "But this call wasn't to her."

"Who then?"

Moretti glanced nervously at Linh Phú, and back again to Dowd. "It appears the call was made to Inspector Phú."

"When? How long ago?"

"Just now, like within a couple of minutes."

Dowd's eyebrows bunched up over his black eyes as he stepped around the desk—his bullying frame towering over Phú. He thrust his hand toward her. "Your phone, now. And your passcode."

The three of them—Dowd, Moretti, and Phú—huddled around the phone to hear the message. Dowd rolled his eyes when McKenna mentioned his lack of physical evidence, then he leaned closer as the recording came to an end:

> ... Anyway, Linh, I suppose I'm avoiding the inevitable. When you get this message, you can come get me. I'm at the warehouse at 168 Russ Street. I'll leave the door...

The captain straightened abruptly, still staring at the phone. Turning to Moretti, he said, "Call Tactical Company, Special Ops and SWAT! Get them rolling to Russ Street. And let them know that if that bastard so much as blinks, they have a green light!"

Then he snapped around to Phú. "And you are confined to your desk." Dowd started to push past her, then stopped at the door. "And so help me God, Phú, if you even think about calling to warn McKenna, it'll be the last thing you ever do in law enforcement."

60

168 Russ Street

I'd never formally met Leo Krumins, though I'd once run him and my captain off the road. And I'd also seen him on TV the morning he reported discovering Inga's body in her apartment.

"I should thank you for doing all this work for me," Krumins said, quietly pulling the warehouse door closed behind him. He motioned toward Elvis who was bound up like a Christmas goose. "Perhaps you could also kill him for me, and then I would have nothing left to do."

I'd started to inch my way to where I'd stashed Elvis's gun, but Krumins pulled a pistol from his coat pocket and leveled it at me. "Over there, slowly." He flicked the barrel in the direction of Elvis.

The weapon was a beefy, black semi-auto. I couldn't identify the manufacturer, but it definitely looked Eastern European—police or military grade. It also appeared to be a 9mm, which most likely used 115 grain ammo—same weight as the bullet recovered from Gustavs Berzins's body.

Krumins held the pistol on me while he checked me for weapons, his eyes daring me to make a move. But the guy had already killed Inga Berzina, her brother Gustavs, and probably had a hand in the others. So I complied with his directions, even though I was mentally kicking myself for not having figured it out sooner. Of course it was Krumins in the black Lincoln with diplomatic plates, he was the top attaché at the consulate and the only one with diplomatic status.

While eyeing me and Elvis, he felt around the loading dock with his free hand—probably looking for a weapon he assumed I had.

Krumins slid his hand under the rag and grinned as he grabbed hold of the gun I'd hidden beneath it. At that moment, the idiot, Elvis, decided to make his move. Still strapped to the chair, he plunged himself forward, ramming his pudgy head into Krumins.

The force drove the diplomat hard against the dock, causing him to stumble sideways toward the stairs. Off balance but now holding a gun in each hand, he quickly recovered.

For once, Lady Luck was in my corner. The trap that I had set for Elvis ended up snaring an even bigger fish.

The fishing line I'd strung out had become tangled around Krumins's ankles, sending him airborne in a spastic tumble. The cartwheel ended with him sprawled on the floor. Meanwhile, Elvis kept driving toward him, chair and all.

The first gunshot came from the ground as Krumins struggled to raise one of the weapons. The round ricocheted off the concrete loading dock, yet Elvis continued bucking and kicking like a bull. He was almost on top of Krumins when the second shot exploded, catching Elvis just below the Adam's apple. The bullet exited in an eruption of bright red blood, discharging from the center of his back like aerosol paint.

That definitely took the fight out of Elvis. He slumped backward, dead, landing upright on his chair like a school boy waiting listlessly for his homework assignment.

I still hadn't moved from where I stood.

Krumins took a few seconds to get off the ground, then he tucked both handguns into his pockets and dusted off his pinstriped suit. "What is all this?" he asked, as casual as a dinner table conversation. "These strings." He waved a hand toward the web I had woven.

"Uh, it's something I put together to trap Elvis." Though my answer sounded lame, the plan had actually worked pretty well.

Krumins nodded. "Did you have any idea what you were getting into when you started this?" He asked. "Inga's brother, Gustavs. That was your investigation, correct?"

"Yes, it was my investigation; and no, I had no idea."

He nodded again, then glanced around the warehouse. "I didn't want to kill Elvis. Not that I give two shits that he's dead, but I had planned to extract some answers out of him first."

"Is that why you killed his girlfriend, Rhonda Pitts?"

Krumins smiled. His manner was much more refined than Elvis's. Almost trustworthy. "Yes. That is why I killed Rhonda Pitts. I had to show those two shameless thieves that I was serious."

"So you killed an innocent woman."

He shrugged. "*Innocent* is a nebulous term. It was her choice to become involved with such a hoodlum, was it not? So, how *innocent* could she have really been?"

"After you killed her, you took her keys and ransacked her apartment—looking for the money they owed you, I assume."

"Very good, Inspector." His grin seemed sincere. "It's a good thing for me you weren't the lead investigator on that case."

I hoped Lou's recorder had picked up that last comment, though I sensed that the dialogue between us would likely be for posterity. Krumins couldn't very well admit all of this to me and then let me live.

I glanced at Elvis's lifeless body, and knew that my fate would be the same as his if Phú didn't get her little ass in gear.

"But then you were put in charge of the park killing," he said. "Inga's big brother, Gustavs."

"Yes." I thought back, picturing the scene. "And you went there that night to meet Elvis and Gustavs. For what? Some kind of *Let's all play nicely together in the sandbox,* meeting?"

"Something like that," he said. "By then, those two buffoons were running scared. They had done the shooting in Oakland, but then after the Pitts girl turned up dead, Elvis and Gustavs had a change of heart. Wanted to pay me the money they owed me, or at least they said they did."

"What happened?"

"I had gone there early," he said. "Scoped it out ahead of our meeting."

"Yeah, I've got your embassy car on film—parked on Oak Street."

"Consulate," Krumins laughed. "Not embassy. They are not the same. Anyway, I saw that fuck Elvis had brought a gun. This gun." He patted his pocket. "Yet I got the drop on them both. But instead of taking it like a man, Elvis ran. Gustavs stepped in front of the bullet that was meant for Elvis. Apparently, neither of them were too bright. And Gustavs didn't have to wear the stupid mask either, because I'd already figured out that Elvis's accomplice was Inga's big brother."

My eyes glanced at the door, wondering if anyone was coming or if this would be my swan song. The only upside to dying here was that Lou's recorder now had enough of the conversation to clear my name.

"I hope the money was worth all of this," I said. "How much could you have really made from a bunch of stolen vodka?"

"You think you've got it all figured out, don't you? Stolen vodka." Krumins shook his head "That was one tiny acorn from a giant oak. You still have no fucking idea."

I didn't like the sound of that. Was he implying that the theft ring was bigger than just the people I had identified? Did it reach higher levels of government than even him? Or maybe he was referring to the money. Perhaps the liquor was more valuable on the black market than I'd thought.

Even though I was seconds away from meeting my maker, my mind still tried to put the pieces together.

"Let's not drag this out any longer," Krumins finally said. "You and I both know how this is going to end. Your comrades will find you here, with your fingerprints all over the murder weapon. And with your, shall we say, dubious history..." He raised his pistol, aiming it at my head.

"Hold on just a sec." My arms went up in front of me in a pleading posture. "Can you just satisfy a condemned man's curiosity?"

"Make it quick."

Suddenly, I couldn't think of any good questions. And worse, I had to take a piss something awful. "Oh yeah, here's one... What about the chief of police? Why was he killed?"

Krumins wrinkled his brow. "It wasn't us. Why? Didn't you do it?"

I shook my head, then remembered my recorder. "Of course not," I said, a little too loudly.

He glanced around, nervously. Raised the gun again.

"Uh, and what about Ruben Ocampo?"

"What about him?"

"Why did you shoot him?

Krumins tilted his head. "Ocampo? The Mexican?"

"Yeah," I said. "He got his head shot off in Alameda."

He shrugged. "Again, not us."

Now, I was frowning. "But a minute ago you mentioned a shooting in Oakland."

"The Customs agent at the port," he said, using the last of his patience. "She was getting in the way. But Elvis and the other two idiots tried to take her out on their own. Screwed it all up."

"The third guy in the van was Ocampo, not you?"

Krumins smiled. "If I'd have been there, the agent would be dead. Anyway, by then Elvis and Gustavs knew I was after them. So they dumped the van at the warehouse and went into hiding."

I tried to come up with another question, anything to stall. But no sooner did I open my mouth when a tremendous boom thundered through the place. I thought Krumins had shot me, and I dropped to the floor.

The room was full of smoke, and my ears rang so loudly that I could only make out the muffled sounds of men yelling. It was total chaos for several seconds, and then as quickly as it had started, it was over. The smoke started to dissipate, though my ears were still ringing.

"Loading dock—clear!"

"Second floor—clear!"

"SITREP for Command?"

"To Command—one down, two in custody."

218

At that moment I felt the plastic zip ties cinch around my wrists. I let out a yowl when they lifted me to my feet and my knee was forced to bear my full weight.

The cops wore face coverings and goggles, but once it was all clear Dowd strolled into the warehouse in a suit—his swagger trumped only by his brash grin. He was about to speak, but I beat him to it.

"Before you say something else you'll regret, Captain, I'd like you to listen to this." I tilted my head toward the cell phone.

He scrunched up his milky face, as if my voice was fingernails on a chalkboard. Just beyond him stood Leo Krumins, whose face held nearly the same expression.

"Right there on the loading dock," I said. "It's my phone, well, Lou's phone, and I've been using it to record these guys. Just listen to what's on there, and it will explain everything."

The room went quiet. Dowd stepped over to the dock and picked up the cell phone. He hit the rewind and then pressed *Play*.

First thing I heard was my voice, asking Elvis about the chief's murder. There was a muffled response, which I couldn't make out, and I couldn't remember who spoke next. Then, the dialogue was clear again.

"What about your guy at the consulate?"

[pause]

"Please give a verbal response."

"No."

"Was he the guy driving the black car with diplomatic license plates? The guy who shot Gustavs at the park?"

[pause]

"Answer verbally."

"Yes, okay? Yes, it was him."

"I hope this damn thing works..."

"You can fast forward through this part," I said with a self-assured nod.

But there was only silence after that. Everyone in the room was looking back and forth at each other, kind of like scratching their heads. Except for Dowd, who was chuckling.

"What the hell is this supposed to be, McKenna? There's nothing more on here."

I suddenly realized that I had stopped the recorder after the first few seconds, to make sure it had worked correctly. Had I mistakenly pressed PLAY instead of RECORD after that?

Son-of-a-bitch!

61

SFPD Homicide Detail

Linh Phú had never received an *ass-chewing* in her life. But she left Dowd's office, understanding for the first time what it meant.

The provisional inspector had realized that the secretive phone calls between her and McKenna could now cost her the permanent position, if not her job. As much as Linh wanted to warn McKenna that Dowd and company were on their way to the warehouse, she couldn't risk contacting him again—no matter the reason.

Sitting at Lou Cassidy's desk, Phú watched the other inspectors return from the tactical operation at the Russ Street warehouse. Doffing their ballistic vests and raid jackets, she listened as they talked among themselves, more openly now, about McKenna. Phú gathered that the arrest of her partner had gone down without him being shot or killed, and for that she was thankful. But it seemed that the inspectors were now even more convinced of McKenna's guilt.

Leo Krumins—the Latvian Consul—had provided Dowd with a written statement, claiming that McKenna, not he, had shot and killed Elvis Lugailo in the warehouse. This was relayed to Phú by Moretti and Lam.

Using an array of disparaging terms, Moretti haughtily described the fact that McKenna's "pregnant girlfriend" was found hiding inside the warehouse during the raid.

"We didn't have enough to hold her," said Moretti. "Refused to give a statement. Had to let her go."

Lam shook his head in disgust. "Protecting McKenna all the way to the electric chair."

"Who knows how long he's been doink'n her and passing along confidential information?" said Moretti.

"Probably since the asshole stole the warehouse keys out of my case file," said Lam.

Linh quietly excused herself, not willing to listen any longer. Walking past the secretary's desk, she stepped into the hall.

"Excuse me, Inspector Phú," Mrs. Ocampo said, following Linh out the door. "Do you have a moment to talk privately?"

The women walked to the end of the corridor where Ocampo proceeded to tell her story. Phú listened with mild surprise as Ocampo told of her son's criminal record, his role in the cargo thefts, and of McKenna's late night visit to her home. "There is a lot more to it," said Ocampo. "All of which I've explained to Inspector McKenna."

Phú nodded, realizing now that her partner had successfully linked several crimes together: Gustavs Berzins, his sister Inga Berzina, Rhonda Pitts, and possibly the death of Ruben Ocampo. "You say your son was killed at the Port of Oakland?"

"Near there," said Ocampo. "At a Customs inspection facility in Alameda." Her eyes pleaded with Phú. "Inspector McKenna was getting close, I think. In my heart, I know that he is a good man and didn't do the things they say he did."

"I agree," said Phú.

Leaving the secretary, Linh quietly returned to her desk to make some calls. The first was to the CBP office at the port. For the second time in as many days, Tim Sanchez refused to give her Sarah Brooks's number.

"I have reason to believe that the shooting of Ruben Ocampo at your inspection facility may be connected with one of our cases."

"That may very well be," said Sanchez. "While I can't comment on our progress, I will tell you that Sarah Brooks is not the investigator. In fact, she was off on injury leave at the time it occurred, and had absolutely no involvement in it."

Linh asked if there was anyone else she could talk to, and Sanchez gave her the name of Paul Bise—the contraband enforcement team supervisor.

"He's coordinating the case from our end," said Sanchez. "Bise witnessed the shooting, and also attended the autopsy."

Bise was dubious at first. But Phú laid out the links to other cases and the fact that Brooks and McKenna had been working together on it. Realizing that his goals and Phú's were the same, Bise agreed to assist.

"I'll reach out to Sarah and pass on what you've told me," he said.

62

County Jail #1
427 7th Street, San Francisco

The holding cell inside the Intake and Release Center consisted of wooden benches lining the walls and an aluminum toilet in the corner. Four of us shared the cell—me, two drunks, and Leo Krumins. A casual observer would have counted three drunks and a sharp looking man in a tailored suit.

After searching me, removing my property, and photographing and fingerprinting me, the deputies took a DNA swab from the inside of my cheek. They told me it was mandatory for anyone charged with murder. Besides being blamed for Inga's death, I had no doubt the second homicide charge would be added once they officially matched my specimen profile to the hair and chewing gum found at Chief Fahey's house.

I was allowed to make a couple of phone calls, but Krumins, who had been booked ahead of me, was already on the phone. He chatted casually, as if discussing last night's game with a friend.

When it was my turn, I realized that my list of friends was almost non-existent. I placed a collect call to my house, and when the phone went to voicemail I was immediately disconnected. It was 2 a.m., and I guessed that Doris and Bridget were asleep. In my heart, I knew that the call wouldn't have been accepted anyway.

Closing my eyes, I leaned back against the greasy wall and thought about the takedown at the warehouse. It's not as if I had bungled a recording of my favorite song, or my wedding vows, or even my daughter's first words. My screw-up had totally wiped out all of the work I had done to clear my name, taking with it any hope of staying out of prison. Now, I was as good as dead.

I remembered standing numbly at the loading dock, staring at Lou's phone and praying that the blank recording was just a terrible dream. Then, a brusque order cut through the silent warehouse, "Hands where I can see them!"

At first I thought they were talking to me, but everyone turned toward the stack of pallets where a SWAT cop was aiming his weapon. "Heads up!" he yelled. "Suspect hiding up top."

The tactical guys rushed toward the pallets and Captain Dowd rushed toward the door. Somebody grabbed me, spun me around and slammed me against the loading dock. I saw Leo Krumins next to me, though he wasn't treated in the same manner. Trying to look back over my shoulder, I was met with a gloved hand—which forced my head down hard.

"Code four," someone called over the radio.

"It's McKenna's prostitute friend," another cop said.

I forced my head back against my handler. "Be careful with her," I yelled. "She's pregnant!"

Dowd had wormed his way back in, and sidled up next to me. Leaning down so only I would hear, he said, "We wouldn't want anyone to hurt *your* little unborn gutter rat, would we?"

They ushered me out of the building right after that, and it's a good thing. Had I gotten my hands free, I think I would have killed Dowd—not that I needed *another* murder charge.

They'd rushed me out so quickly that I never even got a glimpse of Shanay. Realizing that she never actually left the warehouse when they arrived, she had slipped in behind Elvis and stayed hidden on top of the stack of pallets. Which meant that she'd seen the whole thing—the shooting, the admissions—all of it.

Her criminal record would make testifying problematic though, and I knew that juries generally didn't believe people like her. But I trusted Shanay, and even *her* on the witness stand would be better than my twenty minutes of blank tape.

A deputy appeared at the barred door holding a set of keys, and next to him stood Captain Dowd—his rigid posture and narrow eyes looking more like a caricature than a real person.

As the deputy rolled back the cell door, Dowd said, "You're free to go."

I wondered if Linh had managed to contact my wife to arrange bail. If Doris had come all the way into the City to bail me out, I imagined that she must still feel something for me. Whatever the case, I was free to go.

I started to get up.

"Not you, McKenna." Dowd turned slightly to address Krumins. "The City and County of San Francisco apologizes, Consul Krumins, for any inconvenience this brief detention has caused. I'll personally escort you back to the consulate. This way, sir."

My heart felt like it flatlined. Dowd's cruel deception had been unmistakable and intentional. As I slumped back onto the bench, I saw Krumins give me a belittling wink.

I hadn't gotten so much as a second of sleep all night. My knee still ached, but was now joined in its discomfort by my back and hips.

The custody deputies had moved the drunks to another cell and were now keeping me in solitary confinement—protocol, apparently, when a cop is arrested.

One of the deputies mentioned that I would be transferred to the main jail as soon as the transportation unit could arrange it.

Then, from an office somewhere beyond my line of vision, I heard raised voices followed by a door opening and slamming closed.

"What a crock of shit!" Sarah Brooks's words were as bold as a freight train. "Where the hell is McKenna?"

63

Assembly Hall
Mill Valley Middle School

Mr. Martell's 5-B Geometry class was cancelled on Wednesday in lieu of an anti-bullying assembly. It had been difficult enough for Bridget McKenna to make it through her daily classes since the news broke, but she didn't think she could stomach an all-school assembly. The sideways looks, hallway whispers, and ceased conversations—all because of her notorious father—made her feel like an outcast. Bridget's peers had fallen into one of two categories: those who avoided her like the Ebola virus, and those who thought it was cool to be friends with the daughter of a real serial killer.

From an unassuming spot at the top of the bleachers, Bridget sat impassively through the presentation. When her phone vibrated inside her purse, she slyly pulled it out and checked the call. Not recognizing the number, she saw that there was no name on the caller ID. But she knew the 415 area code meant San Francisco.

Bridget slowly worked her way down the bleachers and told Mr. Martell that she had *cramps*. It was the *get out of jail free* card, guaranteeing that she could leave the assembly without any further probing.

In the restroom, Bridget sent a text to the number: *do i kno u?*

Right away, her phone rang again; it was the same caller.

Bridget answered this time. "Hey."

"Is this McKenna's daughter?"

Quickly glancing beneath the stall doors, Bridget saw that the bathroom was empty. "Yeah, who's this?"

"Shanay Moore. I'm a friend of McKenna's."

Bridget thought for a second. "The one from the car?" she said. "The pregnant lady?"

"Lady," Shanay snickered. "Yeah, that's me. Anyways, your daddy in a lot of trouble and you need to help him."

"I, I'm not..." Bridget gathered herself. "That's his problem, not mine. Like, what am I supposed to do anyway? My mom doesn't even talk to him."

"Uh-huh, I see how it is then. You just gonna wash your hands of ol' Pops. You and Mama fat hog'n it in the house he paid for, while he swing'n from the end of a rope. That's okay, then. You have a nice day, girl."

"Wait." Bridget stood there for a minute, thinking. "I'm not even supposed to answer when he calls. Anyway, what could I even do to help him? Like, send him a cake with a saw in it?"

"Ha! Good one, girl. Least that would be something." Shanay lowered her voice. "Is anybody with you?"

"No."

"Okay, now listen," she said. "So, I got this thing that might get McKenna out of jail. Something he don't even know I got. Anyways, I need to talk to him, but they won't let me in cuz'a my record."

"Why don't you just tell one of his cop friends at the department?"

"Uh-uh," said Shanay. "I don't trust none of 'em. They the reason he in jail in the first place."

Bridget didn't say anything.

"Girl, you need to get a ride over here. You know where he works at?"

"Yeah, the Hall of Justice. But how am I supposed to--"

"I don't know," said Shanay. "But you better figure it out quick. Take a BART train, or a bus, or Uber—it don't matter. Just meet me at the coffee shop across the street from the police building. Text me when you get here."

An open hand suddenly slammed onto the sink counter next to Bridget. "Phone, Miss McKenna." Mrs. Lajoie, the assistant principal, stood there with the other hand on her hip. "You know the rules, Bridget. No personal electronics during school, unless being used as study tool under the direction of a teacher. You can pick it up later in my office, provided you bring me a note signed by one of your parents."

The assistant principal pursed her lips as she added, "That is to say, a note signed by your *mother*."

Bridget caught a glimpse of herself in the mirror, then saw the reflection of Mrs. Lajoie—determined and intimidating. Talk about bullying.

Bridget felt a fire stoking inside of her. "I'm sorry, no!"

Lajoie took a step back and cocked her head. "What do you mean, 'no'?"

"I mean no, you're not taking my phone away. And no, I'm not bringing you a note from my mom. When I have a note, it will be from my dad."

"You're going to regret this!" yelled the vice principal, as Bridget dashed past her and out of the restroom.

64

Zuckerberg San Francisco General Hospital
Building 5, third floor, room 1101

Agent Sarah Brooks had badged her way into the intake and release center of the San Francisco County Sheriff's Department. "Let me see if I got this right," she said to the classification sergeant. "You let the murdering son-of-a-bitch go free, just walk right out of here, and then you hold onto the hardworking cop who caught him?"

The sergeant and deputies exchanged looks among themselves, and then he said, "It wasn't our call, Ms. Brooks. This whole matter is in the hands of the SFPD."

Sarah flipped her hand dismissively, and continued past them up to the bars of my cell.

"How did you know I was here?" I asked.

"Your new partner, Linh Phú. She went through a friend to get word to me that you'd been arrested."

I stood there, humiliated.

"Look, McKenna." She leaned close to the bars. "Phú got the evidence report back from the van you seized in the warehouse."

"And?"

"We can't talk here." She glanced around. "You need to get out of the main jail and into a place less custodial, like a hospital psychiatric or medical ward. Somewhere our conversation won't be monitored."

After Brooks left I summoned the sergeant and asked him to take a look at my knee. By then it had ballooned up pretty good and had a fair amount of bruising. I played it up, complaining that I felt feverish, dizzy, and couldn't feel the toes on that foot.

He changed my transfer paperwork, and by eleven o'clock that morning I was being admitted to San Francisco General. In most cases that would have meant lockdown Ward 7D. But I learned that whenever there are less than three prisoner patients, they are put in private rooms on the general medical surgical ward with a guard posted at the door.

Brooks was waiting outside the room, making small talk with my guard. They both sipped from Starbucks cups, which I guessed Brooks had bought to soften up the guy. *Nice touch.*

The transportation deputies cuffed one of my hands to the bedrail before leaving. That, combined with Brooks's eye-batting flirtations, seemed to relax my guard enough to ensure his slothful attention to security.

"Mind if I have a quick word with your prisoner?" Sarah finally asked him. "I've got a few questions related to one of our cases."

The guard dipped his head toward me. "Long as you leave the door open."

Agent Brooks sidled up next to the bed and spoke to me in a hushed voice. "First off, your partner, Linh, is a peach. If it weren't for her persistence, my own agency wouldn't have told me shit."

"Is Linh okay? I haven't heard anything from her."

"And you probably won't." Brooks's upper lip curled in disgust. "Her captain's been monitoring her phone records. Saw that you two have been talking, and he's put the fear of death into her. Anyway, the van we towed from the warehouse came back stolen. No surprise there. But your forensics guys also recovered gunshot residue inside the doorframe, and a spent twelve-gauge cartridge under one of the seats."

"At least now we can positively tie the van to your shooting."

Brooks smirked. "I was already positive."

I nodded. "Before they caught me in the warehouse, the embassy guy, Krumins, admitted that they were the ones who went after you. Said you were sniffing around their stolen cargo racket and they wanted to scare you off."

"Yeah, well fuck him. According to Phú, Forensics also pulled prints from inside the van; Elvis Lugailo's, Gustavs Berzins's, and Ruben Ocampo's."

"Even better," I said. "That links your shooting to my murder investigation. What about Krumins's prints?"

She shook her head. "Didn't find his. But I'm sure he's the one who ordered the hit."

"I don't know," I said. "Your shooting happened *after* Krumins killed the Pitts girl. Their group was splintered by then, battling over money. In fact, Krumins claimed that the Three Stooges went after you on their own."

"Whatever. The little shits are all dead now, anyway."

"And your shooting happened when?"

"Thursday, October 29th," she said.

I sat back against my plastic pillow, trying to figure out the timeline in my mind. The attempt on Brooks's life had taken place three days before Elvis and Gustavs decided to make peace with Krumins. They met him in the park, ostensibly to hand over cash they nipped from the stolen booze. I supposed that the money had probably been in the backpack. I thought for a minute. So, if they paid Krumins what they owed, why would he shoot Berzins? And why go after Berzins's sister eleven days later? I wondered if Krumins had found out that Inga was talking with me. These were all questions I should have asked Krumins when I had the chance.

"Now we've got to find a way to fix your situation." Brooks's words drew me back to the present.

She told me about her and Tam tracking the missing container to an industrial complex in Hayward, but they were never able to locate the exact building where the cargo had been stashed. And then three days later, the Hayward cops found the container sitting empty on the side of the road.

"I need to talk to Tam," I said. "If I can convince him to swear out a statement, and if I can present that along with the evidence connecting your shooting..."

Brooks shook her head. "Tam stayed around for another day or two, trying to develop leads on the cargo. But his boss ordered him back, and he caught a flight out yesterday."

"Shit!" My handcuff pulled against the bedframe. The deputy glanced in. "Sorry," I said. Then, lowering my voice, I told Brooks, "We need more."

"Aren't the forensics from the van enough to clear you?"

I raised my eyebrows. "It shows that my investigation was on the right track, but it still doesn't solve the Inga Berzina killing or the police chief's death. And now, they think I'm the one who shot Elvis last night inside the ware--"

"Dad?"

I jerked my head toward the doorway and there was my daughter.

"Bridge! What are you doing here?"

My guard rolled his eyes, but nodded her through.

"I came to deliver a message to you," she said, extending a cell phone out to me. "It's from Shanay Moore. She told me to say, 'You gotta get with the times, old man.'"

65

San Francisco District Attorney's Office
Independent Investigations Bureau (IIB)
Room #301

The recorder clicked on and the conference room fell silent.

"Please introduce yourselves for the record, starting to my left," said the woman.

"Michael Prowse, Internal Affairs Lieutenant."

"Gregory Dowd, Captain of Investigations, Homicide Detail."

"Bill Rampone, San Francisco Police Officer's Association."

I swallowed dryly. "Daniel Patrick McKenna, Inspector, Homicide Detail."

"Provisional," said Dowd with a sneer.

The woman at the head of the table lifted an index finger to quiet him. "And I'm Marybeth Rigby, San Francisco District Attorney's Office, Independent Investigations Bureau." She then turned her eyes to me. "Mr. McKenna, we are here this morning after having lengthy and hotly debated discussions regarding your conduct, the allegations against you—both criminal and departmental—and your future within the San Francisco Police Department. Before we get started here, do you have anything to say?"

Sure, I had plenty to say. Leaning forward in my chair, I cleared my throat to talk. But Bill Rampone reached across my chest like a seatbelt.

"No ma'am, we have nothing to say at this time," he said.

"Then we'll continue." The DA flipped open a sizable file folder. "With regard to your investigative methods, while I can't say that I condone them, you have successfully brought to closure the murders of Rhonda Allison Pitts—SF homicide victim number sixty-three, Gustavs Berzins—SF homicide victim number sixty-four, Inga Berzina—SF homicide victim number sixty-five, and Elvis Lugailo, also known as Elvis Lang—SF homicide victim number sixty-six."

Dowd's eyes rolled as he yawned his blasé acknowledgment.

"And, to your credit, a clearance in the shooting of a federal agent in Oakland. The murder of Ruben Ocampo in Alameda is still under investigation, and has not yet officially been tied to your suspects."

"What about the Chief's death?" I asked.

She turned to Captain Dowd, whose face looked like he'd just undergone a root canal.

"Yeah, on that," he said, "The Medical Examiner came back with a finding of *no foul play*."

"Can I ask how he died?" I wasn't trying to start trouble, but I had liked the guy. And ever since it happened, I'd been beating myself up over being there that night but not finding him. Maybe if I had been more observant, I'd have spotted him. Been able to help him.

Dowd twisted a kink from his neck, then answered without looking in my direction. "They think it was an accident. Some heart medication he was on." Dowd glanced at his notes. "*Dronedarone*. It's for arrhythmia, they said. Wasn't supposed to be taken with grapefruit juice. Anyway, they think Fahey went downstairs in the middle of the night, drank a glass, and then had some sort of reaction. Combination turned fatal."

I nodded, but didn't say anything.

Then Dowd looked at me. "Still doesn't answer the question of what in the name of God you were doing with your fucking head in the old man's doggie door, McKenna."

The DA held up her hand again. "That aside, Leo Krumins was in possession of two firearms when he was detained at the warehouse; one belonging to the deceased, Elvis Lugailo. The other weapon turned out to be a Bulgarian make, is that right Captain Dowd?"

He let out a sigh as he glanced at his notepad. "Yeah, a 9mm called Arcus 98-DA. So, yeah, the 115 grain bullets it carried could *possibly* corroborate fragment evidence recovered from the bodies of some of the victims. Circumstantially," he grunted.

"And there were the keys," continued Marybeth Rigby, "They were found in Consul Krumins's jacket pocket. Keys to the Pitts victim's car and her house. All of which tends to support Inspector McKenna's assertion of Krumins's involvement."

Dowd rolled his eyes again.

The DA continued. "Additionally, the unwitting confession by Mr. Krumins, which was recorded on video by the witness, Sha Nay Nay Moore, is further corroboration. Not circumstantial." She shot Dowd a look. "Therefore, the DA's office has found the totality of information sufficient to close the previously mentioned homicide cases as *solved*. In doing so, we have cleared you, Mr. McKenna, from any criminal conduct."

I felt Rampone's palm clap my shoulder as I released a long-held breath.

Ms. Rigby gave me a cautionary look. "There still remains in-house issues, not under the jurisdiction of this office." She nodded to the internal affairs lieutenant.

"There are five violations of departmental policy," said Prowse. "Any of which may be job threatening." Then Prowse listed them:

"One, prowling at the home of former Chief Fahey on or about November 8; two, theft of evidence from Inspector Alan Lam's case file—to wit, a set of keys—on or about November 9; three, vehicle assault of Captain Dowd on or about November 11; four, several counts of trespass into the warehouse at 168 Russ Street; and five, unlawful detention of homicide suspect Elvis Lugailo—on or about November 16."

"Unlawful detention!" I said. "Whaa?"

Prowse started to respond, but Dowd bellowed over him. "Yeah, McKenna. We don't normally set booby-traps of chemical filled condoms to catch perps. And we don't condone duct-taping a suspect to a chair in order to force a confession. What's next, waterboarding?"

Lieutenant Prowse continued, "The department has decided to make an offer with regard to these departmental misconduct allegations, which we believe is in the best interest of all involved."

I looked at Bill Rampone, who only shrugged. Across the table, Dowd avoided eye contact with me, which was an indication that he did not like the proposed deal.

"What is it?" I asked.

"You voluntarily step down from the homicide detail, and permanently abdicate your position in the criminal investigations division," said Prowse. "You'll return to uniformed patrol and be reinstated at your previous salary step at a Police Officer III."

My shoulders slumped forward. I felt Bill's hand on my back again but I leaned away. "No. Absolutely not. If I did something wrong, then sure, I should be punished. But if I didn't, then why--?"

Dowd suddenly reengaged. "Listen up, McKenna, I'm not going to have a loose cannon like you working in my bureau. If you have any brains at all, you'll take the deal and hold on to your job. Otherwise we move forward with the internal policy violations, and I guarantee that they'll be sustained and you'll be fired. The way I see it, you have three choices. You can go quietly back to street patrol, you can resign in lieu of termination, or you can roll the dice and fight this thing. Is that what you really want? You want Internal Affairs to pull out all the stops and send this up to the OCC and the Police Commission?"

I sat in stunned silence, trying to wrap my head around what was happening. Dowd hated me and wanted me gone. But if he was so sure I'd be found in violation, then why agree to the deal where I keep my job? Even as a patrolman. There had to be more at play.

"I don't understand," I said. "Seems like I'd still be needed in the homicide detail to finish preparing these cases for court. There are a half dozen witness statements that I need to type up, and I've still got a ton of physical evidence to prepare for the district attorney's office. And what about my testimony at the trial? Leo Krumins's murder cases will probably drag out for months. I'll need to--"

"Well..." Marybeth Rigby glanced at Dowd and then back to me. "That's the sticky part of all this. As Consul of the Latvian Consulate, Leo Krumins has full diplomatic immunity."

I cocked my head. "Meaning?"

"Meaning, he can't be prosecuted for, well, for anything occurring on our soil," said Rigby. "This goes much higher than the SFPD, or the DA's Office, or even City Hall. The diplomatic accommodation afforded Mr. Krumins is dictated by the U.S. Department of State. Our hands are tied here at the local level. The most that's going to happen to Leo Krumins is deportation. In fact, he's being put on a flight back to Riga, Latvia this afternoon."

"So it's all politics," I said. "That's why you guys are so quick to cut a deal with me. You want to shut me up, put me back on patrol, and forget any of this ever happened."

Nobody spoke, except Dowd. "Or, like I said, we can go after you, balls-to-the wall, for each and every violation of departmental rules and regs."

"What if I decide to appeal this?" I asked. "In fact, yes, I want a meeting with Chief Fahey's replacement as soon as it's announced. This isn't only about me losing my position as an inspector--"

"*Provisional* inspector," said Dowd, curtly.

"But what opportunities am I going to have during the rest of my career? Especially with this black cloud over me, guilty or not. No, I want to have an audience with the new chief."

Dowd cracked a tiny smile. "Well it hasn't been made public yet, but the Board of Supervisors has just appointed me chief of police."

I felt Bill Rampone's hand drop limply from my shoulder.

And that was that.

66

Homicide Detail

So much for an objective review of the facts of my case by the new chief. The resignation letter asking for a disciplinary appeal, penned while in the county lockup, may as well have been written on a piece of toilet paper.

I spent the rest of the afternoon in the office, clearing out my things and turning in my department-issued gear. For the most part, the guys in the detail were pretty decent—most stopping by the desk to wish me luck. There were still a few old school assholes who had painted me as a backstabbing criminal, and there was no turpentine strong enough to remove that stain.

Linh Phú was quiet, as usual. Probably didn't know what to say. But she'd been the one person in the entire department who had stood by me.

"I hope Captain Dowd didn't come down too hard on you," I said, "for helping me out while I was on the run."

"Chief of Police Dowd," she reminded me with a smile. "But no, it's nothing I can't handle." She started to turn and then said, "Oh, I nearly forgot. Your friend Curtis Tam has been calling for you. Long distance, I think. He asked me to give you his new number when you got in."

I took the slip of paper and stared at it. There was really nothing Tam could do for me at this point. His focus had always been on recovering the containers of stolen booze, which were no longer on my radar. And now that I'd been cleared, criminally anyway, I wasn't sure there was any point in returning his call.

It was late in the afternoon. Dowd hadn't been around, which was perfectly fine with me. I figured that he was probably out getting the gold stars and other regalia for his new uniform. Anyway, I'd filled out the separation of service paperwork for HR, and was just sitting there thinking.

Mrs. Ocampo's weathered face kept glancing over at me. Her eyes held a mixture of grief and regret. I hoped she wasn't blaming herself for my situation. That got me thinking that her son's murder still hadn't been solved, and I knew she'd been counting on me to do it. I felt in my gut that his killing was connected to my cases, but Krumins had pretty much confessed to everything but that. Said it wasn't any of his people.

Glancing at the note again, I decided to call Tam. It was six a.m. in Hong Kong, and three a.m. in Latvia. But wherever Tam was, he answered with his usual alert voice. I briefly told him what I'd been through—some of which he'd read in the papers—and what loose ends still remained on the other cases.

"I'm hoping I can help you with those *loose ends*," he said. "My client has hinted all along about the existence of another party in play. His theory is that the Russian government, who still disputes my client's rights to distribute the liquor, wanted to even the score with him."

"Russians," I repeated.

"It's just speculation, but my client believes they wanted to kill anyone responsible for benefiting financially from an enterprise the Russians still believe is theirs."

"You're saying that they killed the Ocampo kid?"

"Think about it," he said. "It was a professional assassination. And Brooks saw the shooter getting into a boat with three other people in black clothing. Prior to that, we'd been followed by four black-clad motorcyclists. I believe they were the same people—three men and a woman—who secreted a tracking device in Brooks's purse. That doesn't sound like your Latvians, does it?"

"No," I said. "Nothing they did was ever that sophisticated." I thought for a minute. "Sounds a little far-fetched though. I mean, what would killing Ocampo accomplish? He was just a low-level grunt."

"Who knows?" said Tam. "Maybe the foursome had been sent to take out the people involved in the smuggling ring."

"Wouldn't they have gone after Leo Krumins? He was the damn ringleader."

"Good point," he said. "Anyway, it's just a theory that I thought I'd pass along."

I thanked Tam and told him that there wasn't much I could do with the information anyway. That my career with the SFPD was pretty much over as of today.

"You should think about going into the PI business yourself," he said. "It can be pretty lucrative if you don't mind the travel."

I hate traveling, but I thanked him just the same.

It was the end of the workday, and for me it was also the end of my career as a San Francisco cop. I didn't like the options Prowse, Dowd, and DA Rigby had given me, and I doubted that I'd ever truly be able to repair my damaged reputation within the department. Even if I could, I'd still have to contend with Dowd. The police chief has tentacles that reach down through all districts, divisions, and through all ranks. There would be no hiding from him, or from his ass-kissing henchmen. Guys like Prowse would always be around to do the chief's dirty work. They'd be able to get to me no matter which station I was working out of or which assignment I was in.

It was 5 p.m. on the button. I hugged Linh Phú goodbye and offered the guys in the detail a quick wave.

Then I walked out of the homicide detail and out of the Hall of Justice for the last time.

Epilogue

706 Meadowsweet Drive
Corte Madera

I spent Monday night in a budget motel near Mill Valley. It was quiet, and after the Ocampo bed, the warehouse pallets, and the jail bench, I finally enjoyed a restful night.

Doris, who had continued with her counseling sessions, had gotten word to me through Bridget, that I could retrieve some of my things from the house—as long as she wasn't home when I did it. Doris was busy finding herself, or becoming empowered or self-actualized, or whatever. In any case, she wasn't taking me back.

I'd made arrangements with Bridget to drive her into the city for her final orthodontic appointment. At long last, taking my daughter to get her braces off was a promise that I was determined to keep.

With a few hours to kill before picking her up, I parked my car down at the yacht harbor and gazed out at all the sailboats. The radio was playing some kind of elevator music—which went perfectly with my view. It was the kind of music that helps a guy think.

The news came on rather abruptly, completely screwing up the *zen* moment and diverting my attention from the boats. According to the newscaster, Latvian Consul of San Francisco, Leo Krumins, had been shot and killed inside a restroom at the Frankfurt, Germany airport. The shooting, which was not witnessed, apparently occurred during a layover as he waited for a connecting flight to Riga, Latvia.

The first thing I thought was that they can't blame me for that one. I was here in the United States the whole time.

Then, reflecting on my last conversation with Curtis Tam, I wondered if there was actually some merit to his client's theory about Russian government involvement. It was still pretty out-there as far as hypotheses go, but I wasn't ruling anything out—including my curious musings about the mysterious private investigator. Who was to say that Tam had really headed back to Hong Kong? For all I knew, he could have taken the same flight to Frankfurt as Krumins.

Just for kicks, I called Tam's cell. After several rings, a phone company message came on to say that that number was no longer in service. It was like he had evaporated into thin air—again. Not that any of it mattered to me at that point.

Bridget came down the steps in front of the school as I pulled in to pick her up. She seemed glad to see me. We drove across the Golden Gate Bridge into the City, and I waited in the car while she was inside.

I've always prided myself on being able to figure things out. No matter how long it takes or how complex the clues. My mind just sort of sifts through the facts, distilling them down until there is only one answer. That's what I was doing as I waited for my daughter in front of Westfield Orthodontics on Market Street.

The money thing still didn't add up for me. Why would Krumins continue his little killing spree if Elvis and Gustavs had paid him back what they'd stolen? But according to what Krumins had told me, he still hadn't found the money.

Bridget opened the car door and flashed a smile I hadn't seen in a long time. She was happy to have her pretty white teeth back, and she was happy, I think, to be with me.

I wound my way past the ball park, southbound down to Third Street.

"Where are we going, Dad?"

"I have to take care of something while we're over here," I told her. "Shouldn't take too long."

She looked at me through the eyes of her mother for a second.

"No, no," I said. "I'm not going to hunt down a killer, or run my boss off the road. I just need to make one stop, and then we're done."

The SFPD auto impound yard at Pier 70 was manned by a solo uniformed cop; an old guy I used to work with out in the Ingleside District. I pulled up to the gate and he squinted at me over the tops of his glasses.

"How's it going, Zach?" I asked, hoping that rumors of my resignation hadn't reached him yet. "Just need to double check one of the cars before we release it back to the owner."

Recognizing me, if not by name at least by face, he nodded me through. I zig-zagged through a couple of rows of cars and found the Silver Ford Focus against a fence along the old pier. The rental car was covered in a film of dust but otherwise looked the same as the day I towed it from Oak Street. It had been my first clue of my first case—leading me to its renter, Elvis Lang, who turned out to be Elvis Lugailo, the key to solving the string of thefts and murders.

239

I got out and stared at the Ford, unanswered questions still bouncing around in my head. The interior was clean, except for aluminum powder smudges left by the techs who had dusted for latent prints. Opening the door, I knelt down and swept my hand back and forth under the seat. Nothing.

Then I took the keys, which were still in the ignition, and opened the trunk. It was also clean and appeared empty. Lifting the fabric covered floorplate, I surveyed a vinyl bag of tools, a bumper jack, and an unused spare tire. Unscrewing the wingnut holding the spare in place, I carefully lifted it out of the tire well.

"Humph," I said, stepping back to take it in. "That's freak'n crazy." I reached in and picked up the black daypack that had been stuffed beneath it. Keeping it low in the trunk, so that Bridget wouldn't see, I cautiously unzipped it.

Elvis and Gustavs had never given Krumins the money. Perhaps they had planned to, but never had the opportunity. Maybe Krumins had started shooting too soon, or maybe Elvis had planned to kill Krumins. Like everything else, it no longer mattered. Because here it sat, right in front of me.

Money. A hell of a lot of it.

Arching my head back to look up at the cool blue sky, I sensed the calming arms of satisfaction wrap around me. It felt so good to finally be right.

My next dilemma was what to do with all of this undocumented cash. I'm proud of myself for certain decisions I've made in my life, and there are others that I'm not proud of. This seemed to fall into a gray area somewhere in the middle.

The money didn't belong to Elvis, or Gustavs, or Leo Krumins; they had stolen it from someone else. And they were all dead, anyway. If anyone, it belonged to Curtis Tam's employer—whoever that was. Tam would never disclose the guy's identity, even if I could get back in touch with him—which I couldn't.

So, now what? Turn it in as evidence for a case that will never go to court? Found property? And then when no one claims it after the prescribed waiting period, the money gets cycled back into the local government's general fund? More condoms and syringes for the homeless? Or worse, it goes to one of Chief Dowd's pet projects at SFPD?

I limped around the side of the car, put the keys back in the ignition and slammed the door. I stood there for a long time, staring into the rental car's trunk, thinking. Thinking about what this experience has cost me; my marriage, my career, my reputation...my knee.

Waving to Zach on the way out of the impound yard, I gazed toward the bay. The day was clear and breezy, perfect for sailing. Every now and then my eyes were drawn to the rearview mirror, and the bulging backpack sitting on the seat behind me.

As we crossed over Third Street, I heard Bridget's phone give a short buzz.

"Got a message from Shanay, Dad."

"What does she want?"

"Nothing bad," Bridget said. "She's just texting that she had her baby last night. A little girl."

I drove up 20th Street to San Francisco General. Bridget and I got to Shanay's room just as the nurse was setting the baby in a clear plastic, box-like thing with a pink blanket in it.

Shanay looked tired, so we only stayed for a couple of minutes. Just long enough for me to thank her for literally saving my life. The video recording she had made from her hiding spot on top of the pallets had provided the evidence that even Dowd couldn't ignore.

As we started to leave, I slipped an envelope out of my pocket and set it on the nightstand next to Shanay's bed. It wasn't a thin one, and she eyed it suspiciously before glancing back at me. She smiled and shook her head.

"What?" I said with an innocent shrug. "It's not for you anyway, it's for the baby."

"Thanks, McKenna."

www.ingramcontent.com/pod-product-compliance
Lightning Source LLC
Chambersburg PA
CBHW060315260626
47160CB00007B/2617